RULES OF ENGAGEMENT

ALEX LANE

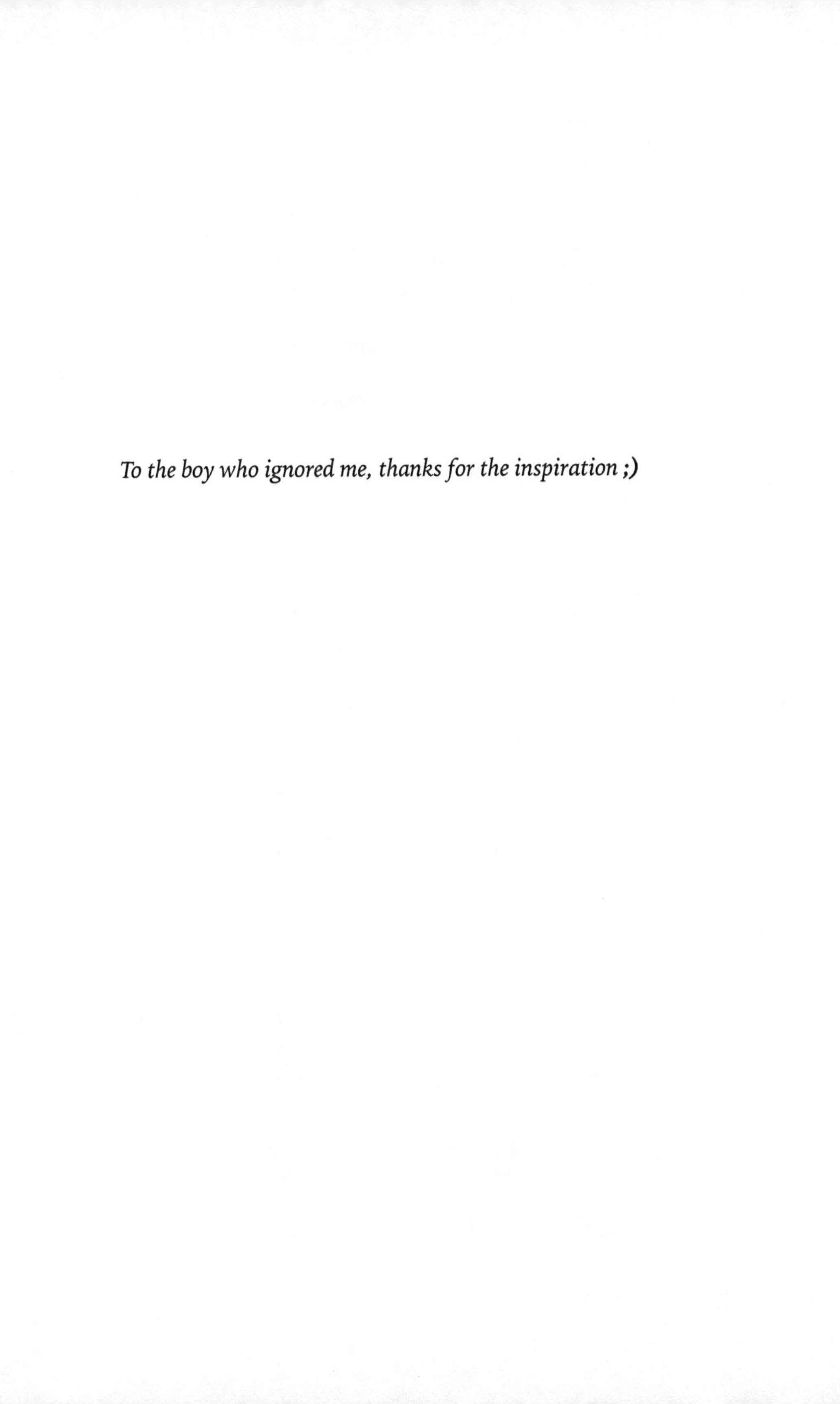

To the boy who ignored me, thanks for the inspiration ;)

1 CLARA

Every operative had the same fear and the same hope: to wake up one day and see the envelope sealed with the signet of Command slipped under their door. This envelope was the call that set an operative apart from the rest. It sent them into their own assignment, separate from those they trained with. It was evidence the operative had a special set of skills the other operatives didn't. It was an incredibly brilliant honor. It was also, more often than not, a death sentence. If not in the original assignment, then in a future one.

When Clara saw the envelope on her floor, adrenaline immediately coursed through her veins. This was not her first assignment like this, and if she survived it wasn't her last. She had gained her status as a high ranking operative over a year ago, and had received more summons than anyone else in her year, almost more than anyone in the division. It had been two months since her last assignment, the longest stint for her and she was completely restless.

Clara threw her clothes on quickly, meticulously lacing her

boots and concealing her favorite weapons. Her trainer had gifted them to her after her first summons. Obsidian blades. Absolutely lethal.

She didn't typically carry beyond those; her role was usually to blend in until it was too late for the person she was after. She had the mannerisms of a spy, but her honed agility and weapons training had given her a level of precision and deadliness few operatives could claim to possess. She smiled into the mirror, her eyes never softening, and she pulled her hair back.

She inhaled deeply. *Here I go.* She broke the seal.

"Clara Richards -

You have been summoned to Command. Join us in the war room at 0900 for your new assignment.

Command"

Clara couldn't keep the slight smile off her face as she walked through the dining line. "What's with you this morning?" Reese, the closest person Clara had to a friend, asked as Clara slid onto the bench next to her.

"Oh, just another one of those mornings."

"So cryptic." Reese stabbed a mini muffin on her plate, waving it on her fork as she added, "You got called into Command again, didn't you?"

Clara did not react immediately. She was trained not to react. But in the safety of the dining hall it was harder to slip into that perfectly crafted role. Reese kept the impaled muffin pointed at Clara. The lack of response was enough for Reese to assume she had correctly guessed. "Of course you did." She deadpanned. "Dude, it's been awhile since you've had an assignment! I'm sure you're thrilled. I know I am. You've been driving me absolutely, positively, incredibly insane."

Clara smiled hesitantly, "So eager to get rid of me."

Reese rolled her eyes, "Get rid of you is a strong phrase. Far too strong since you'll be coming back. Obviously. No, more like I'm grateful you will have the chance to relax and work out some of your stress. Since that's what does it for you. It's weird to me. Really weird to me. But I'm sure you're excited." Reese took a deep breath when she finally finished her rambling train of thought.

Clara allowed a real smile to grace her face, "Yeah, okay. I'm excited. It just doesn't feel like the right thing to admit. I'm sure I'm being sent somewhere extremely dangerous. Again. It doesn't seem like the right thing to be excited about."

Reese didn't hold the same sentiment. "You're not excited because of the danger or because the war is getting worse." She exhaled deeply and popped the muffin into her mouth. Around bites she added, "You're excited because somehow this is where you find purpose. Don't ask me how or why. I'm not a psychic, or is it psychologist? Psychiatrist? Pretty sure it begins with psych. Anyways. You're gonna have to figure that one out on your own."

Clara nodded, shoving a bite of eggs into her mouth. These missions did bring a form of satisfaction to her. It was the knowledge she was furthering her kingdom. She was protecting people. She was standing in the gap in ways the normal population would never know. And the more selfish part, she was proving to herself and everyone else just how capable she was.

Ever since she and Carver were split between disciplines, and then split permanently, she had strived to become the best. She created an identity within her discipline–become the best assassin, until that's all anyone ever saw: a shadow.

As Reese continued to ramble, Clara tried to tune her out. Though she would never admit it, her nerves were becoming more and more on edge from the idea of facing Command. Though she had been in that room many times since they graduated and received their classification, she couldn't walk those hallways without thinking of Carver. It was practically ritualistic. She threw herself into assignments to forget him, only to have his face come to mind every time she was given one.

Following basic training, each person was assigned to continue training as a special operative, or drafted into a military regiment where they became boots on the ground for emerging battles. For those chosen to train as operatives, they were assigned to Ravens, Spiders, or Vipers.

The Ravens were trained to blend into any scenario. Spies — intelligence. The Spiders were crafty and brilliant. Clara had seen some of the weapons they created throughout her own training, and it terrified her to consider what else Spiders might be capable of. She was grateful they were on the same team, and had resolved to never get close to, and never upset, a Spider.

Clara was assigned to Vipers. As lethal as the name suggests, Vipers were trained to be killers. Brutal, awful, terrible murderers.

Clara had been relieved that she and Carver were placed within operative disciplines. Now, she felt foolish for ever believing it was the easy way out. Operatives were pushed until they broke and what was left of their humanity was barely enough to stay sane. The line between brilliance and madness. A tightrope every operative learned to walk. Or didn't.

"So will you admit you're freaking thrilled? Or keep pretending this doesn't phase you?"

Clara rolled her eyes, though secretly she enjoyed the extra attention Reese was paying her.

"Yes, I'm excited. Something I shouldn't admit though," Reese leaned in as Clara dropped her voice slightly. "Before every mission,

I have the same anxious feeling in the pit of my stomach I had the first time."

Reese burst out laughing, the noise shattering the concentration Clara's brain had created. Every noise around her felt louder. Closer. More dangerous. As her anticipation grew, every sense heightened. Adrenaline doesn't know the difference between anxiety and fear, and as Clara had trained, everything around her took on the hue of a threat.

"When did they tell you to go to them?"

"Right after breakfast."

"I'm happy for you, Clara. In all seriousness, I know how hard you work for this."

Clara gave her a tight smile before focusing her attention on finishing her food and keeping it down. Reese couldn't know how hard she had worked for this. No one understood the full price she had paid to reach this level.

There were still operatives within the assassins who walked without the weight of blood on their hands. A feeling Clara couldn't even vaguely remember. She couldn't remember the number of lives she had claimed. All through direct orders. So many prisoners gone by her hand. Diplomats, advisors, generals, and those she knew nothing about except for their name in a list of instructions.

It was part of the training, after all. And Clara had been singled out from the beginning. What he saw in her, she still didn't know. She had been fierce, but after things with Carver ended, she was simply angry. She had a fire that could burn the world down, and no clue how to direct it.

Ferris had singled her out immediately. He claimed she was weak, and that she'd never survive. And he told her from day one he would destroy her. After three months, Ferris realized she wasn't easily destroyed and he flipped his actions. He made her his star pupil, and he, knowing he wouldn't be allowed to stay an operative much longer, taught her his trade secrets he paid too much for to share in a class. He led her through every drill, every practice, coaching her to stay through lunch and dinner, adapting her body to training through weakness. She loved it. She loved the focus. She loved the pain that engulfed her every waking minute. She loved the feel of cool metal in her hands, and the destruction she realized she could wreak.

No one could tell her she was weak ever again.

No one could accuse her of needing a crutch.

Now, here she was. She carried the loss of her innocence as proof of her competence. And she would do it yet again.

"Thanks for the encouragement, Reese," she managed to say through her rushing thoughts. Clara picked up her tray and moved to the door as Reese wished her good luck and goodbye.

Another deep breath as she stepped out of the dining room into the narrow hallway. This is it. No weakness. She focused on the physical reactions she could control as she calmly walked to Command. Deep breaths. Consistent steps. Heart rate slowing.

That's more like it.

The walk to Command was shorter than she remembered. She blamed it on nerves. Command was at the center of the base, with each of the three disciplines sectored off in different directions. Operatives were encouraged, though not forced, to stay in their own sector. Each discipline was different, and what happened if too much cross pollination occurred?

Afraid to become pariahs, most people followed this rule.

Clara, in her path for perfection, of course followed this rule. And so, although she could have passed through and visited old friends from base training, explored a different section, or even come to present a request to Command, Clara only ever walked this way to have her fate sealed. Whatever words were spoken, whatever assignment was given, that was her new destiny. She would execute it regardless of the cost.

She paused before the door, her feet almost stumbling as they broke from their previous pattern. *This is what I've been waiting for. I'm here.* Straightening her already perfect posture, Clara inhaled through her nose, exhaled through her mouth, and stepped through the door.

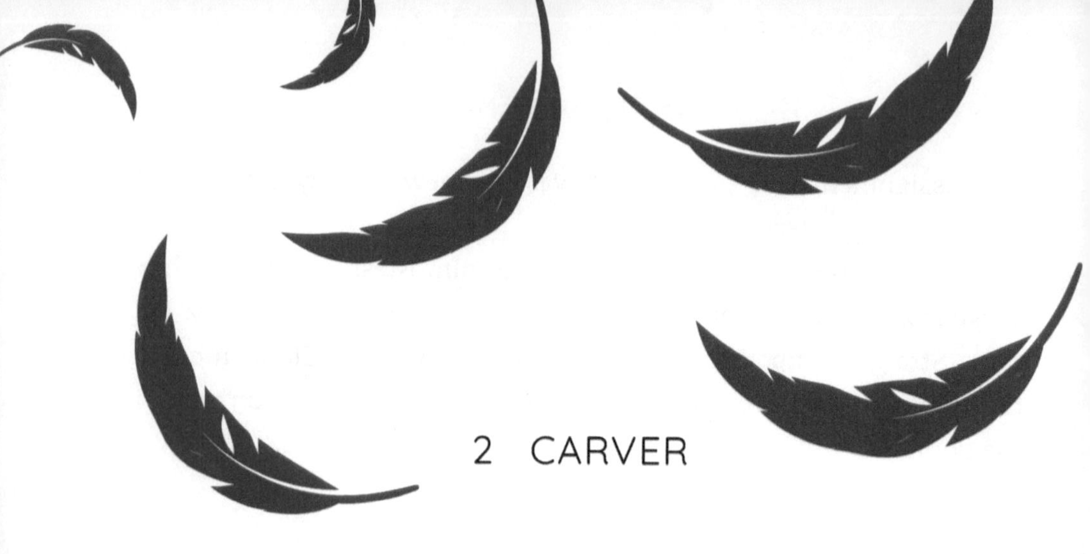

2 CARVER

Carver never understood the fascination with receiving a summons from Command. He loved exciting assignments for the change of scenery, but frankly he just didn't *care*. Yet somehow, he was the best. *Built for it*. So he was constantly told.

He'd been brought before Command for special assignments a handful of times now. Unheard of for the amount of time he'd been an operative, in fact, unheard of in general. He supposed he had proven himself. Command was comfortable with him carrying more information than anyone else in the sector because they knew he, at least, wouldn't break. After his slip up on his last assignment, he was surprised to be called in so soon.

Now he stood before them again, hands clasped behind his back and his eyes scanning the room. They sat in chairs arranged in a crescent shape, and from their stage, they were just high enough to look down on whoever stood before them. There were always five, never the exact same five, but they all had the same presence–icy, unfeeling, robotic. He had been scared the first time he was brought before them, their masks intimidating, their sleeves covering their hands. Now it almost felt routine and he resisted the urge to shift his weight from foot to foot. Couldn't seem too impertinent.

"You'll have a partner for this assignment." Was the first phrase that caught Carver's attention. His eyes snapped forward. This, this was different. He listened more intently as the woman continued.

Her voice was low, her eyes dark, but those were the only distinct features about her. With their masks and outfits, it was impossible to define anything about them. No one knew how many people were actually members of Command, and only those within the fold were capable of identifying other members.

"You've heard rumors of the 'Eclipse?'" His brain spun across the nickname. An assassin rumored to have killed more than any other operative. The rumors say he had never been caught, never failed an assignment. This assignment might end up being more interesting than he had expected. *Why are they assigning me to work with an assassin?*

His gut twisted, unsure about this change in normalcy but he nodded. "The two of you will be partnered for this assignment." The woman looked beyond him to the open doors behind him, "Ah, here she is now."

She. Carver's heart began to pound. It wasn't possible. It couldn't be. He turned slightly, looking over his shoulder. Praying he wouldn't confirm his suspicions. But he was right. He knew he would be. It was her. Her steps faltered for only a beat when her blue eyes met his. She was just as shocked as he was. Carver was glad he was standing so carefully. His lungs no longer wanted to expand, and he was pretty sure his vocal cords would betray him if he tried to speak.

His eyes tracked her as she recomposed herself, far quicker than he could, and walked until she was at his side. Feet away.

Far too close. And way too freaking far. Her posture was straight, and something about her expression sent a chill down his spine.

"Reporting for my assignment." Her voice was careful, unwavering.

It snapped him from his reverie. It was her. How was she the Eclipse? His best friend, lover, then nothing. And now she was a feared assassin. *Of course she is.*

The woman who had spoken earlier looked between the two of them. She obviously knew their history. She was a member of Command, and their relationship, and then lack thereof, had never been a secret. Satisfied with what she saw now, she explained their assignment. "We've received a report that Noxvalis has successfully created an airborne biological weapon that can be used over a long distance."

Carver couldn't stop his eyebrows raising and the surprise that rushed through him. Noxvalis was a violent kingdom, hell bent on destroying all neighboring kingdoms. Their kingdom had been at the top of the list for a while. If Noxvalis had created a biological weapon that powerful, it would end their kingdoms' feud. And cause the death of far too many people.

"We need you to infiltrate Noxvalis, gain access to their labs, and retrieve the weapon."

"Retrieve? Not destroy?" Carver was surprised to hear Clara interject. When he knew her, she was shy, careful to never speak too loudly. And now she was questioning Command.

The woman's eyes narrowed slightly behind the mask and Carver hoped for her own sake Clara wouldn't continue questioning those who held full control over their lives. "We need to study it so we can understand their mechanics and begin developing antidotes. Anything else you wish to *question*, Operative Richards?"

"No ma'am," Clara replied, her tone belying how she honestly felt about the decision.

The woman ignored her and moved on. "Their yearly celebration will begin in five days. Many people from other kingdoms visit for the celebration, and the two of you will enter with them. Once inside, you will meet with our contact. Marsh Harris. She owns a bookstore named 'The Midnight Quill' on the edge of town square. She will give you the information she's collected, and from there it is up to the two of you to get into the lab.

The train will take you within 20 miles of the gates, but you will have to walk the rest of the way, or find a caravan to join. There is no contingency. If you are captured, there will be no extraction.

Both of you have been here long enough to understand the cost of war. I don't have to explain to you how dangerous this weapon will be if it stays in their hands. It must be retrieved at all costs."

She finished, awaiting their response. Postures straight, they both saluted and replied, "Yes ma'am."

"Excellent. You are dismissed to pack and ready yourselves for tomorrow."

Carver turned towards the door, ignoring Clara at his heels.

"Operative Richards, please. Stay one more moment."

Carver looked over his shoulder as Clara turned to face Command again. The woman did not speak again, clearly waiting until he exited. If they were to be partners, why wasn't he receiving the same information she was?

He didn't like it. He didn't like any of this. Was this because of last time?

With no choice but to obey, he waited in the hallway until Clara was finished. He rolled his shoulders back and cracked his neck. The minutes ticked by like an eternity, but he knew it couldn't have been more than five before she stepped into the hallway, a glare on her face before she even spotted him.

As much as he wanted to say something to her, he felt like Clara needed to be the one to break the silence. He was desperate to know what had been said, but he didn't need to ask to know she wouldn't share.

Eventually, after a moment of awkwardness, and with a deep sigh, she acknowledged him. "This is not what I expected from my summons today." The frustration in her voice was clear.

"I'm doing great, Clara. Nice to see you've survived too." Carver spit back with more venom than he intended or knew he had.

Her eyes widened, "Don't pretend this is a picnic for you either. I'm certainly not the one who landed us here."

"You're the one who climbed the ranks enough to be awarded the nickname 'Eclipse' so yeah, you kind of are."

Her face flushed, "I never asked for the name. And what was I supposed to do? I threw myself into training. They didn't think I'd make it, and I proved *everyone* wrong."

Carver's heart wrenched at the way she emphasized everyone. He knew without a doubt that he was included in that statement. He inhaled, exhaling slowly. They had to fulfill this assignment. And they had to do it together. Orders were orders. He couldn't change the past, but maybe he could make this situation a little less volatile. And save the world. And keep them both alive at the same time. That was a long list.

Though the way Clara looked at him, he could survive this assignment and still lose his life. She was an assassin.

"Listen," Carver attempted to slip into a different role, "I didn't pick this," he held his hands up quickly, "And clearly this wasn't your idea either. I guess we should be proud of the fact that we've risen to the top in both of our fields." *Maybe our breakup was worth it,* he wanted to add but wasn't sure she would appreciate that, "We're both here because we love our kingdom." Clara nodded, nervously chewing her bottom lip. "And we both know the cost if we can't accomplish this."

Her face was calmer now, "We will accomplish this." *Success.* Her first admission to a willingness to work with him.

"Yes," he agreed quickly, "But we won't be able to if we're constantly at each other's throats. We have to figure out how to work together and…" he paused, "dare I say trust each other?"

"I don't trust you." He knew the response was coming, still the cold tone felt like a knife plunged in his chest.

"I know," he nodded, "And I share the same sentiments," she looked ready to interject but he held up a hand continuing, "but we are partners for this assignment and must work as such or we—not just we, our kingdom—won't survive."

"So what do you suggest?" She crossed her arms over her chest, leaning back onto one foot. It was a more relaxed position for her, but her eyes still scanned him waiting for a reason to fight.

Carver had expected far more of an argument at his suggestion, but maybe she had matured more than he was giving her credit for. "I suggest we do what they said and go pack." She shifted and looked ready to lunge at him, *maybe she hasn't matured as much as I hoped,* "And then, meet back here after everyone is asleep. That will give us time to process on our own and prepare for the assignment so we can figure out how to work together."

"Fine." Her tone remained curt, though it was at least civil. Carver nodded in response. It took immense effort and self-control to turn and walk away from her again. This wasn't exactly the reunion he had hoped for. Actually, he hadn't dared to hope for a reunion. He always assumed it was a matter of time before one of them ended up dead. And she wasn't supposed to still be here.

Their break-up was a matter of protection. Yes, he had done it under a leader's suggestion. In order to protect Clara. But he wouldn't pretend it wasn't partially self-serving. He couldn't bear the thought of ever having to watch her die. Even now, fear slithered into his chest as he walked back to his room. What was he going to do with this?

"This isn't good," he groaned, slumping against a wall when he was far enough down the hall she couldn't see him. Somehow, somehow he would protect Clara and fulfill this mission. He had to. Both were equally important in his mind, no matter how hard he tried to put his kingdom above her. She would always be a distraction. A perfect, smart, completely lovely distraction.

A distraction he couldn't afford three years ago, and one he certainly couldn't afford now.

3 CLARA

"You will assassinate the king." She hadn't known what to expect when Carver was called from the room. Her perfectionist tendencies screamed trouble. She had done something so atrociously wrong that even sentencing her to work with Carver wasn't penance enough.

That wasn't the case. It wasn't penance. It was an honor. She was being given the most insane assignment. To assassinate the king of their warring nation. It was suicide. And maybe therein lay her punishment. Or her reward.

"Carver isn't being told of this assignment." Clara hadn't needed the confirmation, the fact he was excused before the assignment said enough. "He will get you into the lab. His paperwork will detail a biological weapon he is to retrieve. It is everything we told you it is, powerful enough to destroy our kingdom. But the even greater threat is the king. Once you retrieve the biological weapon, Carver will return. You will remain and wait. Noxvalis will panic and increase safety precautions in the lab, leaving you a brief opportunity to access the king."

She couldn't feel her face. Had the blood left her body? "Will that be too much Operative Richards?"

"No, ma'am." Her voice stayed strong.

Now, Clara wrapped her hands tightly, circling her shoulders to warm up her body. This wasn't what she signed up for. She already had a moment of panic, calmed down enough to pack, and when the lunch bell rang went to the empty training room.

She stayed light on her toes throwing punch after punch, twisting her hips into the motion and relishing the resulting sting on her knuckles. She added in a few kicks, relieved that while her mind was in chaos, at least her body stayed dependable, responding as it always did.

The bag rattled, echoing sound through the vacant room. It was usually pristine, but a few of the weights had been left out by those training before lunch. Clara ignored the small detail, focusing all of her attention on the bag in front of her. She wished she could take this anger out on Carver himself.

Sweat dripped down her spine as she tired. It would be okay. They could do this. It was just an assignment. Assignments always sucked on some level. Clara's personal enemy was now the person charged with watching her back. And she was given an impossible mission.

She snagged her water bottle, and sat against the wall, arms over her knees.

It had been three years. Three long years. She should be over him by now. But he was the reason she trained as hard as she did. He was the reason she was determined to rise through the ranks. He was always the ghost at the edge of her brain. Degrading her and telling her she wasn't capable, then softening and encouraging her to keep going. A pathetic example of intermittent conditioning. And yet, regardless of what form he took, his memory hurt far less than seeing him.

She closed her eyes tightly. Could she be dreaming? Is this just a nightmare from which she will soon awake? No, she was, in fact, leaving on an assignment with Carver. *Carver.*

"You need to grow up! Stop being so weak. It's pathetic. I can't do this anymore." The last anger-fused words he said to her before he turned and walked away. Three years ago. The day they received their operative groups. The day she lost him.

She had been stunned. What could she have said in response? The love of her life, her best friend, and he ended things with her with an insult.

She had stood there, her eyes fixed on where he had stood moments before She didn't react. It had hurt too much for her to do anything except stand there and wish the pieces would come back together.

In a lot of ways, he was right. She had been weak. Two years of basic training, but it was his constant presence that kept her moving forward. The last three years, it was his absence that kept her pushing herself harder and harder. The things she would never admit to him.

As her breathing slowed, she unwrapped her hands, re-rolling the fabric as was habit. Her knuckles were bright red, split across her pointer and middle finger. She flexed her fingers, watching the cuts release a little more blood.

She could do this. She was strong.

Carver expected her to be the same girl. But she wasn't. She was brutal, cold, uncaring. She was the top assassin for a reason. She had to keep that in mind.

The day passed in a blur, both too quickly and too slowly for Clara's liking. She ran through training exercises with her group, met with a former trainer, ate, listened to Reese's banter and decided against telling her best friend about Carver having the same assignment, and finally, finally ended up pacing the floor of her room as she waited for the time to meet Carver. He was smart in suggesting they meet after everyone was asleep. She didn't want anyone else to know how weak she still was when it came to him. She had, as Carver discovered, made a name for herself. She wouldn't sacrifice that on the altar of past affection.

Almost time. Clara looked around her bedroom. The thin mattress on a narrow frame. The blanket her mother sent her when she graduated, embroidered with a reminder, "Stay Alive." So far, she had. This next assignment could change that. Yeah, it would probably change that.

She felt a sliver of fear at the thought of abandoning her mother, but she shook it off. She could come back. She would.

Her wooden dresser was bare aside from the sketchbook Reese gifted her almost a year ago, and the three books her father left her when he went to war. The covers were worn, pages beginning to fall from the bindings. She could recite every page of all three books. She was tempted to pack one as a reminder of her long-gone father, a reminder that she had to stay alive for the sake of her mother, but she realized the sentimentality was more foolish than anything else. A memento wouldn't keep her safe. It would be one more thing she was afraid to lose. One more thing she felt desperate to protect.

Clara paused in front of the mirror on the back of the door. Vanity was frowned upon in all the sectors, but as Clara had proven herself a serious operative a mirror had been her one request, so an allowance had been given. She still couldn't say why she had wanted it so desperately. But the image the mirror showed reminded her of how far she had come, and how far she still had to go.

They would succeed.

Then she could go back to her life where Carver was nothing but a haunting memory. How lovely.

With one last look, noting the harshness her features developed over the last three years, she began the walk to Command.

Carver was nowhere to be seen when she arrived, and Clara debated turning around. Would he use her decision to show up as proof that she was still weak? Would he again berate her? Remind her of what was at stake and the price they had paid to receive this responsibility that now weighed on their shoulders? She was well aware. She knew exactly what she had paid. She knew what was at stake, and she refused to let him yell at her again.

She slid down the wall at the entrance of the hallway to her sector, plopping down unceremoniously. She could see the opening where he would eventually appear, if he chose to appear.

She leaned her head back, debating between closing her eyes or continuing to stare. She decided it wouldn't hurt to relax a little. When she opened her eyes, only a few minutes later, he had materialized in front of her. She almost jolted, but caught herself just in time to avoid a reaction. He was a spy, this was as much his MO as hers, she reminded herself.

He held out a bottle like an apology, his eyes softer than she expected.

"What's that?" She practically barked out, inwardly cringing at the harshness of her own tone.

He shrugged, sheepish, "I thought a drink might take the edge off and make this conversation a little easier."

She grabbed the bottle from him, and quickly took a gulp, almost coughing at the burning sensation as it ran down her throat. The feeling after wasn't as unpleasant. "Thanks," she handed the bottle back awkwardly, attempting to move on from her original opening.

"You all packed?" Carver looked back and forth between her and the wall on the opposite side of the hallway, ultimately sitting across from her. His legs were long enough that in the narrow hallway his feet reached as far as her knees. She resisted the urge to move away from him.

"Yeah. You?"

He nodded, gulping from the bottle. He grimaced as he swallowed. "Nothing like a strong drink." She only stared in response. Her heart already pounding as they sat in the hallway. He handed her the bottle.

She resisted the urge to scan him. To commit every inch of him to memory, replacing the old version that haunted her. Did this Carver have the same easy-going smile? Did this Carver brush off the things that hurt him until the door was closed? Was he the life of the party? Everyone's favorite? Her turn to take a drink. Since he grimaced, she didn't.

More importantly, was this how the coming weeks were to go? Each of them pretending the person in front of them was a stranger instead of someone they knew intimately?

She didn't think she could pretend that long.

"We have to come up with a plan or this won't work."

"What won't work?" He asked with another drink, handing the bottle back to her.

She practically rolled her eyes as she took it. "You know exactly what I'm talking about. Us. This. We won't be able to work together if we're constantly on egg shells." Clara inhaled deeply, trying to ignore the way the shadows cut across his jawline, "We can't pretend the past away."

Her next drink of liquor went down smoother, and it had been long enough since she'd had a drink that she could feel the effects already. Carver nodded, contemplating her statement.

She took the moment to note all the changes the last three years had on him, allowing herself to view him the way she wouldn't only moments before. He was leaner than she'd ever seen him. Every line of his body perfectly carved and toned. It looked like he hadn't eaten enough recently, his cheeks slightly sunken. His jawline cut so precisely her heart fluttered. Because of the alcohol, of course. Only because of the alcohol. She hated him. No way in hell did she find him attractive.

She couldn't tell if the circles under his eyes were from lack of sleep or just the shadows playing tricks on her. For some reason she couldn't identify, she hoped it was the latter. Though she spent the last three years killing every positive emotion she had towards him, some emotions refused to die. It was those rebellious thoughts that wouldn't let her wish hell on him. She hoped he hadn't paid the same price she had. Foolish thinking.

He noticed her examination and met her eyes. Clara held his gaze, contemplating the phrase, "the tension could be cut with a knife." She certainly felt that way now.

"I have an idea," he said, keeping his voice low. Instinctively, she leaned forward from the wall to hear him better.

4 CARVER

"You've seen rules of engagement paperwork, right?"

Clara nodded, and Carver took a second to formulate his ideas. He motioned for Clara to hand him the drink, and she obliged. After downing another gulp he continued, "Rules of engagement define what degree of force is allowed within a specific mission. Basically, how the soldiers are allowed to handle combat." He spoke the words carefully, as much for his benefit as hers.

"Again, well aware." Sarcasm dripped from her tone, and he wondered why he was trying so hard to keep his own tone neutral, "What's your point?"

"We need to create our own rules of engagement. If we have to work together, and spend all this time together, we need to have a set list of how we'll cooperate. The past is in the past; like you said we can't pretend it away, and the one thing we agree on is that we both want to succeed on this mission. Right?"

Clara bit her bottom lip, (and *dang* Carver needed to focus), hesitating before she responded, "Agreed."

Carver grinned, surprised at the pride that welled in him with her agreement; he forced his eyes to focus though the alcohol was starting to make that difficult. He should stop drinking, and he should not have skipped dinner. "Excellent. Rule Number 1. No matter what the circumstances, you cannot undress in front of me."

Clara almost choked, "Of all the requests, that's the one you're starting with??"

One shoulder went up in a half defensive shrug, "Hey, I'm male. I didn't make the rules on how my biology works."

He received an eye roll in return. "Fine. Rule Number 2. No winking. Ever."

"Really? That's what's a problem for you?" Clara leaned across the hall and swiped the bottle from him, "Rule 3. You can't look at me like I'm someone who's hurt you."

"I don't look at you like that!"

Carver raised his hands, "I didn't say you have, I'm saying you can't moving forward. Who knows what the next couple weeks will bring out of us, and we both know we can't afford any distraction."

It killed him to call her a distraction, and though she quickly masked it, he didn't miss the look of hurt that crossed her face. It's how he had explained being better off without her after they received their operatives assignments. He had told her she was a distraction he couldn't afford. Belittling their relationship to that of a mutual benefit. Not love. He couldn't admit how much he loved her. So he told her she was a distraction. A stupid distraction as he was crawling his way to the top.

"Rule 4," her tone was colder again, her walls erecting in spite of the alcohol in her system, "No matter what the circumstances, you cannot go out of your way to defend or protect me beyond what you would do for a normal comrade."

"That's a long rule. But I agree, though that one should go for both of us." He leaned back pressing his head against the wall, watching her carefully as he formulated the next rule. "Rule 5. We don't discuss the past."

"I agree with that one," Clara said slowly. She paused and he waited for her to continue, "Honestly, I feel like we should summarize these rules a little more professionally. Most of the ones we've created wouldn't work as actual rules."

"What exactly did you have in mind?"

"Do you have paper? Let's write it down."

He didn't, but he volunteered to retrieve some from his room, leaving the bottle with her as he jogged away. He wouldn't have admitted it, but he needed a second to compose himself without her eyes on him. The years must have been brutal for her. She no longer had the sparkle in her eyes he loved. She didn't smile. She had maintained an aspect of femininity throughout her basic training, now even that was gone. The bodycon outfits designed for movement no longer covered a curvaceous body.

His heart ached as he imagined what she had been through. He thought he was protecting her by pushing her away, forcing her to become her own person to survive, but in doing that it seemed he had indirectly destroyed who she was. He could never forgive himself for that, but he could at least keep her alive now.

He grabbed a notebook and pen from his room and rushed back. His head felt a little fuzzy, and if he didn't wrap the conversation up soon, he would admit something that would only be harmful in the light of day. He had hurt her enough. He wouldn't do that to her.

Better she believe the lies he spewed three years ago. Apologies would not make things better now, so best to just move forward.

He handed her the notebook without comment, ignoring the pinkish tint the alcohol had brought to her cheeks. She opened the journal, and a folded piece of paper fell into her lap. She started to open it, but Carver panicked and said, "That's not for you!"

He snatched it out of her hand, shoving it into his pocket. He didn't apologize for his outburst, though he knew he should.

Like she had earlier, she chewed her lower lip, waiting for him to sit on his side of the hallway before she said anything. The page was the journal entry he had written earlier. He tore it out to burn it, but got distracted and left it in the book. It was all of the thoughts he had about her. She could never see and never know.

"I think if we do this, they should legitimately be rules of engagement. The rules should have more to do with our ability to complete the mission than…us."

"Okay," Carver answered softly, feeling guilty for yelling at her.

"Rule 1, the mission comes first." She waited for him to respond, and when he nodded, she added the first rule to the book.

"Rule 2, no flirting."

"With each other," Clara added.

Carver shook his head, "No. No flirting with anyone. Each other or anyone else. The mission will go better if we agree that flirting won't be a part of the trip in any way."

She silently weighed the idea before nodding and writing the second rule.

"Rule 3, no physical contact."

"That's a given," Carver interjected.

"Still making it a rule."

He scoffed but didn't comment waiting for her to finish writing. Once she looked up he said, "Rule 4, no mention of our history–like we talked about earlier."

"Yeah." That rule was as much for him as her. If she asked him why he had ended things the way he had, the truth might come out. He had done too much to her already; he didn't want to add that to the list. "Rule 5," her eyes snapped up to his, daring him to challenge what she was about to say, "No defending the other person beyond what is necessary for the mission."

He felt his heart sink a little. He knew beyond a shadow of a doubt he would do whatever it took to keep her alive. But she was asking him not to. She held his gaze, her eyes hard, waiting for him to agree. He knew he had to, so he nodded yes. Relief washed across her face and she wrote the rule. She certainly was determined to fulfill this assignment.

"Rule 6, if there's only one bed, I'll take the floor."

Clara rolled her eyes, clearly forgetting his earlier comment. "That's not a rule. If there's only one bed, *we'll take turns* sleeping on the floor. Don't try to be chivalrous." She didn't give him a chance to respond before writing the rule the way she had decided it should be.

When Clara was finished, she handed him the journal to approve. He nodded. "I feel like we should sign this in blood or something," he quipped.

She shrugged. "Works for me." She pulled a knife out of her boot—he hadn't even known it was there—and sliced a small cut in the tip of her finger. She held her finger up, letting the blood pool and handed him the knife hilt first.

He took it gingerly. Though he had been trained with weapons, the part of being a spy he enjoyed the most was that he rarely ended up in combat. He forced himself not to flinch as he cut. He met her eyes, and they pressed their fingers to the page, careful not to brush against each other, sealing their agreement.

"Feel better?"

"Yeah," Clara responded. "See ya tomorrow." Just like that she was gone, leaving Carver still sitting in the hallway holding the blood sealed page in front of him. He read the rules again, sighing deeply as he realized just how hard he would have to work to abide by them.

Rule 1: The mission comes first.

Rule 2: No flirting.

Rule 3: No physical contact.

Rule 4: No mention of our history.

Rule 5: No defending the other person beyond what is necessary for the mission.

Rule 6: If there's only one bed we take turns sleeping on the floor.

5 CLARA

Clara practically ran back to her room. She closed the door carefully, holding the doorknob until she could slip it in place soundlessly. Completely alone, she slumped against the door, sliding to the floor and almost knocking her mirror off in the process.

She couldn't do this. She couldn't spend the next couple weeks around him. Not like this. *I have to be strong.* She reminded herself over and over, but she felt like all of the work she had done in the last few years evaporated in his presence. And when they sealed their rules, she caught his scent and it threw her back to all those moments wrapped in his arms. She had almost hesitated.

Had almost given into weakness and leaned into him. She wanted to. God knows she wanted to. "Okay," she whispered to herself, "This is just a test, right? A hard assignment to once again prove your worth. You've done this before." She paused, pulling down her ponytail and letting her hair fall around her shoulders. It would be smart to cut or shave it; she would have if she were a soldier, but for her purposes she kept it long to blend in. And because she liked it. "Well, not this exactly. But you can do this."

Her speech did little to encourage her, but it did keep her from completely giving up. As she had so many times before, she pulled down one of the books her father had left her. She traced her fingers over the lines in the pages, running one gently over her father's hastily scrawled notes on the edges. This was why she fought.

Because he fought. Because he died fighting. And though it may damn her, she was her father's daughter. A fact both her mother and Carver had reminded her of through the years. Strong-willed, rebellious, but she had never been as strong as him. He had been a spy, like Carver. She wondered for a moment what her father would think of his daughter having so much blood on her hands. Would he be proud she attempted to follow in his footsteps, or disappointed in the number of lives she had taken?

She put the book back, and pulled the sketchbook onto the floor with her. On her hands and knees, she reached underneath her bed and tugged out a small box. It was filled with the braided bracelets Reese gave her each time she left for a mission. A reminder that someone wanted her to return unscathed.

Clara opened the sketchbook to a new page, and took a pencil from the box. The scritch-scratch of lead across paper helped to slow her heart rate, and she drew until her eyelids grew heavy and her lines were no longer precise. She'd give it to Reese in the morning. A sketch for a bracelet. A bond the years hadn't broken.

She almost fell asleep slumped against the door, but managed to return the pencil to the box and slide it back under her bed before turning the light off and slipping between the covers. This was the last moment of peace she'd have for awhile, and she didn't know how well she would sleep in the coming weeks with Carver so near. If today was any indication, even his presence was a bane.

She was relieved to awake from a dreamless sleep. It made it easier to ignore the anxiety spiraling in her stomach. She dressed carefully, again meticulous in the storage of each weapon. She braided her hair back, leaving it hanging over her shoulder. Today was just transportation. She wouldn't need to have her hair back yet.

Clara joined her class in the mess hall, being cautious to keep her expression neutral. She didn't want anyone to know just how much she already hated this assignment. She forced a smile when Reese plopped down across from her.

"So?? You were super quiet last night, but you leave today. I want to know everything. Well, everything you're allowed to tell me." Reese's enthusiasm comforted Clara, not everything had changed. Though it felt like her life had been suddenly upstaged, in reality everything was the same.

She shrugged, finishing her bite of food before responding, "I was given an assignment with a spy. We're heading to enemy territory, but that's all I can say."

Reese's eyes widened, "Oh my gods. A spy? Isn't that where..." her voice trailed off, her eyes searching Clara's face for the answer to the question she wouldn't dare ask.

Clara forced herself to calmly take another bite of food. Her stomach churned, but she willed herself to keep it down. "Yeah." She admitted.

It didn't seem possible, but Reese's eyes widened further. "And is he..." Another question she couldn't quite bring herself to ask.

"Yeah."

"Well crap." The confession stunned Reese into silence, and though it only lasted a few minutes, it was the most silence their table ever had. "Why would Command do that to you? They have to know your history."

"Maybe it's another test," Clara responded, but there was no conviction in her tone. "As if we haven't proven ourselves enough already."

"I can't imagine that's the reason. It must be because they think individually you're both the best equipped for this. I'd ask you how you're feeling about *him*, but I know you're not exactly big on talking about feelings. Sooooo maybe I should just change the conversation?"

Clara shrugged, unwilling to share anything that could further the appearance of her weakness. She had become so strong, but *him*. Him.

Reese hesitated before changing the conversation, and spoke animatedly about the interaction she had with one of the newer guys yesterday. She raised her eyebrows suggestively as she repeated their conversation, and Clara figured this was Reese's newest conquest.

Reese had the bubbly personality of a cheerleader, combined with a decent amount of brain power and daddy issues. It was the perfect combination to find a new bed mate in this sector. Interesting enough to wrap them around her finger, but careless enough to end up in their sheets. Clara had too much melancholy and darkness hidden in her soul to go that route, but she would be lying if she said she didn't enjoy hearing Reese's stories.

All too soon, it was time for her to report. Reese wrapped her arms around Clara's waist. She was significantly smaller, and Clara's head practically rested on top of hers as Clara hugged Reese back. Clara missed Reese on these trips. Even if most days it seemed she suffered through the endless chatter, it was usually a welcome respite from the constant droning in her own head.

Reese pulled back, fixing Clara with a glare. "Come back alive. Okay? You have to come back alive. You aren't allowed to die. You hear me?" She pulled a bracelet from her pocket, slipping it over Clara's wrist.

Clara allowed a small smile to slip out from her mask, "Okay Reese. I promise. I'll come back alive. And when I'm back, you'll have to tell me all the progress you've made with the new kid. Garrett, right?"

Reese grinned, twirling one of her many braids around her finger. "Yep. Be safe."

Reese pulled her into one last hug, "Oh, I almost forgot." Clara handed Reese the folded drawing. Reese grinned, but didn't open the page. Their tradition. Each exchanging small pieces. The reminder that neither was actually alone.

Clara walked out of the mess hall, heart pounding but footsteps sure. She stopped by her room to grab her bag, checking her appearance again to make sure everything was in place. She carefully replaced the book she read last night on the stack, making sure the three were perfectly aligned before she left.

She would never admit it to anyone, but the details helped her stay focused. Everything had to stay in place. Everything had to stay perfect. Otherwise her grip on reality might slip. Slowly at first, and then it all became chaos. She had developed routines. Tendencies that she hadn't had before that were now a part of everyday life. Without conscious thought, her blankets were folded perfectly and the books were aligned. She just did it and looked around her room, satisfied with the returned order.

She threw her bag over her shoulder and began the trek to command. Her heart thundered, every beat trying to throw off the breathing rhythm she was determined to keep. This was what she had wanted. The recognition, the assignments. This is what she had worked for. The favor, the eventual power. This was who she was now. The Eclipse. This was just another assignment.

Liar.

6 CARVER

He hadn't slept at all. He had a feeling he wouldn't. His dreams were rarely kind to him, and after the day he had, he knew they would be worse than usual. It wasn't just the fear that kept him from slipping beneath the sheets, but the restless energy that surged through his veins as he tried to solve this problem.

Clara. The one problem he could never solve.

He thought he had solved it. He pushed her away, believing it was best for both of them. They could live their separate lives and she could stay alive. At least in his mind. She was never supposed to remain an operative. When she did, at least their sectors were separate enough he would never have known if she didn't survive. He was okay with that. It was better to assume she was still alive than to know she wasn't.

And now she was back in his life. On the most dangerous assignment he had ever been given and he had sworn *not* to protect her. *Like hell I won't.*

This endless circle of thoughts landed him in the training room, sprinting until he couldn't breathe anymore. He hoped the lack of oxygen would stifle the increasingly stressful thoughts, but instead it seemed to perpetuate them. His body's desperation for air, and his desperation for something to be different combined and left him feeling even more panicked.

"I thought I might find you here." Carver snapped to attention as his mentor walked in. Nate shook his head, dismissing Carver's posture. Carver slumped back against the wall as Nate approached.

"This isn't a normal assignment." Nate often received more information than Carver would receive from Command, and some form of friendship, loyalty or responsibility let him break the rules and share what he wasn't supposed to.

"Just because of Clara?" Pain stabbed his chest at the feel of her name when he spoke, but he didn't let it show.

Nate paused, "She received a different assignment." His eyes skipped across the room as he stepped closer to Carver, "I'm not sure what she was given, but the two of you aren't being sent because of a biological weapon."

Carver wanted to ask more questions, but Nate silenced him with a look. "Command has a history of this. Most operatives don't live long enough to understand the conniving behind the scenes, but you're reaching that point."

"They don't want us to succeed?"

"Oh, they want you to succeed. They're right in thinking you and Clara are the best equipped for this. They also want to see if you'll break. You'll either return victorious and be brought into leadership, or you won't. They're fine with either option."

Nate shook his head. "I don't know what you saw on your last assignment, but they weren't thrilled about it." Carver opened his mouth but Nate held up a hand, "I don't want to know. I'm only here to give you a warning."

He placed his hands on Carver's shoulders, "Be smart." A better benediction than most people's be safe. Then Nate left, leaving Carver's head spinning even more.

He skipped breakfast, a habit he too often fell into. Instead, choosing to lie on his mattress and stare at the ceiling. What had Clara been told? Was this assignment retribution from his previous one?

He left his blankets bundled at the foot of his bed, and ignored the clothes still on the floor. He had thrown together what he needed, and the rest would still be there to deal with when he came back. No need to deal with it now.

He was at Command long before the instructed time, leaning against the hallway wall, watching the doors. They wouldn't open until it was time, but still he stared. He kept waiting for this to be a nightmare. He was hoping his eyes would open, he'd wake up and discover he was on the mission alone. He wouldn't have to live out his worst fear. He wouldn't have to watch Clara die.

She wouldn't die, of course. He told himself this over and over. It became a resounding anthem in his head. *I will keep her alive.* Whatever the cost, whatever it takes. *You promised you wouldn't,* the more logical voice whispered back. *Technically,* he argued, *I only promised I wouldn't protect her more than I would protect someone else. She doesn't know how I would protect someone else.* The logical voice continued to disagree, and though he looked calm to any passerby, his inward war continued to rage.

It only grew louder when she stepped into view. She stopped when he saw her, and he could have sworn he stopped breathing. Such a stupid reaction, but there it was. She was in full gear this morning. Black leggings grooved to conceal weapons, black jacket with armor across the shoulders and chest, dark brown straps across her body to hold more weapons. All complete with a dark hood, which was currently left down around her shoulders. He closed his mouth quickly, hoping she didn't notice the way his jaw dropped at the sight of her.

He had never seen her in full armor before. That was no excuse for his reaction, but *damn,* she was stunning. Even if she was looking at him like he was the target. Maybe especially because she was looking at him like he was the target.

She approached him, never relaxing her perfect posture. "You're here early." She shifted her bag on her shoulder before setting it at her feet.

He shrugged, "Blame it on excitement?"

Her lips twitched, "I'm sure it's something like that." He couldn't tell if she was resisting a smirk or a scowl.

Carver wanted to ask how she slept, how she felt about this trip. He wanted to ask about the past three years, fill in the blanks he himself had created between them. He wanted to understand what she had been through to become this shadow of her former self. Or the her he remembered, at least. But he wouldn't.

They hadn't even left for the trip yet, and he was already struggling to follow the rules. *This is gonna suck.* Plus, he already knew Clara was hiding things from him—whatever Command told her when he was ushered out of the room.

Instead of any of the things he truly wanted to know, he merely commented, "This should be fun." In a way he meant it: if your definition of fun was burning yourself just to tear the blister off.

"It will be something." She met his eyes, "I'm assuming you brought the list?"

He nodded, lightly patting the pocket over his chest. Fitting, that the list was so close to his heart. It would serve as a reminder of what he had to keep caged.

They stood in an awkward silence, neither daring to offer something that could be so easily shot down, until the doors opened and they were summoned in. Carver watched her throw her bag back over her shoulder, resisting the urge to carry it for her. Old habits die hard. She was more than capable; that wasn't the issue. But there was something in him that wanted to do whatever it took to make her life easier.

The same woman from the day before stared down at them. Her eyes were softer this time, as though she knew she was sentencing them to death, or something far worse. What other option did any of them have?

"Are you both ready?" Her voice was also softer today, and that, more than anything else, gave Carver the first sliver of fear. *Just keep her alive. That's all you have to do.* A reminder to himself, but he stopped himself from looking at Clara. How could he keep her alive when he didn't even know what she was told to do?

They nodded, and Carver forced the thoughts in his brain to slow down enough to focus on the moment in front of him. Nothing bad was happening yet. They were simply beginning their transport.

"Remember, the first two days will be spent on the train. Then you will have two days to trek the final 20 miles and make it into the city on time." She pursed her lips, "If you succeed, you will both come back as heroes." Carver saw Clara straighten her already straight spine out of the corner of his eye, "If you don't, well, I don't need to tell you how things end. We wish you the best of luck. May the gods be with you."

An old phrase. No one actually believed in the gods anymore. If they ever existed, they were long dead or content to avoid all things to do with humanity. But Carver understood the sentiment in the statement. If there is some greater power, may they assist you in every aspect of the journey.

He would need help from the gods to keep Clara's rules of engagement. He would need help from the gods to keep her alive.

They saluted Command and were each handed bigger backpacks

with materials they needed for their journey. He stopped long enough to put his smaller bag in the top. They walked in silence to the train. The rain fell in slow, massive droplets. He would have shivered had it not seemed emasculating.

Clara turned her face up to the rain, letting the drops fall across her cheeks like tears. He didn't know why he made that comparison. She looked far calmer than he felt as they boarded the train. The train was designed for carrying cargo, and they were put in one of the back cargo cars with a singular window. The glass was thick, keeping the inside of the train dark. A few crates were stacked throughout the train, as well as pillows and blankets that were added specifically for them.

There was no huge farewell as they boarded, no farewell as they left everything behind. It felt anticlimactic to have the large door closed. Everything felt like it had changed, but it was just another assignment. *Just another assignment.*

Carver continued to stare at the door long after it was sealed. The train jolted, causing him to stumble so he belatedly sat down. Two days. Two days in this box with Clara. If there were gods, they must be desperate to have him pay for his mistakes.

7 CLARA

Clara learned the cost of high expectations at a young age. The world didn't care how hard she worked, or how desperate she was for a certain outcome. No, the world spun the same way it always had and expectations were only good for creating disappointment.

By the time she trained as a Viper, Clara had lost all expectation of the world. Her only expectation was of herself. To survive and become the best. She worked hard, knowing that eventually the work would pay off, and having this gut feeling that her life would change. She had to admit, she was right on one part. Her hard work did, in fact, change her life. But the way it changed her life felt like a cruel joke in comparison to what she secretly wanted.

Now, she wanted to remain as far away from Carver as she could. It wasn't a rule, but subconsciously it became one. The second the door slid closed, she moved towards the back of the car, grabbed a blanket, and climbed on top of one of the boxes. She wouldn't admit it, but in the moment he stood there, she replayed the interactions from the night before.

Including the split second she considered embracing him. A bad idea, of course–possibly the worst.

When he stumbled as the train lurched, she covered her mouth to avoid laughing. He didn't look up at her, so she allowed the smile to remain another minute, enjoying the thought of how things could have been.

Then it hit her. Things could have been different. They could have gone on this assignment *together*, as true partners in crime. They would have climbed their ranks, still gotten married, and eventually been here, but so much better. Stronger together. But they weren't. They weren't. Because of the choice *Carver* had made.

She hated him for it. He decided and she could do nothing except pick up the shattered pieces.

He broke the silence first, "We're stuck here for the next two days. We should try to converse or at least be civil."

"Wasn't in the rules." She bit back.

He rolled his shoulders to relieve tension, and the muscles rippled under his thin shirt. He had already shed his jacket, and truthfully, Clara wished his jacket had remained on. It wasn't fair that his well defined physique was clearly visible through his clothing. *Damn, maybe that should've been a rule*, she thought salaciously.

"It's not against the rules either. And we did agree that we would have to figure out how to trust each other for the sake of the assignment."

"Fair," she conceded. She wanted to talk to him. Well, truthfully, she wanted to yell at him. She wanted him to know exactly how much he'd hurt her. She wanted him to know that he made the last three years of her life hell. She became reckless, blaming him for half the scars scattered across her body.

Simultaneously, she wanted him to believe that he didn't have an effect on her, that with or without him she would have become this strong. He didn't get to hurt her.

"What do you want to talk about?" She deadpanned, giving him all the freedom to begin.

"What was your favorite part of training to be a *Viper*?" The question caught her off guard, and for once she didn't have a snarky remark.

She combed through the memories as they rushed by in a blur. The training, the blood on her hands, her body, the hollow eyes of those she had killed, the fear, the rush, the adrenaline. Nope, none of that. She could say any one of those, but none of those things were her favorite. She could at least answer him honestly.

"My trainer hated me from day one. He forced me to go harder than anyone else. He wanted me to break; he actually told me he was trying to break me. A team is only as strong as its weakest unit, and he was absolutely convinced I was the weakest unit.

One day about three months in I finally won a fight. The other girl was bigger, and everyone thought she would destroy me. But I was faster. So fast that I took the advantage, and she had to be helped to the healing room." Clara smiled at that, "A strange thing to be proud of, I know. But it was the first time my trainer looked at me with anything other than derision. The next day, he told me he was wrong about me and he was proud of how seriously I was taking training. Everything changed after that moment."

She didn't tell Carver that she'd felt capable–the first time she'd actually felt strong because she was strong. No outside force had helped her. She had done it herself, and there was a confidence that came with that capability. She didn't think Carver could understand that. He had always been strong. He had always been so brilliantly perfect in every discipline. School, basic training, making friends. He was always everyone's favorite. It felt nice to be on her own and be someone's favorite.

He didn't respond for several minutes, and she couldn't help but wonder what he was thinking. Would he mock her for her favorite memory?

"I'm proud of you, Clara." He replied softly.

She clenched her teeth instinctively, feeling like he'd hit her. "You don't get to say that to me."

He nodded, agreeing, and it fueled her anger. She wanted to fight. She wanted to scream. She wanted to yell and say all the things she said to him in her dreams. "You don't get to say that to me," she repeated more harshly. "You don't get to pretend we're okay and you're my friend now." She chose her words carefully, but allowed her tone to stay as angry as she felt. She wouldn't be the one to break the rules. "We're on an assignment. We're working together. That's it." She felt her heart break as she said the words; she forced her voice to stay strong and not do the same.

"You're right." He admitted, sounding tired. "I'm sorry."

She wouldn't accept his apology. Wouldn't give him that courtesy. Instead, she wrapped her blanket around her shoulders and pressed herself further into the corner on the crates. She was done talking to him.

8 CARVER

It's my own fault for asking. Carver knew that. His question was an attempt to glimpse the last three years of her life, an unrealized hope that he might mend what he had destroyed. He shouldn't have asked.

He knew her too well. He knew her well enough to understand why her trainer singled her out–knew her well enough to know the first few weeks she showed up with dark circles under her eyes and irises rimmed in red. He knew how the backlash would have inspired her to push harder.

He didn't lie to her. He was proud. She had become so much stronger than he thought she could be. But was it worth the price she paid? The price he forced her to pay? He had kept her alive, so he had kept his promise. Until now, at least.

She pretended to sleep for the next couple hours, and Carver was honestly relieved she didn't ask him about his favorite memory. It was for the best. After all, he couldn't give her an honest answer. He would have told her some BS story about the first time he was called into Command.

It had, of course, been a defining moment in his career. As he stood before them, he knew his father would have been pleased with how far he had come, and he was grateful his mother couldn't worry about where he was headed.

The train slowed to a stop. They were in a smaller town, far outside the city walls. He stood up and stretched, trying to roll the tension from his shoulders. "Where do you think we are?"

He almost shrugged or replied snarkily, but if she was willing to talk to him suddenly, he wouldn't waste it. "I'm not sure. We've been traveling for at least a few hours. We're at least three hundred miles outside of Quorath."

"I'm sorry I snapped at you earlier." She murmured.

He looked at her from the side of his eye. They both stood, facing the door, waiting to be released. She still looked stern, but unless he was going crazy, she did at least look a little softer. "Don't worry about it," came his easy response.

Inwardly, he felt victorious that she was actually talking to him again.

The metal squealed as the train door opened. "Conductor said we'll be here for about an hour. A good time to do your business and get some food."

Carver nodded in appreciation, "Thank you. We'll do that." The boy walked away as soon as Carver acknowledged him.

He turned to Clara, unsure what to do next.

Would Clara want to stay with him as they entered the city? Or would she want to do her own thing? He knew Command must have given her the same package he received as they boarded. A package with dried food, iodine for cleansing water, money, and a few other items he hoped he wouldn't need. There was also a note he hadn't bothered to read yet. It would be specific instructions for the mission and he wasn't ready to prepare for that.

He secretly hoped it detailed more of what Nate mentioned to him–that Command wasn't blindsiding him the way it felt like they were. Why would they cut Carver out? He was the most trusted spy. What had Clara done to warrant more trust than him? Or was this another test for him individually?

Carver's mind ran circles; he debated asking Clara to get food with him, or going his own way. He didn't want to ask, but he did want her to know he wouldn't mind her company. His deliberation was a waste of time. Clara hopped down from the train, and disappeared into the crowd without a second look. He shouldn't have felt disappointed. They were partners on this assignment, not friends–never friends. They couldn't be friends again.

He desperately wished things could be different. The list of reasons replayed in his head, the ever ongoing battle.

Carver stepped down from the train car, and slipped right into the crowd. No one gave him a second look as he walked down the road glancing at the different shops. He found a small inn that promised a home cooked meal. If he had an hour, he'd stop for food.

The inside of the inn was dark, and the lights flickered slightly, but the food smelled amazing. He was ushered from the front to a seat, and he nearly cursed when he passed Clara. He was seated at a table directly behind hers, and she glared at him as he walked by.

The second the waitress walked away, Clara turned in her seat. "Stalking me now?" She asked gruffly.

It took him a second to formulate a response. She had never been harsh. She had barely been able to stand up for herself. And now? This new version of her was kinda hot. He smiled lightly, attempting to appear far more relaxed than he actually felt. "Actually, I had no idea where you went. I saw the advertisement for home cooked food outside, and decided it sounded good. Running into you was mere coincidence." His smile grew a tiny bit at her frustration. She could be angry with him all she wanted as long as she kept talking to him.

"Uh huh. You just happened to end up in the same room, one table behind me."

He shrugged, "Coincidence. It's not a very big town in case you didn't notice."

She continued to glare at him, "We're already stuck together on the train."

"Is that so? I hadn't noticed. If you're going to keep talking to me, you might as well join me." The second he said it, he kicked himself for offering it. They were already sharing so much time on the train, and the more time he spent with her, especially unrequired time, the harder it was for him to follow the rules.

At first, to his relief, she looked ready to object; but she stirred slowly and begrudgingly sat across from him. They slipped into silence as both stared at the menu in front of them. Carver kept his eyes glued to the page.

Somehow the sarcasm and sass she used to *hate* from him is what caused her to sit with him now. He wasn't entirely sure what to do with that information, but if that was how she wanted to play this he could oblige. The waitress returned and if she had any questions about the two of them joining each other, she kept them to herself. "What can I get for you today?"

Clara placed her order first, and then the waitress turned to Carver. "And what about you, love? What'll you have?"

The waitress tilted in his direction as she asked, the neckline of her outfit low enough to provide Carver with a direct shot of her cleavage. He kept his eyes on her face, and ordered the roast beef with carrots and potatoes. "Is that gonna be all for you, love?"

"Yes ma'am, unless you have anything else, Clara?" Clara shook her head no, handing her menu to the waitress.

The waitress took her menu, and then reached for Carver's,

intentionally brushing her hand across his. "I'll be back with your food shortly."

Clara laughed, the sound so reminiscent of times past that Carver almost flinched. "We've barely started our trip and you're already getting hit on. That has to be some kind of a record. Good job with not flirting back by the way." She raised her water glass to him in jest.

He smiled lightly in return, though his entire body felt tense, "So she **was** flirting with me."

Clara rolled her eyes, "There's no way you couldn't tell. She all but forced you to look down her shirt. Don't tell me you didn't notice that."

"I'm not a saint; I noticed." He mumbled, heat flaring into his cheeks. He rolled his shoulders backwards as he grabbed his water.

"I don't think that takes from your sainthood. You did a better job at looking away than I would have." He shifted uncomfortably, not sure how to respond.

Their food arrived, and they spent the rest of the meal alternating between semi-comfortable silence and insignificant banter. It scared Carver a little how much easier things were between them already and he worried they could easily slip into old habits. Even with their history, the break-up, the pain, it seemed the walls of protection were already being dismantled–word by word, laugh by laugh. It had to stop. They'd built the walls, and Carver needed them to stay there. For Clara's sake.

He ended things for a reason, and that reason was just as valid today as it was three years ago. Yes, he wanted her to forgive him. Selfishly. So selfishly. He only needed her to trust him enough that he would be able to keep her alive.

He hadn't bargained for how quickly they became familiar with one another again. He had to stop it before it was too late.

9 CLARA

The second Carver finished his food he excused himself. Clara didn't see him again until they were both on the train. "Food was good." She commented as she climbed back up to her perch on the boxes.

Carver grunted in response. He was already lying on the ground. His eyes flickered closed, and he added no further comment, ending her attempt at conversation. He had tried so hard to converse with her at lunch in an effort to be a tad friendlier, she thought–for the sake of the assignment, of course.

It surprised her that he was unresponsive now. Surprised her, and offended her. It was stupid to think he had changed or they could be friends again. *We can't be friends again.* She reminded herself. Too much had happened between them. She couldn't just forgive and forget. *I won't.*

She kept her eyes open this time. The small window provided enough light, but the glass was smudged and scratched so she couldn't see any scenery. It was all just a blur. Like the past three years. It all felt like a blur.

And now, in the same space as Carver, everything felt more real. She could hear his every breath, feel his presence in the atmosphere. Though it grated on her nerves she couldn't shut the awareness of him down. She knew she could only lie to herself for so long, and at some point she would have to address the reasons she hated him so much. But for now, she re-focused on the assignment.

The packet Command gave her included a journal and map. She ran her fingers across the locations, using the name she had spotted at the previous town and her limited knowledge of train routes to guess where they were. If her guess was correct, they were making better progress than she thought.

She continued to trace her finger along the page until she reached Noxvalis. Even on the map it looked formidable. The walls surrounding the city were massive and marked by small, heavily guarded, gates. They would never have a shot at entering the city if it wasn't for the party.

Clara pulled out the page that had her identity. She was recorded as Clara Brown. A basic name that wouldn't draw any attention. Her occupation said she worked in the clothing industry, and was coming to view the fashions from her homeland Calyndor. She knew Carver's paperwork listed the same homeland. They couldn't avoid being seen together, so it had been decided their cover was a married couple.

Command had sprung that final edict this morning. She had almost scoffed–had almost begged them not to make her do that. But she was a soldier. She would do as she was told.

As if executing the most notorious ruler wasn't enough of a challenge.

A sealed envelope fell out of the journal. She lifted it carefully, glancing down to make sure Carver wasn't watching as she broke the seal.

"The Raven has the details on how to retrieve the weapon. Your job is to kill everyone who witnesses your entrance into the lab."

She bit her lip. Blood on her lip, more blood on her hands.

"As instructed, you will leave the Raven in the lab to find the biological weapon. You will determine how to best draw the king out to assassinate him after the initial assignment. The vials must be retrieved; the king assassinated. Once inside, the Raven is no longer your concern."

No longer my concern. In other words, if she could escape with the vials, she didn't have to bring him with her. She could leave him to his own devices.

She stared at her hands then shifted her gaze to Reese's bracelet. The black and white strands intertwined, and she twisted it around her wrist. Reese usually gave her colorful ones, but Clara thought this one may be her favorite, a wistful thought that the world could be black and white.

Carver turned over in his sleep, and Clara's eyes caught on his face. She expected him to look restful in sleep, but his face contorted–eyebrows scrunching together, jaw set firmly, muscles randomly twitching. She looked back to her paperwork, her stomach churning.

She jumped when he cried out, desperately scrambling from the boxes to reach him. Her mind didn't process what she was doing, it was just instinct. She banged her knee on one of the corners and swore under her breath.

She paused as she reached him, hands hovering over his shoulders to shake him awake. *No physical contact. It's one of the rules.* She reminded herself, pulling her hands back and intertwining her fingers in her bracelet as he cried out again. "Carver, Carver?" She said his name softly at first, then louder until he awoke. "Carver?" She said again as he squinted up at her. The second his eyes opened, he scrambled back from her, bracing himself on his forearms.

His breaths came in quick bursts, and Clara was concerned he would hyperventilate. "What happened?" she asked, keeping her voice as soft as she could. Her eyes scanned him, looking for any kind of damage beyond the terror in his eyes.

He shook his head, trying to shake her questions away. "Just a nightmare," he answered, falling back into his normal look of nonchalance.

"You cried out in pain."

"It was just a nightmare." He emphasized like it meant nothing. Like her heart wasn't still racing from watching him writhe in his sleep. "I get them sometimes. It's not a big deal."

"Sometimes?" She questioned, knowing she shouldn't press this, but unable to see him in pain though she'd never admit it, "Is that why you have dark circles under your eyes? Do you ever sleep normally? Is *this* normal for you?"

"Don't ask questions you don't want the answer to," he warned, his voice gruff and frustrated. Frustrated at her. For gods sake she was just trying to help.

Clara quickly backed down. Of course she got in trouble for trying to help. Once again, it's far better to be standoffish than to put yourself out there and get rejected. "Sorry for asking." She said sharply, and turned her back to him as she stepped toward the crates.

He exhaled deeply. "That's not what I meant, Clara." She paused, but didn't face him. The sound of her name on his lips sent a forbidden electricity through her veins. "I just meant, we agreed not to talk about our history. Or there being an us. So you can't take care of me."

She understood his confession, and knew she would have

reacted far worse than he if he had seen her weakness. She nodded, still not turning around, and climbed back to her perch.

Carver pressed the heels of his hands into his eyes, stretching out his neck as he did so. "I'm sorry I disturbed you with my nightmare." He met her eyes, and she had to look away.

"No problem." He was right, obviously. They had to stay professional. She couldn't take care of him, no matter how much she wanted to.

She collected all of her paperwork and brought it down to sit next to him, slipping the note back into her journal before he saw it. "We should create a game plan. We'll be here for one more full day, then two more stops. A stop tonight and a stop tomorrow afternoon before they drop us off. Then we'll spend the two days walking. It will be easier to plan now, here, than when we're walking across the wilderness."

"Good idea." Carver reached behind her for his pack, and she held her breath rather than risk catching a hint of his musk.

"I looked at the map earlier, and I think the main gate will be our best bet for getting in," Carver began. "It will be heavily guarded, but more people will be passing through so they won't check everything as thoroughly."

Clara nodded, "Agreed. How tall are the walls? Will we be able to leave over them?"

Carver shook his head, "No. They're over 20 feet tall, and each section of the wall is guarded. They also have snipers on all of these points," he pointed to sections just above the gates, "So that anyone who tries to escape can be easily shot down."

"Then we'll have to leave the same way we enter–with a group of people and pray they don't look at us too hard." She didn't explain she wouldn't be leaving with him. There was a reason Command hadn't told him she would stay.

"Pretty much," Carver admitted. "Unless our contact knows a way that isn't detailed on this map. Maybe there's a smaller gate."

"I don't like how much power one person has in this mission." Clara twisted the bracelet around her wrist until she noticed Carver staring. She clenched her hands into fists and put them in her lap.

He shrugged, gaze shifting from her hands back onto the maps. "It was her intel that sent us on this trip anyway."

"And we trust her?"

"Do you trust anyone?"

She could tell he meant the question genuinely, but she hated him for asking it. How could she trust anyone after him?

She spun her bracelet around her wrist again as they continued to pour over the map. There were so many details they had absolutely no control over. She couldn't control this assignment. All the plotting in the world wouldn't guarantee they came out alive.

10 CARVER

Carver wished he could have stopped the nightmare before Clara saw it. Not because of his pride, no, he couldn't care less if she thought he was weak. He didn't need to earn her affection. From the way she looked at him, he already had too much of it to be a good thing.

He didn't want her to see an episode because she couldn't help but care. Even now, after everything she had been through, her instinct was to care for him. And that terrified him. It terrified him to wake up from a dream where he watched someone torture her and see her standing over him, eyes wide, trying to help him. She needed to keep her distance. He *needed* her to keep her distance.

He couldn't explain that to her. He couldn't explain the reasoning behind all of the his choices. Not without breaking the rules. It was his duty, his highest purpose, to keep her alive. She was never supposed to end up here: the highest ranked assassin, stuck on a train with him for the riskiest mission he'd ever encountered.

He'd made a deal. They'd assigned her to assassins because she was weak and would be weeded out. Then she'd be safe. Outside of the war. Back with her mom who had begged him to do something. But that's not what happened. Clara proved them all wrong. He hated her for it, everything he did to keep her safe rendered worthless. But *damn.* He also loved her for it.

He didn't miss the note she slipped into her journal. Though curiosity plagued him, he ignored its throb, focusing instead on what she had asked of him.

Carver kept his back straight as they ran through potential plans, careful not to lean into her. He kept his own contingency in the back of his mind. He was fully willing to sacrifice himself if it meant getting her out alive. "I think only one of us should go into the labs. The other one should wait here," he pointed to a spot between the city and where the labs should be, "To keep guard and be ready for the escape."

He felt Clara stiffen beside him, "You're trying to protect me." It wasn't a question, and any defense he gave would only make him seem guiltier.

"There's no need for both of us to go into the lab." A logical response, but even he could feel its frailty. She weighed this, her blue eyes stormy in the darkening train car.

"No, I think we should both go in. We'll need each other to get the weapon out. They didn't tell us how big it is, or how we can conceal it." He was sure the details he was missing were on his note, but through his insane bout of stubbornness, he was still refusing to view it.

His mind scrambled to think of a rebuttal, but *screw it,* she was right. "You know I'm right," she prodded. Carver inhaled sharply. "You can just admit it." Admitting she was right wasn't the problem. The problem was he didn't want to put her in more danger than she had to be in. And she seemed all too willing to dive into the thick of it. Was that another thing he had created?

Was her reckless impulsivity a product of the hurt he had inflicted?

"We agreed," her voice was softer now, as if sensing his inner struggle. "The assignment comes first. For the sake of the assignment, we both need to go in. You can't protect me. Rules of engagement."

Carver wanted to shake off his frustration, to make a joke about how he was trying to be efficient, or that he would be the one to stay outside. But every idea he had seemed illogical and revealed too much. She couldn't know how much he cared. So instead, he patted the folded set of rules, "It's a rule for a reason," was the only response he could generate.

Clara fell silent for a while, and Carver attempted to collect his thoughts and figure out how to keep her safe. "Is this harder than you expected?" Her words came out as a whisper. He couldn't help but feel it was a question asked against her better judgment. That was a sentiment he understood too well.

"Yeah," *if only you knew how brutally hard this is for me. If only you knew that I want to throw you off this train to keep you safe. I would damn myself to death if I could keep you out of the lab. This was never supposed to happen.*

They never should have ended up here. If only she had followed the stupid plan. The plan he had crafted to keep her safe. To keep her from ending up here. She should have just stayed weak. Looking at her now, her raw strength and beauty, he was conflicted. She was too perfect. In danger, but perfect.

"Command had to have known. So why us?"

"We're the best. We've been trained so intensely we're past the point of emotions." Or, they should be past the point of emotions. He wasn't.

"I mean, I knew it would be hard," again, her words sounded

stilted like the admission was out of her control. "But," she exhaled, "How the hell did we end up here?"

"That's not a question we can explore." He emphasized where the rules were hidden. Something flashed across her eyes. His statement snapped her from her reverie.

"Right." She pulled the map up into her lap, examining it more closely. Carver watched as her walls went back up. Relief flooded his body as her cool composure returned, as she lengthened the distance between them in a single breath. He also felt disappointed, but that wasn't fair. They had to follow the rules.

Carver dozed off again at some point, and drifted back from sleep as the train slowed. "Next stop?" He asked. Clara shrugged, barely visible in the mostly dark train car.

The single light in the corner of the train flickered to stay alive. Its hazy glow cast moving shadows across the walls. "Do you think we're supposed to sleep here? Or get a room wherever we stop?"

He was trying to extend some form of olive branch, keep the communication open enough to protect her, but still professional. All in order to protect her. At least that's what he told himself.

"I'm sure we can do either." She stretched, pulling her arms over her head. Her shirt came untucked just enough to show her abdomen. He quickly looked away before his mind spiraled down the rabbit trail of other things that could happen to that shirt. "I, for one, wouldn't mind sleeping in an actual bed before things get serious."

"Fair."

Once again, the heavy metal slid aside to release them. "The conductor says we'll stop here overnight. They're loading cargo first thing in the morning. We'll head out at 7am sharp."

"Thank you," Clara replied. The boy nodded and walked further down the tracks to deal with other cargo.

"Should we find lodging then?"

"You can do whatever you want." The sharp edge was back in her tone, "I'm finding a room." Once again, she left him standing in the car as she walked into the town. Carver waited a few minutes, taking deep breaths and reining in his thoughts. He had to be careful. He cared too much, and she could tell.

She asked if it was harder than he expected, and the honest answer was…So. Much. Harder. She had moved on in her life, becoming strong, powerful, infamous, even. And he had become a far less version of himself. A brilliant spy, yes, but weaker in so many ways. She was the fire that burned in his life, and without her all that remained were ashes.

He dreamed about her every night. Always brutal. Always painful to watch. He'd seen her die more ways than he wished to recount.

He didn't know exactly what had triggered the nightmares. They started the week after he broke up with her. She had taken a piece of his soul he didn't know was expendable, and left him with the pain of processing every decision. He knew better than anyone, some decisions haunt you forever. The ones you can't unmake are the scariest.

11 CLARA

Clara was relieved when Carver didn't follow. She needed space and time away from him. She needed to breathe without his stifling presence. It was torture, bloody torture, sitting in the train with him. She was all too aware of what they could have been and what they weren't because of an entirely selfish decision on his part. Commitment issues. Sure. That's what everyone said to avoid the truth.

You're not good enough for me. Resounded through her head in his tone of voice. Why hadn't he just admitted it? He danced around the truth, and she hated it.

At least it would have been honest. But no one wants to say that. No one wants to explain they've decided they're better off alone. So they make up an excuse. "It's not you, it's me"; "I need to focus on myself right now"; "There's someone better out there for you"; or Carver's favorite, "You need to grow up." It was a realization he discovered five years into their relationship–a lie to cover what he actually meant.

He didn't stop there either. He emphasized her weakness and

inadequacies and blamed her for the end of their relationship. Too weak to continue. So desperate to be with him she followed him to the army. A mile long list of delusions, and he expected her to bear the weight.

It was true, she had followed him into the army, but he wasn't the reason she stayed.

The air tickled her skin, and she lifted her face to feel its caress. She didn't realize how hot the train car had become over their journey. The gentle breeze blew her hair back, so she took it out of the braid and enjoyed the relative quiet of the evening. Walking deeper into the town, the noises grew as the night hours turned the peaceful streets into a line of rambunctious bars.

She found a small inn, and approached the counter to request a room. The woman grimaced, "I'm sorry, ma'am, my last room was just reserved. You could try the bar across the street. Sometimes they have a room above available."

Clara was about to try her suggestion when a familiar form in the dining room caused her to pause. "You got the last room?" She didn't mean for her voice to come out so loudly, but she was exhausted and screw him. *Screw him.*

He shrugged, "Beat you here, I guess."

"You're insufferable."

He grinned, "All part of my charm."

"Charming me is against the rules."

He instantly sobered, "So it is. Well, then, call it my lack of charm perhaps? Anyways, good luck." He fake saluted her.

Her hand slipped down to the side of her waist, and she braced her palm against the knife hidden there. If only, if only. She could do it. He couldn't respond in time. She could put him out of her sight forever. Her heart clenched at the thought of him no longer existing. She could so easily pin him though. And then...too many options in that scenario. Could go either way, infatuation resurfacing or anger winning, and that was a risk she couldn't take.

He watched her, never taking his eyes off her face. He studied her face as if he could read her thoughts, and she stared back determined not to flinch.

She pulled her shoulders back, breaking the moment, "Sleep well," she said as genuinely as possible and stormed out before she had a chance to do anything else–especially anything involving her hands on him.

The second she was outside, her shoulders slumped. She was stronger than this. She had to be. In the past three years, she hadn't let anyone provoke her the way he just did. He so seamlessly slipped under her skin. He targeted her in a way no one else could. What she didn't understand was why.

Why had he broken up with her? Why had he pushed her away? Why, now, was he playing this game of back and forth? Pull her just a tiny bit closer to push her farther away. It was all a game to him. She wouldn't lose. She could play too, make him want her back and then refuse him.

The bar was full of half drunk men, and she kept her palm across her knife as she maneuvered to the counter. Thankfully no one attempted to intersect her. Anger was bubbling beneath her skin, begging for release and she might have stabbed someone for the hell of it.

She paid, and caught the key the bartender tossed to her. He immediately turned his attention to his other patrons, not bothering to see if she found her room, or even giving her the room number. The key had "11" carved into it, the marks half rusted and barely visible.

The steps were uneven. Most of them had begun to sink in. Clara stepped carefully, avoiding the dingiest spots. She curled her lip in disgust at some of the stains, at least she hoped they were only stains, spotting the floor and hallway.

Room 11 was near the end of the hall. The lock rattled as she tried it, and it took more than a couple grunts for her to actually make it inside. The door closed behind her easily enough, leaving her in a dark, unsanitary room. She thought through her options. She could sleep here, she could go back to the train and sleep out in the cold, she could…no. She definitely could not ask Carver for his help. That's one thing she would not do. She could sleep here. She would.

The bathroom at least had running water (she shouldn't have been surprised, but from the state of the building she wasn't sure anything had been updated in the last 100 years). Though when she turned the faucet on, it sputtered with a milky red liquid before cleaning out and running clear. She grimaced, staring at the stream, reluctant to touch it.

Again, she weighed her options. She could go back to the train. It was clean, if nothing else. This wouldn't be comfortable. She seriously wanted a shower. Pulling the curtain back, she almost gagged, 99% sure the giant splotch on the back wall was blood. She'd seen enough of it to know. She glanced at it again, hoping it would fade a little more. Clearly, it hadn't been cleaned well enough. She imagined running her finger nail over it, and cringed at the idea of the dried blood flaking off into her hand. Killing marks was one thing, showering with blood of an unknown origin, another.

She shuddered, her stomach churning.

While not usually squeamish, the chaos from the bar downstairs, her exhaustion, and the disgusting condition of the room began to overwhelm her. Things needed to be in order. They had to be in order.

Her stomach rumbled and her mind flipped over too many ideas. It was a weird feeling not knowing what to do. She went through each of her options again and again, still coming to the same conclusion. Her available options weren't good enough.

She could start with food then. Surely the bar had food.

The men were more drunk and raucous than before, and she had to resist slicing through someone's forearm as he tried to grab her when she walked by. She could have done it. She wouldn't have felt guilty. He clearly deserved it. But she didn't want to draw attention to herself.

There was only one spot open at the bar, and to Clara's vast relief it was at the far end of the counter. As secluded as she could possibly be among the number of wasted bodies. She sat, pressing herself against the wall. A slight shift in her seat and she could see the entire bar.

"What'll ya have?" The bartender finished drying a glass, throwing his dish towel over his shoulder as he moved in front of her.

Her brain spun as she tried to come up with something that sounded like a possible order. The drink she had with Carver the other night was the first time she had consumed alcohol since her one and only bad experience with it. Reese still hadn't let her live down that night. Her attempt at dancing on a table had not gone well.

"Vodka?" She knew how unsure she sounded.

He looked at her, assessing. "Want that in a mixed drink?"

She shook her head no, and he raised an eyebrow before grabbing the glass and pouring the shot.

"Do you have food?" She asked, cautiously. She had never been to a bar before. She felt conspicuously out of place, waiting for someone to come in and rip her away. She felt wrong, like the enjoyment people had in this place was too foreign for her to even witness.

He set a menu down in front of her, and served a couple of other people as she tried to read the faded words. She thought it was a fairly decent list for an establishment that specialized in liquor. She ordered the first thing that sounded filling, and picked up her shot glass as the bartender walked away.

She held the clear liquid in front of her face, peering quizzically into the glass. She knew a couple of her friends, well more Reese's friends, snuck off base to drink regularly. Reese had convinced her to join only once, and Clara had sworn she would never do it again.

The other night with Carver was a desperate attempt at normalcy. The drink had kept her from wrapping her hands around his throat. She wasn't certain what prompted her to try this tonight. She sniffed it, resisting the urge to down it. After a moment's hesitation, she took a tentative sip and coughed.

12 CARVER

Carver reveled in the satisfaction of having beaten Clara to the room for a full thirty seconds before his worry kicked in. He couldn't send her to the far less safe bar and let her stay there alone. He wouldn't. He was too much of a gentleman for that, even if Clara wouldn't acknowledge it.

Unfortunately, as soon as she walked out, the food he had ordered was set before him. Fine. He would eat, and then find Clara. He had to make sure she was okay. He had passed the bar on his way to this inn, and he wasn't a fan of what he'd seen inside. One man was thrown out only moments after he had passed. He could only imagine what they would think of her.

Her slender figure made her appear an easy target. And, even though she glared most of the time, she was still stunningly beautiful. At least in his eyes. Any number of drunk men would think she was an excellent catch. He couldn't force her into that.

He finished his food quickly, burning his mouth in the process. The taste lingered on his tongue, but as his feet hit the dirt road he couldn't remember what he'd ordered. He marched across the street, suddenly desperate to find her. What was he thinking prodding her into staying at the bar? He should have immediately offered her his room. It was his job to protect her. *Technically, she doesn't want your protection.* He tried to remind himself. But it didn't work. It *was* his job to protect her.

He stepped into the bar, eyes scanning the room quickly, but there was no sign of her. Maybe she was already in a room upstairs? Maybe she had given up on this idea altogether? He took another step into the room, ducking to the side as a giant man barreled toward him carrying more drinks to his table of inebriated friends.

"Crap, Clara," Carver muttered, all the more desperate to find her.

Finally, he saw her. His lungs fully expanded for the first time since he had turned her away at the inn. He walked towards her, but stopped to watch her instead. She picked up a shot glass and didn't seem to know what to do with it.

He smiled as he watched her deliberate. She sniffed it, grimacing, and it was the cutest thing he had witnessed in so long. He felt his heart tighten, and knew more than ever the only job he had on this assignment was to protect her. Command had asked him for enough. His kingdom was worthless to him if she wasn't in it. And after what he'd seen on the last assignment, his loyalty to Quorath was already strained.

She gingerly took a sip, and Carver laughed as her face contorted and she coughed. The bar was too loud for Clara to hear his laughter, and he shook his head as she attempted a second sip. It was either perfect timing or just luck, but the bar stool next to Clara emptied as Carver headed towards her. He quickly grabbed the vacant stool.

"You're supposed to take it as a shot, you know." He commented without looking at her, not needing to see the surprise and anger, maybe frustration, that appeared on her face.

"Because you're the expert on drinking?"

He shrugged. "Had a dark year. What can I say? Just another man who tried to find solace in the bottom of a bottle." Though, he had been relatively sober for the past year. Minus the drink with Clara the day before.

She set the glass on the counter, eyeing it with disdain. "I don't think this is for me."

"No, I wouldn't think it is. I was surprised you took the drink I offered you yesterday."

"Desperate times, desperate measures?"

"What can I get for you?" The bartender asked, pausing their conversation.

"Surprise me. Nothing frilly."

"You got it."

The bartender brought back a glass with a massive ice cube, and an amber liquid swirling around it. He offered the glass to Clara, "Want to try it?"

She shook her head. "I think I'm a one and done when it comes to alcohol. What are you doing over here anyway? I thought you were so happy in your nice, warm, cozy inn room."

He didn't miss how she emphasized the adjectives; her room here must not be any of those. He nodded, taking a sip of his drink and biting back his own grimace. He liked the harsh taste, but it had been awhile since he'd had anything quite this strong. "Yeah, about that," he tried to think through what he could offer as an excuse. She wouldn't just agree to stay with him. Plus, he couldn't stay with her. That was a terrible idea–a terribly fun idea. No, a terrible idea.

"She misread her room list. They had one room left and she accidentally overlooked it when you came in. By the time she realized, you were long gone. But she witnessed our interaction, asked if I knew you, and offered to let me reserve the room for you." The lies fell from his mouth so naturally he barely thought once he started talking. He slipped his hand into his pocket, removing his room key, "I reserved the room for you. Here's the key." He set it in front of her.

She grabbed the key, faster than he expected. "Wait really? I can't believe you did that for me." The look in her eyes encouraged him far more than it should have. She leaned in to whisper, closer than he was comfortable with. He could feel his body reacting as her breath touched his cheek, "The rooms here are bloody awful."

One statement and she leaned back, restoring the space between them and calming Carver's frantic heart, at least a little bit. He took another drink. He had to stay cool. He couldn't want her. He had to lie to himself about what he was currently feeling. It wasn't his fault she was so hot.

"I can only imagine," he responded, completely casual. Smooth was his middle name. "If you want to give me your key, I'll return it after you leave. I'm staying here to drink for a bit."

Her food arrived in front of her, and her eyes expanded with excitement. "This looks amazing." She took a bite and Carver stared back at his drink. It was too much like old times. She was so different from the girl he had loved, and yet, she was still the girl he loved. Time hadn't changed that the way he had hoped. "Was that your way of telling me I should eat and leave? Is my company that awful?"

She accented the statement with an eye roll, and it took everything in Carver not to grin back at her. "No, your company isn't that awful. Only partially awful." Then he did grin, hiding it behind his glass as he took another drink.

She balked at him, "Still such an asshole."

If she had omitted the word still, perhaps the flirtation would have continued a little longer. Perhaps Carver would have poked her like he used to, or she would have laughed, leaning a little too far into his space as she did so. But the word "still" was all it took to sober Carver up. He couldn't love her. He wasn't allowed to.

As if she noticed the change in his posture and attitude, Clara honed her focus on her food, not commenting to him again. He downed the rest of his drink, and immediately requested another one. She paid for her food, and hesitated as she stood.

"I'm finishing my drink." Carver remarked without looking at her, trying to get her to understand he wouldn't walk over with her. "I trust you're capable of making it across the street without my help." He put as much edge as he could into his tone, knowing she would jump on the challenge and leave him.

If she had something else she was planning to say, she chose not to. She walked away from him with a glare and stormed out of the bar. He stared straight ahead as he took another sip. He should be pleased. He still had a way of getting under her skin.

Carver finished his drink within a couple minutes, and decided to check out the upstairs room before he resigned himself to sleeping in the train. He had a feeling it was the best bet for him.

One look into the room, and he knew he wouldn't sleep there. He couldn't believe Clara was stubborn enough that she would have stayed there. Well, he could believe she was stubborn enough. But he still couldn't believe she would *actually* stay in that room.

He ran his hand through his hair and used the bathroom, as awful as it was, before making the brief trek back to the train car. The train was cold and hard, but he'd much rather be there than have Clara stay in that awful room.

13 CLARA

Clara woke up before the sun. She laid there for a while, the remnants of her dream still spinning through her mind. She hadn't dreamed about him in years. Most of her dreams consisted of training, scenarios, and the deaths she had witnessed or executed. It didn't bode well for the future that two days in his presence and her subconscious was already manifesting him through her dreams.

He truly was an asshole. How dare he.

She slid out from under the sheets and went through a basic stretching routine. She focused on her breathing. In and out. Forcing her body, and her mind, to relax. Her muscles screamed at her from the day on the train , and she decided that today she would be more active even if it was pacing in the train car.

She dressed for the day and braided her hair back loosely.

She stepped out of the room and her stomach growled at the smell of food. She had planned to walk directly to the train in an effort to beat Carver, but, she couldn't resist ordering a couple of burritos to-go. She debated getting one for Carver. He was kind enough to bring her the key to this place.

With that in mind, she took her food and walked briskly to the train. It wasn't raining, but a gentle mist still hung in the air. Clara breathed in deeply, exhaling all of the stress she had woken up with.

She wasn't still in love with Carver. Couldn't be. After all, she hated him. *He's an annoying, arrogant, perfect, insufferable asshole.* She knew part of her was lying. She had, against her better judgment, gotten him a burrito. Well, technically, she got herself three burritos. But she also knew she'd never be able to eat more than two.

He was already on the train when she reached it, and she was frustrated she hadn't beat him. He leaned against a crate of some new cargo, but he stood up as she approached. How long did he even sleep? The sun was just barely peeking over the horizon, still sending out rays of orange and pink.

The circles under his eyes were darker than the day before. His hair stuck up at weird angles and he yawned as she approached. He squinted, as the rising sun behind her bathed her in an orange glow. Had he slept at all?

"Drink too much?"

He yawned again, sat back down and leaned against the crate. "Define too much." He closed his eyes, crossing his arms across his chest.

Clara sat cross legged leaning against the wall a few feet from him. "Whatever you had," she muttered, unwrapping her first burrito. She sighed as she took her first bite. It was so worth stopping, and she was grateful she hadn't skipped getting the burritos.

Carver opened one eye, lazily glancing her direction. "You got food?"

"Of course." It didn't take her long to polish off the burrito, and as she unwrapped the second one she said, "These were bigger than I thought. I can only eat two. Do you want the last one?"

He fully glared at her for that statement, and she was a little surprised. "What, did you poison it or something?" *That is a brilliant way to complete this mission. I don't hate you enough to damn our kingdom.*

"Poison it?" She asked flatly, trying not to give him the satisfaction of a true reaction. "Who do you think I am?"

"I don't know, maybe the most renowned assassin?"

"You know what, jerk? I rescind my offer."

He went back to fake sleeping, and she angrily finished her burrito. She was tempted to eat the third one as well, just to prove something to him, though what it would prove she hadn't figured out yet. But it would definitely prove something. Unfortunately, she was too full for that.

A few minutes later, the man walked back, and glanced inside to make sure they were both there. He closed the door to the train car. The train rumbled to a start, and they were off.

"I shouldn't have picked a fight." Carver said softly, eyes staying closed.

"No, you shouldn't have." She glared at him, feeling safe doing so since he wasn't looking.

"Can I still take you up on the offer for your last burrito?"

"Seriously? You think you can yell at me and still have my food?" She answered harshly, and held out the last burrito.

He walked a little shakily as the train rumbled. Taking it from her, he answered, "Yeah, just like you know you would."

He stepped carefully back across the train to sit. "Thank you." He answered with direct eye contact, and after a couple seconds Clara had to look away. He was still so attractive to her. Even with how much weight he had lost and the circles under his eyes.

The unkempt hair? Well...that was actually an improvement over his perfectly gelled style. She wondered for a moment what it would feel like to run her fingers through his hair now. They wouldn't get stuck anymore, and he probably wouldn't even be annoyed at her for messing his hair up this time.

He caught her looking at him and raised his shoulders in a silent question. She could feel the heat rush to her cheeks. "Good burrito, right?" She pulled the journal out of her bag, pretending she was focused. She started drawing on the first page, trying to get her thoughts together. She couldn't look at him like that. She definitely couldn't imagine touching him. Rule 3. She certainly wouldn't break that one. An avid rule follower, she couldn't break any of them.

The train ride eventually smoothed out. Once she started sketching, she didn't want to stop. It was very simple at first. A sketch of the training room, the punching bag centered instead of in the corner. But then the edges grew darker, and weapons filled the room. A dark splotch of blood consumed the right corner as if someone had died just off the page. Morbid, but she felt calmer with the darkness outside of her mind instead of bouncing around the edges of her brain.

"I didn't know you could draw."

She pulled the journal to her chest protectively as she looked up to see Carver. "I can't." She bit back, though the retort was weak.

He looked unamused. "Clara, I saw what you drew. You can draw."

She didn't bother with a second rebuttal. "It's not a big deal. I'm not even that great."

He raised his eyebrows and she felt her jaw clench in an effort to ignore how cute that look was on him. *I don't like him. I don't like him. I don't like him.*

"You're pretty great. I sure can't draw like that."

"Oh, yes, and you're certainly the measure of success."

He grinned, "Absolutely. Have you ever known me to be bad at anything?"

Her mind spun. He was so frustrating. And, no, she couldn't

think of anything he sucked at. But she sure as hell wouldn't tell him that. Then it hit her. "Yeah, I can."

"Oh?" He enjoyed the back and forth, waiting for her to come up with something random she could barely accuse him of. She had more than he expected and she knew that.

"You're extremely bad at relationships."

The humor evaporated, and she watched pain flare in his eyes before he masked it. "Low blow."

She shrugged. "Yes, yes it was." She was dangerously close to addressing their history, but again, the rules. She needed Carver out of her space. Right. Now. "Will you sit down so I can get back to drawing? Or will you keep standing there, staring at me like an idiot?"

He gritted his teeth, and she wished she hadn't noticed the sharp edge of his jaw again. Nothing about him was actually helpful for this situation. *Except his personality,* she had to concede. But even that was hit or miss. She was either more desperate to have him, or desperate to make sure no one else ever had him. By, you know, killing him, of course.

14 CARVER

Carver sat down without another comment. She was absolutely ridiculous. She was right, but ridiculous. How they ended wasn't his fault. At least not entirely. She never should have followed him to the army. That's where it all started. If she had just stayed. Stayed with her mom. Stayed safe. Stayed away from him.

He was the one with something to prove. He was the one with a chip on his shoulder. The war had taken his father, and as a consequence his mother. One of his father's best friends, who became Carver's mentor, drafted him in long before he officially signed up. He could still see the shock on Clara's face when he told her he had enlisted. Tears filled her eyes immediately, but she was too kind to respond with anger in the moment. Anger came after the news fully processed and she didn't speak to him for almost a week. They lived on the same property, yet she wouldn't deign to acknowledge him.

When the week was over, she came back with an entirely new attitude. Things were back to being good. He loved her, told her so, and told her once basic training was over for him, he would propose. He bought a ring the week before basic training, and stored it with his clothing the day he left.

He never expected to see her in the line up. The first day of basic was mostly paperwork; men and women were separated. Clothing was issued, rooms were assigned. It was strategic, and preparation for the difficult training about to ensue.

Day 2, they lined up and met their commanders and training groups. Training groups included men and women, and somehow, whatever form of fate existed put Clara in his group. He almost screamed at her there and then. She wouldn't look at him. She held her head high, and the look of utter confidence was one he'd never seen her wear. Damn her stubbornness.

Even then, he thought it would be a matter of time before she dropped out. But she had done something he never expected of her. She not only survived, she thrived.

Carver pulled out his own journal, and jotted down some of these thoughts. The train car lurched and he cursed under his breath as his pen slid across the page leaving an ugly line behind. He noticed Clara stand out of the corner of his eye, but didn't look as she stretched. Watching her would not help his thoughts be more constructive.

He kept writing, losing himself in the words. When the train rolled to a stop, he was surprised by how much time actually passed. Like habit, the door was opened, and Clara hopped off without comment.

He got off long enough only to get food, and then resumed his writing. It helped bring some clarity to the thoughts he had too often. He hated this war–hated what it had taken from him. His father, his mother, Clara. Everything he loved, taken from him because of Noxvalis.

Noxvalis was more scientifically advanced than Quorath, and they desired world domination. They remained peaceful only to the kingdoms that were as advanced as them, or offered a trade they couldn't resist. It was people from these kingdoms that would attend the festival.

The kingdom of Calyndor, for example, had offered one of the royal daughters in marriage to the prince of Noxvalis—cementing the alliance between the two kingdoms. The girl was queen now. She married in only months before the prince succeeded his father. It was all political, all about power. And he hated it.

He glanced up, and since Clara wasn't back to the train yet decided he should read the note from Command.

"Carver -

As usual your mission is to retrieve the item. It is labeled DF23, and should be a bright purple color. Intelligence tells us there are 10 vials, and it is vital all 10 are retrieved. You run point on this mission. Clara will have your back.
You will enter the city together, as instructed. You'll find rings in the bottom of your bag to complete the husband and wife ensemble.

Command"

No mention of the previous mission. As a spy, he was never supposed to see the intel he collected. On the last mission, a single piece of paper fell out on his return. It shouldn't have been damning. He shouldn't have read it. He didn't read it–not fully. His eyes just glanced over the page long enough to see "creatures" and "bioengineering."

His mistake was asking Command if they ever heard of "creatures." Their response was a blatant dismissal, followed by, "If you want to keep your position, we suggest you follow the rules, Operative." They knew. Nate confirmed it later, and Carver waited for weeks to find out if he would be punished.

Now, he was here.

Clara got back on the train only a few minutes before the door was closed, and he hastily folded the note and shoved it in his bag. She would hate that he was the one in charge of this mission. She would hate the rings even more.

He didn't think she would speak at first, but once the train chugged to a start, she did. "I'm sorry. I shouldn't have said what I did."

"Doesn't matter."

"But it does. We agreed to trust each other enough for the purpose of this mission. I shouldn't have been a bitch to you. Not to mention, I came a little too close to breaking one of the rules." She said the last part with a gentle smile, and he knew he had to offer what she was looking for, regardless of how he felt about it.

"It's okay. Don't worry; we're good." None of it felt true, but she didn't question his sincerity.

She nodded. "What were you writing?"

My feelings about you. My feelings about this mission. All of the feelings I'm not supposed to freaking have. I'm trying to figure out if this is my punishment from Command. But he wouldn't say that. So he just shrugged the question off. "Writing helps me think."

"Drawing does the same for me." It felt like mutual ground–a thin line of connection he was terrified to break. An admission from both of them. So basic, and yet for them it was a massive step.

"How are you feeling about the assignment? We're getting closer."

"Yeah. This is our last day on the train. They're supposed to drop us in the closest city we can travel to, right?"

"I think so."

She stood, back to her stretching. This time, he decided to join her. "This isn't at all what I expected when I was called into Command."

"Nor I." He agreed.

"You've done a list of assignments for Command before, haven't you?"

"Yeah, but never with someone. They were always intelligence based. In and out. Just me. I work best alone."

"Hey, thanks."

He sighed, "That's not what I meant, and you know it."

"Sureee. I think you're enjoying my company more than you're willing to admit."

She bent down to touch her toes, facing away from him. He looked away, *you have no idea.* "I don't know what you're talking about."

The train lurched suddenly, and Clara lost her balance, crashing into him. He managed to catch her before she hit the wall, and stood there awkwardly with her in his arms. Her hair smelled familiar, even better than he remembered, and he resisted the urge to pull her against his chest the way he would have before. Instead he held his arms out aloft, providing her the security she needed to regain her balance, but not holding her.

She quickly got her footing back, her cheeks pink from the encounter, "Sorry," she murmured stepping away from him.

"Breaking the rules, I see." He teased.

She glared at him, "That wasn't my fault."

"I know. But it's fun to tease you all the same."

"I swear I wasn't trying to break the rules."

Carver paused at the defensive tone in her voice, "I know," he emphasized. "That's why it's funny. If you were intentionally breaking the rules, we'd have a *different* conversation."

15 CLARA

Clara pulled her shirt down around her waist as she recovered from crashing into Carver. She could feel the heat in her face, and was further frustrated she looked as flustered as she felt. The blush deepened as she wondered what exactly Carver was implying with his emphasis on *different*.

Fortunately, the door slid open before she had too long to ruminate. The boy's eyes were wide, his face bright red and panicked. "There's been a..." his voice trailed off, gaze darting between the two of them. "A malfunction. This is as far as we're able to take you. We have to repair the train before we can keep moving."

Clara almost looked at Carver to give the response, but instead stepped forward and said, "What do you mean this is as far as we can go? Where are we?"

The boy scratched the back of his head. "We're approaching Hillcrest, the second to last town on the map. About 15 miles from the town we were supposed to leave you in."

Carver jumped in, "So we have to walk an additional 15 miles?" The boy's eyes widened at Carver's tone, and he swallowed hard before nodding. "Can you tell us what kind of 'malfunction' occurred?"

The boy shook his head and walked away before Carver could ask additional questions. Carver looked at Clara questioningly, "Well, I guess we should get our stuff and start walking? Maybe we can make it before dark?"

She squinted at him, "15 miles? Before dark? Maybe. We'll have to start soon though. I want to find the conductor and see if we can find out what's happened and if this affects our mission, though."

Carver nodded, "If you want to do that, I'll go into town and get water and food for our now far more exhausting trip."

"Sounds good."

She jumped down from the train and walked to the front. The sun was out, and she was glad she had left her leather gear behind. It wouldn't have fared well in the direct heat. Her boots crunched against the dirt and gravel, and she paused. There were no other sounds. This town should have been fully active. There should have been all of the usual noises.

She unsheathed her knife, holding it at her side. Though not immediately visible, it was immediately usable. She didn't see the boy as she walked to the front. The conductor wasn't there. She went car by car, searching for others. She couldn't find a single person.

What the hell?

She picked up her pace, head spinning. There was no reason she could think of to explain this. She almost ran into Carver. He caught her, hands warm even through the fabric of her sleeves. She shrugged him off, and he quickly removed his hands like he'd been burned. "The weirdest thing," he began.

She cut him off. "There's no one. We've been abandoned."

He nodded, eyes growing even more concerned as the reality of their situation set in. "But, why?"

Clara turned in a circle as she focused on the abandoned town. The windows of all the buildings were boarded over. A breeze stirred up the dirt, and all of the porches, window frames, and other available surfaces had been coated in a layer of the light dust. "It wasn't recently abandoned."

"No, it's been like this for a while." Carver confirmed.

Clara closed her eyes taking deep breaths. She felt terrified. Yes, she had been involved in executions, but everything had been sterile. Planned. Expected. Even the assassinations. She knew every detail of every routine and was in and out before there was even a chance of suspicion.

She was supposed to be on the train for another day. They were supposed to have one more day to plan. What did they do now?

"My guess is the war reached farther than our intelligence showed."

"Or, we've been sent into a trap." She gnawed on her lip, not quite splitting it, but close.

"Or we've been sent into a trap." Carver ran his hand through his hair, giving Clara another unhelpful detail to try not to focus on.

She took a deep breath. "Okay. Does this change anything? Aside from the amount of walking we have to do?"

He tilted his head side to side, his hair just long enough to fall towards his eyes before he pushed it back. "I'm going with no?"

She exhaled harshly, an attempt to push the stress for her body. A metallic taste filled her mouth, and she licked her lips trying not to let Carver see the blood blossoming on her lip. Her own fault. "You sound so confident."

"It's not like I've been here before, Clara."

She paced, not able to look at him and think clearly while she was already fighting the urge to panic. This was not ideal. Sweat dripped down her spine, and the idea of walking an extra 15 miles was beyond frustrating. "Think, think," she whispered to herself.

She stopped pacing and said, "Okay, there's still a biological weapon. We're still in charge of saving our kingdom. So we need to get our stuff and start heading towards Noxvalis."

If Carver was surprised she took charge, nothing on his features revealed it. In fact, to Clara's great surprise, he immediately nodded and began walking to their train car so they could grab their stuff.

"Wait," Carver paused mid step. "We still haven't figured out what happened to the conductor and the boy with him."

Clara thought for a second. "I'm not sure," she admitted. "I walked around the train and didn't see them."

"Let's make one more lap around? I'm sure they're still here somewhere. Maybe under the train if they're having to repair it to turn around?"

"Listen," her tone was sharper than she intended and inwardly she grimaced, but honestly it was irrelevant. "We have to walk 15 miles, hopefully before the sun sets. That needs to be our focus. Not what happened to two people whose names we don't even know."

"Cory." Carver said quietly as she passed him.

"What?" She asked over her shoulder.

"The boy's name was Cory. I'm not sure about the conductor."

Clara stepped into the train car, taking stock of what cargo was left to see if any of it was useful. Unfortunately, none of it was. "How did you know his name?"

Carver shrugged. "I asked him the first day. He's apprenticing to eventually be a conductor. I'm a little annoyed about the fact we can't find him. He's only 14. This is not a good place for him to be lost."

Clara didn't respond, guilt pooling in her chest for not knowing the name of the boy who had helped them and now disappeared. She almost suggested they look again, but that wouldn't be prudent. Time was of the essence. So instead she gathered her things.

Carver picked up his bag, and began stuffing his journal, map, clothes, and everything else in. No particular order. Didn't fold his clothes. Didn't even fold the map. Clara bit down on her lip again, determined not to lash out at him. But what the hell? What kind of psychopath stuffed a map into a bag? Maybe she was better off without him.

Clara, on the other hand, perfectly folded the clothing she had removed, and the map. She put it all back in the bag in the same order it had been in when she received it. She found some dried food packages in one of the crates and threw a few of them to Carver. The rest she added to the top of her bag, tying it off and slinging it over her shoulder.

16 CARVER

She put everything in her bag neatly. Precisely. Perfectly. Everything was in *the exact place* it was when they received the bags, with her personal bag on top. How?? It took a few minutes, but Carver realized he couldn't figure out how Clara managed to keep everything so organized. A couple years before, he might have tried to stay more organized, but now he just didn't care.

His only priority was to keep Clara alive. To hell with how his bag looked. Sure, it was far harder to tie off than Clara's was. And sure, his clothes wouldn't be as presentable, and the creases in the map would be annoying. But it was still readable. And fine, he cared more about his bag than he was willing to admit. It was irrelevant. He wouldn't repack or ask Clara for help.

He stuffed the dried food packs into the top, and after two tries was able to close his bag. Clara pursed her lips like she wanted to comment, but maybe he was only assuming her to be judgemental.

"Ready?" He asked her.

"Ready," she gave him a hesitant smile.

His eyes caught on the small split in her lip, but she hopped down from the train before he commented. He noticed her chewing on it, and wondered if perhaps she wasn't quite as confident as her status implied. Or, was it too much to hope *he* was the one who unnerved her that much?

The ground was hard as they began the trek. They both kept a steady pace, and it wasn't long until the train faded from their view. In front of them, the landscape was mostly untamed, browning grass on the edges of the tracks, forest on either side. They walked next to the train tracks, the unspoken agreement it was the fastest and most direct route.

He glanced back over his shoulder at the abandoned town as he tried to make sense of it all. Command's intel would have known the town was abandoned. At least they should have. If that intel was bad, what else was bad? Or, had Command kept them in the dark intentionally?

"So," the lamest conversation starter ever, but it was all he had. "How'd you get nicknamed the Eclipse?" Carver hiked his bag higher on his shoulder, ignoring the sun beating down on his head. At least it wasn't raining. Small comfort.

She almost tripped, but quickly regained her balance. With a shrug she answered, "How does anyone get a nickname? They earn it."

Brilliant. Completely enlightening. But he played along. "Okayyyy, how did you earn your nickname?"

"You don't want to know."

"If I didn't want to know, I wouldn't have asked. Duh." He kept his tone light, contrasting the harshness in hers. She was so annoyingly frustrating, but he could be the bigger person. He would be the bigger person.

"Just drop it. Okay?"

Carver weighed the options in his mind and decided dropping it was not the one he preferred. In fact, he didn't mind the idea of pushing her. Maybe he would learn something. "And if I don't?"

"Maybe you'll learn the reason."

He sighed dramatically. "Believe it or not, I asked because I'm *trying* to learn the reason."

Her hands clenched at her side, and Carver wondered if there was a darker reason behind her name than what he suspected.

"Have you ever killed someone?" Her voice was soft, and barely carried to him over the wind and sound of their boots.

He mussed his hair, already uncomfortable with the direction this was headed. "Um," he chuckled nervously, and she glanced his way out of the corner of her eye. He had to be honest then. "No. I haven't."

Her lips pressed into a thin line, and somehow Carver felt like he had given the wrong answer. Wasn't there only one right answer to that question? But in times of war, perhaps there was valor in having a body count. (The death one, not the other one.) He only knew a few spies who could claim a body. For their sector, killing someone meant there had been a mistake. They weren't trained as soldiers, or war machines. They were trained in espionage. Carver didn't have to ask to know that Clara's sector functioned differently.

"I was only six months into the program," she whispered, not slowing her pace. He leaned his head in her direction to hear her words, and was grateful the wind was calming. He waited for her to continue, but moments passed and she didn't say anything.

The forest tapered off, and Clara paused, "Sounds like a river." Carver stilled to listen, and could barely hear the sound in the distance.

He nodded, "We should fill up our bottles."

They left the train tracks, and trekked down the slight incline to reach the river in the forest's valley. Though they could hear the louder sounds of water, presumably from a waterfall somewhere upstream, the water here ran far more gently.

He filled his water bottle, adding a drop of iodine and sealing the lid. The stream looked clean enough, but he wasn't willing to take the unnecessary risk. Clara did the same.

Carver splashed water on his face, enjoying the frigidity against his sun warmed skin. Clara perched on the balls of her feet a couple yards away from him, fully focused on the stream.

He smirked to himself, and before he had time to categorize whether it was a good or bad idea, he reached into the water and splashed her. She gasped and jumped back stunned, and an apology was on his lips before she reached down and splashed him back.

He blinked the water out of his eyes, "Okay, that was somehow colder than I expected. Like, I already splashed my face. Why was it colder when you splashed me?"

She didn't smile, but he could see the mischievous glint appearing in her eyes. In that moment, it felt like nothing had changed. The wall crumbled and she was still the innocent girl he spent his life protecting. The one he would lay his life down to save.

He scooped up a handful of water, letting it drip through his fingers, an obvious threat. She squealed, and scrambled back. He splashed some water her way with minimal effort so it landed about a foot from her feet.

"We still have to walk, I don't want to be soaking wet," she said with a smile.

He stalked towards her, "Oh yeah? Soooo throwing you in is a bad idea?"

"Very bad." she laughed as he stood over her. His heart pounded at the sound and he knew he would do anything to hear it again.

"That's not much incentive for me to *not* do it. In fact, I'm starting to think I should." For once, his smile didn't feel forced or like an act. For once, he felt happy. He felt *happy*.

"I really don't think you should," she was still smiling, and Carver stepped closer to her, preparing to throw her in. He paused above her, her eyes stopping to meet his. He dreamed about her almost every night, but in this moment he wondered how he could have forgotten how beautiful she was.

Sunlight filtered through the leaves, splotching her face in light and shadows. Her bright blue eyes dared him to continue, but he knew if he did she would retaliate. He didn't care.

He leaned down about to grab her, but faster than he could have prepared for, she kicked his hand away from her, and moved into a standing position. "Don't you dare start breaking the rules." All mirth was gone from her voice, and his heart stilled within him. She held her hands in front, ready to defend herself if he took a step forward.

What the hell was he thinking?

The sounds of the forest raged again, and the moment passed as though it never happened.

"I'm sorry." Carver clenched his hands at his sides, and turned to gather all of his stuff so they could continue on. She did the same, and they walked in silence back to the tracks.

17 CLARA

The silence remained unbroken as they walked, and Clara was relieved that Carver didn't push to start a conversation. She didn't want him to keep probing into her past, and she didn't want the flirtation to continue. Well, she did, but that wasn't fair or good. They had to fulfill their assignment and then go their separate ways. A flirtation would only break her heart again, and he didn't get that privilege.

Her eyes darted across the scenery, and it was hard for her not to comment on how tall the trees were. How green everything was. Most of her missions had been within cities–high value targets: politicians, generals, anyone with enough power they needed to be taken out.

Though she was given missions, and often in charge of executions, her specialty was interrogations. There wasn't a single prisoner who thought she was capable of what she inflicted on them. They underestimated her, but they quickly learned to look at her with fear. What would Carver think of her if he knew?

She wasn't weak anymore. No, she was worse. She was cruel.

The sun began its descent, and even the trees closest to the tracks started to blur together. "How close do you think we are?" Carver interrupted her running thoughts.

"We've kept up a good pace; we shouldn't be far." She stumbled over a branch and Carver reached out to steady her but she jerked her arm out of reach.

"Our theory about the town's abandonment having to do with the war?"

"Yeah?" Clara watched her feet more carefully, unsure where he was headed with this question.

"Well, if the war *had* reached that far, this town we're headed to is even closer to Noxvalis..." He trailed off and she quickly filled in the blanks.

"We have no idea what to expect. It could be abandoned like the town before, it could be occupied by enemy troops, could have been destroyed. This could be another small attack to fuel the feud, or the beginning of something bigger."

"Exactly. We'll see the edges of it soon, though the darkness will limit our vision."

"What do we do if it is occupied by soldiers?" Clara didn't like the hint of fear in her voice. She didn't like not having the answer. She didn't like that she trusted Carver enough to give an answer, and to follow him. She didn't like the way she unconsciously shifted closer to him as if he could provide the comfort she needed.

She subtly stepped to the side giving herself more space. She was fully independent, she reminded herself.

His response was calm, "We'll camp in the woods. Maybe steal some supplies in the morning. We're not close enough to the festival to get away with our identities."

"Makes sense."

They fell back into their voiceless rhythm, footsteps and breaths staying even. Eventually Clara admitted, softly enough he leaned his head in her direction to hear, "I've never been undercover like this before."

He stood straighter, and even in the twilight she could see the look of suspicion on his face. "Clara, everyone has heard the rumors that follow the 'Eclipse.' How is it you aren't familiar with espionage and the roles played on assignment? You've never pretended to be someone else?"

She shook her head, her braid whipping across her back. "They used me for in-house operations, primarily. That's how I earned my reputation. The assignments I was sent on were almost always high-level targets, and my job was to be in and out without anyone spotting me. No espionage, no interactions."

"In-house operations?" He questioned.

Clara wondered what she could say to explain. How could she phrase it so she wouldn't seem as much like the monster she had become? A monster he created by constantly doubting her. That wasn't entirely fair, but she didn't care.

"I helped them with…sensitive matters regarding prisoners." At least, most of the time they were prisoners. One or two of the aristocrats had been placed under her purview as well.

"Sensitive matters," he deadpanned, and she could feel his gaze tracking her.

"Don't push it."

"Okay…" he paused, and in that pause she feared everything he could ask her. Did you torture people? How many people have you killed? And a thousand offensive statements he could pin to her. But instead he said simply, "Is this you asking for my help in espionage?"

"No," she replied way too fast and he immediately laughed at her. Her heart thundered, still waiting for her worst case scenario to play out. "Kind of?"

"You might want to make up your mind. Double mindedness doesn't play well in intense situations."

She huffed, "Yes, I'd like a few pointers." She may be ahead when it came to actually killing people, but she didn't know how to interact with them. At all.

"You have to get in the mind of the character you are playing. It's all an elaborate ruse, right? The more you create a character and understand the inner workings of that character, the easier it is to become them."

"Basically, it's like a game?"

"Kinda, but it's more complicated than that." He kicked a rock and it bounced across the ground a couple times before coming to a stop. "You have to fully understand what you're doing. Think about it. People's intentions aren't always clear, but you can tell enough from their body language to understand the direction they're heading. Like I said with double mindedness, if you're having to convince yourself to tell a lie, it's a lot easier to pick up on than if you have already accepted the lie and are presenting your reality."

"Huh?"

"Basic psychology. Why do you think psychopaths and narcissists get as far in life as they do? They, at least in part, believe the reality they are selling to other people. It's the same concept for our mission. We are the people on the identity cards they gave us. Our past aligns with that. How would those people act? What would they think? That is who we have to become."

"Are you finally admitting you've always been a narcissist?" Clara tried to listen to the breakdown he gave her, but truthfully, she checked out after psychopaths and narcissists.

Carver exhaled loudly. "Ouch. I give you a whole explanation to try and help you and that's your takeaway? What the hell, Clara, I was just trying to help."

She rolled her eyes. "I know, I know. Sorry. Shouldn't have said that."

"Did you learn anything from what I said? If we end up participating in the festival, you have to act...normal..." He cringed away from his last statement, and she assumed it was in preparation for her response.

"Normal?" She questioned, giving him a chance to correct his statement. She acted perfectly fine, thank you very much.

"Yeah, no offense, but you're not exactly good at socializing." Clara clenched her fists at her side to avoid smacking him across the face. *I won't break the rules; I won't break the rules; I won't break the rules.*

"What's that supposed to mean?" Again, another opportunity for him to change his statement, and he would if he knew what was good for him.

"How many friends have you had in the last couple years? Do you go to parties? Do you talk to people regularly?" Anger welled in her chest. How dare he.

"I have friends."

"Yeah? And are they nice to you? Are you nice to them? Would you confide in them?" She opened her mouth to yell at him, but he held up a hand, "My point is this. We're supposed to be from Calyndor. Girls from there aren't usually trained warriors. They laugh. They smile. They have a lightness about them that, quite frankly, you don't have." His eyebrows drew together, and Clara didn't appreciate how serious he looked.

"Wonder why." If he wanted happy and carefree, maybe he should have made better decisions. Her heart ached as once again, that fateful day flashed before her vision.

"I'm sure there's a million reasons why I don't know. I'm not trying to start a fight."

"Well, apparently you don't have to try." Another biting remark was all she could offer to keep from crying.

"Clara, that's not—" His frustration bled through every word, but what right did he have to be frustrated?

She cut him off, "Just shut up. We're approaching the town. Stay focused."

18 CARVER

Carver felt the tension the second he started saying things he should have hidden. He knew better. He watched her shoulders tighten, her fists clench at her sides. He was honestly surprised she didn't swing at him. He can't say he would have complained if she had tackled him–the evening would have been a lot more interesting.

But she restrained her fury, and he had to give her some measure of credit for that. He didn't want her to be angry at him. If she didn't figure out how to act well for this assignment, she would be the death of them–a reality she didn't seem to fully comprehend. He hoped she listened to at least some of what he said, and maybe once the anger faded she would see the validity and change enough for it to work.

Fat chance. She was a woman after all.

He could barely make out the silhouettes of the buildings as they exited the forest. He felt too exposed, and both slowed their steps. There were no lights or movement in the town, but that didn't mean they were safe.

They approached the back of the first building, pressing themselves into the shadows as they waited for anything they couldn't see. Clara moved gracefully, checking the edges, "I'm going up," she whispered, motioning along the side of the building. His eyes moved to scan the roof, and he nodded his approval. Catching her eye again before she began climbing, he moved his finger in a circle to show he would walk the perimeter.

She was gone as soon as he finished the motion, already scaling the side of the building by the water pipe. He crept along the edge, careful at the corner and the alley between two buildings. Nothing moved and he relaxed a little.

He froze when he heard a rustle, and almost jumped when a mouse scampered out and darted around his feet. He blamed his jumpiness on the lack of sleep from giving Clara his room. That's the only reason he startled.

He stood still when he reached the front of the building, staying in the shadows but observing as much as he could of the town. The stillness felt unreal. Shutters creaked from the wind, and branches blew across the town. Clouds filtered in and out across the moon casting constantly moving shadows. But there was no sign of life, so even in these movements the stillness was overwhelmingly heavy.

He did flinch when Clara soundlessly landed beside him. Even with her bag slung across her back and hair blowing in the wind, there was nothing to alert him of her presence.

"Dang it, Clara!"

Her teeth gleamed in the moonlight, "Jumpy much."

He groaned, knowing she wouldn't let him live this down easily. He thought about trying to find something to throw back at her, but decided the best course of action was changing the conversation altogether. "I think it's abandoned."

"Obviously. From the roof I still couldn't see anyone. I guess it's technically the best case scenario."

Best case scenario. The words floated through his head, taunting him. Nothing about this situation was the best case scenario. Having her here was like preparing to live out a scene from his nightmares: to have her in front of him, close enough to touch, then watch her be ripped away by something he's not quite strong enough to protect her from.

She looked at him, observing him so closely he wished he could turn away. Instead, he stared back at her with the same intent, daring her to be the one to break away first. After too long, she did, eyes moving back over the landscape. Carver breathed a quiet sigh of relief. Too many thoughts ran through his mind under her stare. The small distance between them, the all encroaching darkness, the complete solitude with only the two of them to break the silence. And he knew a few ways they could break that silence. However, none of the ideas were helpful to their situation. And, he thought Clara would reject all of them–except maybe the one that involved fighting. She might be convinced into that one.

"So." It was both a statement and a question. Her turn to begin the conversation with the worst starter ever. He almost smiled.

"So," he repeated, wishing to continue the phrase but unable to find the words. *So, this is awkward. So, how about that assignment. So, are you thinking about my body as much as I'm thinking about yours? Definitely not.*

"Where do we want to sleep for the night?" *I, for one, would like to sleep in your arms,* half of his head said. The other half instantly shot it down with cries of *not helpful.*

"Preferably a building with bedding that's entirely devoid of rats or other small animals?" He suggested.

"Squeamish much?"

"Only thinking about you, my dear." She threw a glare his way, and he assumed it was part for the comment and part for the sarcastically given term of endearment. He grinned in response. *Damn.* She was *stunning.*

He followed her as she scouted out buildings. The first she opened released enough dust to give both of them a coughing fit. The second, a much nicer home, seemed like it worked until a rat ran out, and of course, scurried across Carver's foot.

He stomped, frustrated, and only grew more so when Clara lost it in a bout of laughter. "Thought you weren't afraid of rats?" She dropped her voice as low as it could go, "Only thinking about you, my dear."

"Will you shut up and find us a place to sleep?"

"Hey, I opened the last two houses. Your turn to pick a place." She laughed again, and Carver's frustration dissipated with the sound. He tried not to dwell on it, but if he was honest all he wanted to do was find more ways to trigger that sound again and again and again.

Instead, he turned back to the row of houses and muttered, "Fine," like his heart wasn't racing, like blood hadn't rushed to his face with her laugh. Like he wasn't desperate to hold her and make up for the past three years.

The moon provided enough light to see the outlines of the buildings, though the clouds often obscured more than he would like. He walked toward the center of town, determined to pick one that worked, if only to hold it over Clara.

Carver passed through the center of town, and didn't stop. He found a street which at some point held perfectly manicured homes built in rows. Now, the grass had grown up, weeds choking out the picket fences. "I'm betting one of these will be better than the work buildings you were looking in."

"Are you going to find out? Or are we spending the rest of the night walking in circles?"

He opened the picket fence gate to the first house, "You know, you should be nicer to me. The attitude is completely unnecessary."

"Attitude? This is just my personality jackass."

Carver paused, his hand on the door knob as he turned to face her. "Well, maybe you should learn how to have a better personality."

Whether she was stunned into silence, or simply focused as he threw the door open, Carver would never know. Either way, they both stood on the porch in front of the open door, waiting for something to come out at them–another cloud of dust or rat, or something far more sinister.

Carver counted the beats of his heart, waiting for the racing to slow. He grinned back at Clara, "Ladies first?"

She turned behind her, making a show of looking for someone else. "I don't see any ladies, so why don't you go ahead." This time, Carver was the one who rolled his eyes.

He stepped through the threshold, adrenaline racing. Every instinct told him something should go wrong. The floor should fall through. The door should slam behind him and lock him in. An army should step out guns blazing. But none of these things happened. The exhaustion was clearly making him paranoid.

Clara dug into her bag as he called for her to follow him. After a couple minutes, she pulled out a flashlight. "Dang Clara, why didn't you tell me we had flashlights?"

He squinted as she walked through the doorway, flashlight pointed into his eyes. "What, you didn't sort through all of your supplies?"

"I looked through most of them," he mumbled, mentally telling himself to thoroughly sort through the rest sooner rather than later.

"Maybe next time you should look harder." She moved the beam across the room.

They were in someone's living room. Photos were still in frames on the fireplace, furniture was still fully intact. Aside from the layer of dust coating everything, it looked like someone still lived there.

"What makes an entire populace leave without taking any of their items? Who would leave behind family photos?" Clara asked softly, brushing her fingers across a child in one of the photos.

"I'm not sure, but the stillness of this place gives me the heebie jeebies."

"Heebie jeebies." Clara deadpanned.

"Yeah? You know, like ants in my pants, uncomfortable and waiting for something to go wrong." He shifted from foot to foot, trying to convey the mental picture. She continued to stare at him, eyebrows raising and one corner of her lip quirking up. The look could almost be read as amusement.

"Heebie jeebies." She said again, still questioning.

"Is the phrase really that strange to you?"

She didn't answer, instead walking into the kitchen. She flicked the light switch, but nothing happened. Carver wasn't surprised. While news may have not reached them of the towns being abandoned, it certainly wasn't a recent enterprise.

"We should find a bed and crash." Carver said, inwardly cringing at the fact he said "a bed," and not "beds."

He fully expected Clara to either clarify his statement or give him a hard time for it, but instead her voice remained soft as she replied, "Don't you want to know what happened to everyone?"

"I mean, yeah, but an empty kitchen won't tell us that. Unless the walls start talking, there's not a lot of investigation we can do here."

She straightened, and he realized how harsh his tone had sounded. "You're right. Let's find somewhere to sleep."

She rushed past him, and Carver immediately wished he had fostered her curiosity. Yes, it would have been pointless, at least if the point was finding out what happened. But had the point been making himself less of an enemy in her mind...helping her would have accomplished that nicely.

19 CLARA

Clara kept her posture neutral as she searched the house for a bedroom. What she actually wanted was to slip the brass knuckles out of her bag and see how well Carver could talk after a solid hit to the jaw. But she kept her hands unclenched, by her sides, hopefully the picture of innocence.

Thankfully, after his last comment, they fell into silence. The first room she walked into was a dining room; she walked out of the other side to see a bathroom and under-the-stairs closet. *Upstairs then*, she decided.

Her footsteps, while soft on the steps, echoed throughout the house. She was too tired to care, and no one was around. She was a little miffed at how soundlessly Carver trailed. She couldn't even hear his breaths. While her soundlessness required a lot of mental focus, his seemed to be entirely natural. It was unnerving.

The first room was decorated in shades of pink, a crib centered on the far wall. For a moment, she forgot Carver was behind her as she trailed her fingers gently over the baby blankets left behind. The life she once dreamed of flashed before her eyes. She could have decorated a room like this. Could have held her baby close to her chest, rocked her to sleep in the rocking chair.

She closed her eyes for only a second before reality launched back in. That life was no longer something she could have. She worked too hard, was promoted too high to ever just up and leave. There would always be prisoners, always new assignments, always battles for Clara to fight, and she wouldn't drag a child into that.

Carver cleared his throat, rather awkwardly she thought, behind her. "It's interesting to see how people live," she explained softly.

"You know how people live." The confusion in his tone was clear, but she didn't have an answer.

It was true, she realized as she walked into the next bedroom. She did at one point have a normal family. Lived a relatively normal life. Both parents loved her, home life was stable, everything was in its perfect place. But things changed suddenly, and the idea of that kind of normality now felt foreign.

The second bedroom had vehicles painted on the walls, and sported a single twin bed. "If we don't find anything better, you can always stay here," Clara said with a grin.

Carver lifted an eyebrow at her, proceeding to motion to his 6' frame. "I don't think I fit in a child's bed, Clara."

"Ohhhh, you only think like a child." She bobbed her head smiling, "Makes sense."

"You're such a brat." He snapped, "Can we speed this up? We need to get some rest if we're going to make it to the festival in time. That means you can't pause and observe every single thing in every single room."

She scoffed, her smile instantly falling, and stomped into the next room. It appeared to be a guest bedroom, and had one full size bed. "Dibs." she immediately said.

"Not how this works," Carver droned. He was exasperated with her, and Clara was loving every minute of it. Good, let him be at least a little miserable. He deserved it.

She sat her bag on the floor, and plopped on the edge of the bed stretching her hands across the comforter to either side as she leaned forward. "Is that so? Looks like I'm here. I'm sure there's a master bedroom you can take over somewhere. Or the car room looked like it would be a good fit, at least personality wise." She watched him in the dim light of the flashlight, the shadows creating even harder lines for his figure.

He clenched his teeth, a muscle in his jaw flexing as his eyes flashed. She wondered what he was thinking about saying back. Was he considering breaking the rules? She had considered violence more than once already, had she driven him to the same point? If he was allowed, after all these years, would he tell her the truth of how he saw her? Or would he continue to lie to her face as if she couldn't see through it?

"Fine. Sleep well." He muttered and continued down the hallway.

Clara's shoulders dropped, from relief or disappointment? She wasn't sure, but she couldn't believe the latter to be true. She didn't want Carver back. She didn't trust him, didn't need him, couldn't be herself with him, and didn't love him. The last one might have been a lie, but it was too late at night for her to decide for sure.

She rolled her neck, stretching out the places of her body that were sore from their trip thus far. She didn't want to wake up unable to move in the morning. She aligned her breathing to each movement, determined to be calm and go to sleep easily. Carver didn't get to disturb her sleep. She might not be able to control her dreams, yet anyway, but she could at least control her thoughts. Most of the time. On a good day.

"Clara," she heard him whisper sharply, and waited as his

silhouette appeared in the doorway. The windows streamed moon-light and provided a slightly creepy back light. The shadows entirely obscured his face, and it bothered her that she couldn't read him.

"Yeah?" She whispered back, but what she wanted to say was *leave me alone, it's time to sleep.*

"Oh, you are awake." He stopped whispering and continued, "Do you have a feeling that this assignment will be a lot harder than they even prepared us for?"

She groaned inwardly. She knew this could only be harder than she expected. The note she read before they were even out of sight of Quorath was enough to tell her that. Plus, hadn't they already had this conversation? "Yes."

"It's weird, right? These towns, the conductor and Cory not staying to give us more instruction. Like what's next?"

"Mhm," she agreed, but truthfully, she was exhausted and fading quickly.

"Do you think sleeping in separate rooms is a good idea?" That jolted her fully awake–for multiple reasons. She sat all the way up as he kept talking without giving her a chance to argue, "If some-thing else happens, I don't want us to be separated."

"We're not sharing a bed. It's in the rules."

He shook his head harshly, "No, no, not share a bed. I'll drag in one of the mattresses and sleep on the floor."

"Really. You're abandoning the comfort of sleeping in a bed, to take up a guard post at the foot of mine?"

"I'll still be on a mattress. And I'm not *guarding* you."

"But you think I shouldn't be left to sleep alone."

He inhaled deeply, and she almost grinned at how well she could annoy him. "Are you going to continue to deliberately misin-terpret my words?"

"Are you going to continue to bring me satisfaction by becoming annoyed?" She forced an overly sweet tone, and could've sworn he was trying not to launch himself at her. She could only imagine how many ways he wished to harm her at that moment.

"If worst comes to worst," he gritted out carefully, "We should be together so we can finish the assignment. We will have more success together than apart. That is all I am saying." He paused, dragging his hand across his face, his exhaustion seeping into his posture. "If you would prefer, you can drag a mattress and sleep on the floor of my room."

Clara sat daintily on the foot of her bed. "I think I'm good here. But I will *allow* you to sleep on the floor."

"Brat," he whispered as he turned but she caught it.

To further annoy him, she replied cheekily, "Throw terms of endearment like that around and we might end up having problems."

20 CARVER

For the sixteenth time, Carver rolled over, fluffed his pillow, and fell back into it. His body barely moved from exhaustion, but his mind was aware of everything. At the moment, it was fixated on Clara's breathing. Not the fact that she was breathing, per say. More the fact that she was in bed, sound asleep, most likely looking adorable.

And instead of being asleep next to her, he was trying to get comfortable on the mattress he set up on the floor.

There was nothing wrong with it. Actually, it was very comfortable. Much better than the night before he spent on the train. But knowing she was there, so close, and yet, so far, made something inside him desperate for her. He was desperate for the one thing he could never have.

She hated him more now than she had when they first met almost 10 years ago. His dad passed when he was 14. Carver's dad had served under Clara's at the front lines for the attacks; they were soldiers, not operatives, and they had stayed close even after their terms ended. When his dad died, Carver and his mom had been invited to move in with the Richards.

Clara's family had money, and behind their gorgeous house was a cottage-like building. Carver and his mom moved in there. From the beginning, Clara hated having another person around her. It was a bold case of only child syndrome, and when her dad was killed by an explosion only a few miles away from the base, she seemed to hate Carver even more. Somehow, he was the one she blamed for the loss of her father. It took him months to win her trust. Now he had completely lost it. Good.

He tossed and turned, his mind running rampant and refusing to calm down. After every decision he had made to protect her, would this assignment destroy her anyway?

It felt like only minutes had passed before a hand on his shoulder was shaking him awake. He launched himself up, and Clara swiftly moved herself back. "We need to start walking," she said apologetically. If she was that apologetic, he must truly look awful.

He groaned, "You're right."

Guilt clouded her face, and he paused to ask, "You okay?"

She inhaled deeply, "Sorry for breaking the rules. It's just I've been trying to wake you up for the past 5 minutes and you wouldn't budge."

He tried to smile, but it felt more like a grimace. "Don't worry about it."

"I looked through the kitchen for food, but there's nothing left. They didn't board windows here, but it seems they packed just as meticulously."

He nodded, yawning widely. He was too tired to consider the possibilities of what that could mean. "Is there still running water?" He asked.

She shook her head no. "But we shouldn't be too far from the stream once we're out of town. We could walk until the sun is a little higher and then break by the water." She looked him over again, and he wished more than anything he could read her mind for a moment. "I'm already packed, so I'll wait downstairs for you."

She was gone before he could reply, and he was again impressed by her fast movements. He wasn't sure what to do with this person she had become, but it was becoming more and more obvious he was proud of her. He wouldn't vocalize it though, he'd already made that mistake once.

Yawning again, he worked to untangle his legs from the blankets, and almost fell off the mattress. He let out a breath of amusement, grateful Clara hadn't been there to witness and mock him.

"Hurry up!" She yelled from below.

She could certainly be a pain in the butt. "I just woke up, give me a second!" He shouted back.

"Well, whose fault is that?"

"Well, whose fault is that," he mimicked under his breath. There were a few other things he wanted to add to the conversation, but he refrained. It was too early to start a fight. They had too far to walk, and would certainly be at each other's throats later in the day. It was best to prolong that as long as he could.

He stomped down the stairs, "Ready," he said as joyfully as possible. His joy increased when she rolled her eyes.

She hoisted her bag over her shoulders, and he did the same. Carver closed the door to the house when they walked out, and repeated it with the picket fence gate. "I don't think anyone is coming back." Clara said.

"I don't think so either." He lifted one shoulder, "But it feels wrong to leave it all open. At least it should be closed and left undisturbed."

"Minus the beds we messed up and the mattress now randomly left on the floor. That will be a fun one for them to figure out."

"Maybe they'll think the house is haunted."

She laughed, and he thought maybe spending the day walking

wouldn't be so bad. "Yeah, we're so awful we've already become ghosts."

"That's not what I meant." If Clara had the opportunity to become a ghost, then he had failed. The idea of her dying felt like a knife to his chest. He wouldn't let that happen.

"I know. But it's funny to think about." She dropped the volume of her voice, "People would probably like me as a ghost better anyway."

"I doubt that's true."

She glared at him. *What did I do to deserve this already?* He wondered, flipping back to his original opinion of how the day would go. "You've even admitted I'm not that likable."

He opened his mouth to rebut that, closed his mouth before he said something else she could twist, and after some debate replied, "I didn't say that exactly, what I said was—"

"I know what you said," she cut in. "You didn't have to say it for me to infer that."

"Clara—"

"I didn't get to be likable."

"If you would stop interrupting me I could explain what I meant!" His voice was loud enough it startled a flock of birds out of the trees on the other side of the tracks, and he took a deep breath.

"I know what you meant." She rolled her eyes. "It doesn't matter. You didn't have to say it. I know I'm not likable. I don't have friends. Aside from Reese, and I'm not sure how or why we're friends. But she's the closest thing I have." Clara was finally opening up to him, and he didn't dare stop her, even though he did still want to defend himself. "It was hard, you know? Coming out of...well...everything. I didn't know how to deal with anything. My instructor seemed determined to cut me out. He didn't succeed though." She smiled, looking very far away as she ran through the memories.

"When I completed the first three months and he took me under his wing, I thought the hard part was over. I survived. I was through basic training, and the initial cuts in what is arguably the hardest sector." She glanced at him from the corner of his eye as if daring him to fight her.

"I can agree with that," he said slowly, not wanting to say anything that would derail her story.

"I was stupid. I hadn't reached the hardest part yet. You said you've never killed anyone." Her voice trailed off again.

"I haven't had a reason to yet," was the only explanation he had.

"I was given a reason to six months in. My first in house assignment. I had been working him the past three weeks. We had gotten quite a bit of intel from him. Everyone was impressed. No one thought I would have the stomach for it. I threw up immediately after the first couple times, but at some point, my stomach stopped churning and I grew used to nightmares."

"And by work him you mean…"

"Torture. I thought that's all they were requiring of me. I knew I was trained as an assassin, but I thought that would be somewhere a lot further down the road. I walked in one day, ready to continue the…questioning…but they handed me a gun instead. He was tied to a chair, eyes on me the entire time."

She paused, chewing her bottom lip as they continued walking. Carver looked over his shoulder. The town was already far behind them. "It clicked then what being an assassin meant: killing anyone they told me to. I don't know. Maybe I shouldn't have done it, but orders are orders, right? I still remember how cold the metal of the pistol felt in my hand. How heavy it felt in the moment I picked it up, and how light it felt after the action was completed. The amazement and disgust I felt that something so small could accomplish something so horrendous.

The bullet went straight through his forehead. And that was

that. They were shocked at how well I handled it. I guess they expected me to run from the challenge or throw up or something. But I didn't. They decided then they could trust me, and they brought me into the rooms for higher level prisoners and more risky assignments. I didn't train as often after that, and they started calling me the Eclipse at some point. I think it started as a joke. Because most of them never saw me anymore or something.

A few Vipers found out that a couple of the reported assassinations had been at my hands. Then the nickname became one of honor and esteem. I was never quite sure what to think of it."

Carver attempted to process this information, but he had absolutely no idea what his response should be. A murderer. He was walking next to a *murderer*. He was trying to protect a *murderer*. Yet, she wasn't a murderer. She was still Clara. Still just the girl he loved.

He tried to reconcile her words to her, but he couldn't. This girl next to him couldn't have killed anyone. She couldn't be what she claimed to be. The girl he grew up with felt guilty when she killed a bug. She couldn't have grown up to be a murderer.

21 CLARA

Now he knows what a monster I am. She thought, but there was a relief in that knowledge. Now he could stop pretending that he had to be any kind of chivalrous or take care of her. Regardless of what he claimed his motivations to be until this point, between bringing her a key, dragging a mattress in, and everything else, she knew he was attempting to protect her and she hated it. She hated that he still saw her as defenseless, weak.

Carver's silence seemed to stretch into eternity, and though she wanted to fill the gap, she had done enough. It wasn't until they reached a clearing, and paused to stretch and survey their surroundings that he responded. "I," she looked up, almost startled as he cleared his throat. "I don't know what to say." *Clearly.* "I'm sorry that you went through all of that."

Somehow, it wasn't what she expected to hear him say and his apology unlocked fury within her. "You're sorry? You weren't the one who asked me to put a bullet in a man's head."

"No, but I am sorry—"

"Carver, you don't owe me an apology. For anything. I am *not* your responsibility." Ah, that's where the anger was coming from. Even now, he was still trying to protect her, still claiming her as his responsibility. Hadn't he figured out by now that she didn't need him?

"I didn't say you were, I just meant—"

"Just stop it! Stop trying to explain what you meant! I don't care about your good intentions. We're getting too close to the line and it has to stop. Far too close. Okay? It has to stop. We're not friends. I shouldn't have told you any of that. We are, at best, partners in this assignment only, and that has to remain our focus."

"Can you not interrupt me just one time?" He matched her intensity without matching her volume, "I'm allowed to be sorry that you had to *murder someone* without it meaning anything more than I think it's an awful thing to have to do! If you had told me your friend, what was her name? Reese? Had to kill someone, I would have had the same reaction. Stop assuming you're special."

He was breathing heavily, hands tugging on strands of his hair, and now it was Clara's turn to have no response. He was right. She did assume everything he had done until this point was because of their past. But if he was following the rules, that wasn't the case and she was the one who was nearing a breaking point with them.

"You're right, I'm sorry." Anger still welled in her chest, but she was doing her best to keep her tone calm. Her *partner*, not ex, didn't deserve her anger in this moment.

"Wow," he shook his hair out, dropping his hands back to his sides. "Never thought you were capable of those words."

"Don't push it," she warned, feeling the anger flame a little brighter, "You still have the rules, right?" He nodded, patting the pocket over his chest. "Why don't you pull it out and read it? I think we could both use the reminder."

He cleared his throat dramatically, unfolding the page. "Rule 1. The mission comes first. Rule 2. No flirting."

"Which includes throwing water at me." She interjected.

"Can I add a rule that you're not allowed to interrupt me? I really don't appreciate it." She rolled her eyes, and Carver continued, "Rule 3. No physical contact. We've done okay with that one," he shrugged.

"Yeah." As long as they didn't mention her shaking him awake that morning. But it didn't need to be brought up, so she agreed with his statement.

"Rule 4. No mention of our history. Rule 5. No defending the other person beyond what is necessary for the mission." Clara gave him a pointed look, and Carver threw up his hands in defense. "I haven't defended you. Not once. I haven't done anything except keep us both alive *for the sake of the mission.*"

"If you say so."

"I do say so. And you can't read my mind, so you have no choice but to believe me."

"There's always a choice." She muttered, purely for the sake of argument.

"Just let me finish reading." He closed his eyes momentarily, and Clara almost smiled at how well she pushed his buttons.

"Fine. Hurry up."

"Stop commenting and I could! Rule 6. If there's only one bed we take turns sleeping on the floor. Or, in my case," he grinned widely, "Learn to enjoy sleeping on the floor and always choose that."

"You didn't have to sleep on the floor." Clara started walking again, and Carver folded the page, less carefully than she preferred, as he caught up to her.

"Not a big deal." He shrugged it off, "Truthfully, without knowing what happened there, that town made me a little nervous. I'm glad we're out of it."

"How far can we follow the tracks before we need to divert more towards Noxvalis?"

Carver hooked his thumbs through the straps of his bag, and for a moment Clara envied how carefree he looked. His hair shone in the sun, and his skin, practically glowing from their amount of sun exposure, looked vibrant. Glancing down at her own arms, she could already see the pink forming, and freckles had begun to dot her skin from the day before.

"We should check the map when we stop for water. When are we doing that, by the way? You seemed to want to be in charge of the journey, so I will leave our stops to your discretion." He tilted his head towards her mockingly. If it had been allowed, she would have shoved him. Hard. And hoped he'd trip over something and land on his backside.

But it wasn't allowed so she focused her gaze straight ahead. "Soon. Are you thirsty already?" They had drained their bottles a ways back, but she was still okay. The sun beat down on her head, and she knew they needed water quickly, regardless of how they felt at the moment.

"I'm good right now."

"Let's keep walking for a little while then."

"Yes ma'am." This time it was a fake salute. Clara looked out across the other side of the tracks so Carver wouldn't be able to see her smile. She missed his goofiness, far more than she realized. For the last three years, she had learned to hate every memory of him. She rewrote every thought of him in a haze of red, changing what he meant or his tone.

Now, he was here. And she couldn't rewrite this moment. Not yet, anyway.

"What was training to be a spy like?" She asked after a while. Her face warmed from the sun, and she knew they should stop for water. Her stubbornness was still louder than her parched throat and she didn't want to lead them off course yet. A distraction would help.

"Is this something I'm allowed to talk about?"

"I asked, didn't I?" She smirked.

"I didn't ask for your attitude." He said flatly, the ghost of a smile gracing his lips.

"No, that came for free. You don't have to share if you don't want to. I was just curious."

"You told me yours," he sighed, "I suppose it's my turn to tell you mine. There was a lot of physical training in the beginning. Unusual physical training. We even did a stint in ballet."

"Ballet?"

"Yeah. Sounds weird, I know. But it worked. I learned more about footwork and how to stay quiet from those training sessions than anything else we did. I also learned balance and discipline. It was a lot harder than you would think."

She laughed, "I'm sure it was."

"No, really. It was." He chuckled lightly, "I had bruises on my feet for weeks because of the shoes. By the time we moved on, I could move without a sound."

"So you became a *fabulous* dancer."

Now he fully laughed. Clara couldn't help but smile at the sound. It was another thing she had missed from him. "Not at all. I learned what I needed and forgot the rest." He pointed at her, "So don't you dare ask me to pirouette."

"Oh c'mon, that was my next request." She groaned.

His smile faded, "Those kinds of things were fun. The physical training part I enjoyed. Yeah, it sucked sometimes, but you learn to love the pain after a certain point." Clara nodded, understanding that feeling way too well. The pain was her only escape. "But we're spies. So while you learned to kill," he grimaced as he glanced at her but she didn't react, "We learned to lie."

"That doesn't sound too bad," she said carefully, but could tell it was headed somewhere she wasn't prepared for.

"That's what I thought too. I think all of us thought that way in the beginning. It was endless lie detector tests, endless betrayals. They assigned us stories we had to keep from our friends. And then it was actions." He inhaled deeply, "Stab your best friend in the back, not literally of course, then make sure they would still trust you to protect them. It messes with your head. After a couple months, you learn not to trust anyone. Everyone becomes insanely brilliant liars, and it's absolutely terrifying because *every*one is good at it. There's no one left to trust."

Clara stayed quiet. Another feeling she understood. Though, she also learned how to rebuild trust, at least partially. She could always trust Reese to have her back. Same with a couple other assassins. To have no one? To wait for everyone to try and take you out? She couldn't quite imagine that.

Carver's eyes scanned her face, and they softened when she looked at him. "Not a fun idea, right?"

"Not at all." She whispered back.

"Okay, I know I said I would let you decide, but I think we should go ahead and stop for water." His tone was jovial again, but Clara wondered just how many scars he hid. She wore hers proudly, the anger, the ferocity. Every scar was displayed as a dare to mess with her.

He seemed so unchanged from who he had been. He was still the life of the party, still perfect, still the person everyone wanted to be around. His words stunned her more than she wanted to admit. Did he trust anyone? How could he hide that kind of damage and still seem so...happy? She certainly wasn't.

"Earth to Clara." Carver waved his hand in front of her face, and she jolted. "Water?"

She swallowed, recognizing how dry her throat was. "Good idea."

He turned off to walk down into the forest towards the stream. She carefully followed, wondering what else she would discover about him. One thing was certain. He wasn't the same man who had broken up with her. She hadn't yet figured out if that was good or bad.

22 CARVER

They refilled their water bottles, neither saying a word. The threads of unspoken conversation brushed across Carver's mind and he desperately wished something would ease the tension, and mend the bridge between them. What if things had been different? What if things were different now? If he explained himself, would she forgive him? Did he want her to forgive him?

The reality was harsh but he clung to it, desperate not to lose himself in possibilities. His reasoning three years ago was just as valid now. He couldn't have her back. He still needed to keep her safe. *He* wasn't safe–not for her.

He glanced at her out of the corner of his eye. Man, he missed her. Her hands swung at her sides, and it took a brutal amount of restraint to avoid wrapping her hand in his. Truth was, he still loved her. He never stopped loving her. But she would never know that.

The day passed slowly, the sun never wavering in its attempt to bake them. As the sun moved lower, Carver suggested they double check the maps and ensure they were headed the right direction.

Clara traced her finger against the line they needed to follow and looked around. "We should leave the tracks and begin heading straight east towards Noxvalis."

"Or, should we head northeast and hope to encounter a caravan we can ride in with? Will it look less suspicious if we are surrounded by people instead of showing up from the wrong direction looking harried from our trip?" He knew this was the better option. Obviously, two people claiming to be from Calyndor would not arrive from the most direct path. They needed to find a caravan. He needed Clara to come to that conclusion on her own. Otherwise, he would be attacked for trying to take control.

She gnawed her lip, "If we do that, we'll spend a couple extra hours traveling. It will end up being a slightly further distance."

He shrugged, his muscles aching with the motion. "Doesn't matter that much, does it? We're both in good shape." He started to poke her bicep but caught himself before he broke the rule. He dropped his hand awkwardly, uncomfortable with the way her eyes traced its path the entire time.

"Okay." Her eyes stayed on his hand, "Let's keep walking then."

She took off, and he struggled to put the map back as he trailed after her. "Hey, stop a second," he requested. She obliged, clearly frustrated by the request. He returned the map to its spot and pulled out a compass so he could keep them on track. "I have a feeling I'm better versed at using this than you are. I'll keep us on track."

"Sounds brilliant."

"You don't have to be rude."

"I don't have to be, that's true. But it's so much more fun." Her tone remained dry, and she hiked the straps of her bag further up her shoulders.

"You're clearly exhausted. How much further do you want to

walk tonight?" He flinched once the question was out. She wouldn't receive that well.

He was correct. "I can keep going." She snapped, picking up her pace.

"I know you can," he presented as a peace offering, and her face calmed slightly. "I was just suggesting that for the sake of longevity we decide on a time to rest."

"For the sake of longevity." She pulled her braid over her shoulder and picked at the ends of it, refusing to look at him. "I think we shouldn't stop for at least another hour. Maybe stop when we find a relatively sheltered area of the forest to stay in?"

"Works for me." His pride would never let him admit it, but he was as exhausted as she was, if not more so. The idea of sleeping on the ground out in the open sounded absolutely miserable, but at least he wouldn't have to fight Clara on whether or not they should stay together. It was a small benefit to the great outdoors, he supposed.

After a while, Clara's steps grew heavier. She tripped over a branch, a rock, and then what seemed to just be air. Carver didn't comment, determined not to irk her so late at night. His own feet faltered a couple of times, and he was grateful for the litheness drilled into him through extensive training. Eventually, she tripped in a way she couldn't quite brush off, so he pointed, "Look, those trees over there provide a relatively decent amount of shelter. Why don't we crash there for the night."

Her eyes scanned the landscape landing on where he pointed. The moonlight filtered through the trees just enough to show the outlines of everything. "Okay."

Wow, she must be tired, he thought when she didn't put up a fight. It was so unlike her. They carefully sat their bags down, and Clara rubbed her eyes.

Carver yawned as he opened his pack to pull out the blanket. He only had one, and no pillow. He folded one of his jackets to use as a pillow, and laid his blanket out in a way he hoped would work to use it both for bedding and as a covering. Clara did the same.

"You know, if it wasn't for the rules, I'd be suggesting we use one blanket to lay on and the other to cover us." He could feel the heat of her glare even in the darkness, and he was glad she couldn't see how pink his cheeks were at the suggestion he offered.

"You're exhausted, so I'll let the comment slide." She replied quietly, tiredness coating every word. "But continue to make comments like that, and I will have to consider it a breach of contract."

"Breach of contract," he yawned again. "You get so professional sounding when you're tired."

"And you sound like an idiot."

"That's not very nice," he pouted.

"Go to sleep. Long day tomorrow." Clara laid her head down, and managed to pull the blanket over half her body.

"Yes, Mom." He replied.

The night air was cooler than he anticipated. He'd worked up enough of a sweat walking he had barely noticed the temperature dropping. As his heart rate slowed, he noticed it more and more. It wasn't exactly comfortable.

He glanced Clara's way and saw her shivering in her lack of covering. He was pretty close to doing the same. "Is this going to work?" He whispered.

"What do you mean?"

"We're both shivering, and there's an easy solution." He paused, contemplating how to present his suggestion. "The mission comes first, right?"

"Right," she answered, rolling to her side to look at him.

"And we can't finish the mission if we freeze to death." He

appealed to her logic, hoping she would agree with him—purely for the sake of the mission.

"I don't think we're in danger of freezing to death," she attempted to rebut, but her chattering teeth belied her statement.

"You know what I mean. Technically, we could share without breaking any of the rules."

"Oh?" At that comment, she looked willing to listen.

"Well, we'd be sharing a blanket. We can each stay on our side and avoid any physical touch. The rules say if there's only one bed, we take turns sleeping on the floor. Technically, we're both on the floor already, so we wouldn't be breaking that rule either." A brilliant loophole, but would she accept it?

She contemplated it for a moment, but as her shivering grew worse, finally consented.

Carver spread his blanket out over the ground, and laid on the far side. She laid down on the other side and they pulled the blanket over both of them, managing to cover far more than the single blankets had.

Clara immediately closed her eyes, and moments later her breathing evened and Carver knew she was asleep. With that knowledge, he gingerly turned to his side so he was facing her. He did so slowly, careful not to wake her. He knew it could be considered creepy, but asleep she looked like the girl he had fallen in love with. She looked peaceful again, untouched by the horrors of the world. As if, once again, her biggest worries were choosing the right outfit or planning dinner.

He fell asleep quickly, in spite of the forest noises. The day had taken its toll.

He woke with the sunrise, Clara still asleep beside him. For the first time in years, he had no nightmares.

23 CLARA

Clara woke to find the spot next to her empty. She rubbed the sleep from her eyes and scanned the area for Carver. She thought she would see him quickly, where would he go anyway? Panic set in when she couldn't spot him.

"Carver?" She called softly as she pushed the blanket back and stood up. No response. "Carver?" She called a little louder. A bird tweeted a response, but nothing came from him. She stood, spinning in a circle to look throughout the clearing. No sign of him.

For a moment she wondered if he had abandoned her, decided he was better set to accomplish the mission without her, and slinked away. But no, his stuff was still here. He couldn't have left his bag, map, papers, clothes, and everything else behind, and still have a shot at completing the mission. There was a minuscule amount of comfort in that.

So where was he? Did something happen to him? Was he hurt? It was fitting, she supposed, that her initial assumption was he had abandoned her, not that he was hurt. Her mind spun frantically, and she didn't know what to do. She couldn't leave their stuff to go look for him, but she had to know what happened to him.

She started packing her stuff, less carefully than she had the day before. "Good morning, sunshine!" His voice was far too carefree for the stress she felt, and truly she wanted to punch him. She did spin to face him.

"Where were you?" He looked confused by the anger in her tone, but chose not to question it.

"Nature calls?" He raised an eyebrow as he took in her posture. Feet spread as though bracing for impact, arms crossed over her chest. Even she could feel how prepared for a fight she was. She exhaled, relief flooding her veins. She dropped her arms to her side, shaking her head at him before resuming her packing more calmly.

"Why, were you worried about me?" He teased.

Clara, however, was not in a teasing mood, not with the anxiety still working its way out of her veins from his disappearing stunt. "No." She replied sharply as she took the blanket from her bag, folded it in a perfect square, and then returned it to her bag.

"I think you were concerned," his singsong tone only frustrated her more.

"Like you said, we need to stick together. How do you think I felt when I woke up to see you were nowhere to be found?"

"Clara, you're overreacting. I had to piss."

She clenched her fists at her sides. "Don't you dare tell me I'm overreacting."

"But you are. You're acting like I've committed some heinous crime. All I did was pee!"

She rolled her eyes, beyond frustrated. "Did I actually scare you that much?" Carver asked after a few minutes. She finished packing her bag, and glared at him as she waited for him to gather the last of his things.

"Yes," she admitted. She couldn't believe she had admitted that to him, but he was her partner. It was her job to keep him alive. *I only care because if you die we can't complete the assignment.* She tried to convince herself that was the full truth, but as good as she was at lying to herself this one fell short.

"I'm sorry." His tone was sincere, and she waited for the punchline or sarcasm that never came.

"Apology accepted." They started walking, falling into step. "I may have overreacted."

"May have?"

"Okay, okay," she smiled slightly, a little lighter now than she felt moments before. "I overreacted. I'm sorry. I woke up, you were nowhere to be found, and I feared the worst."

"You worried I was hurt or dead."

Actually, I'm selfish enough the worst I feared was you leaving me. "Something like that."

Clara tucked her hands into the sleeves of her jacket, enjoying the feel of the brisk morning air as they started to walk. "Technically, this should be day two of our walking journey. Hopefully, we find people to join today."

He nodded. "I personally think we've made good time. We don't have an exact way to measure distance, but we've kept a good pace."

Clara chewed on the inside of her cheek. In her opinion, everything mission oriented until this point was easy. Sure, they had a lot of physical activity, but she was used to that. It was this next part that truly terrified her–the part where she had to become someone else. She didn't know how to do that.

"Um," she inhaled deeply, not wanting to actually say the statement out loud. "Do we have our stories straight? For the, uh, the parts we're playing? That's what you called it right? The people we become and the characters we are."

"Well, we're both from Calyndor. What do you know about

Calyndor?"

She scrambled to remember the history lessons she had been taught. She vaguely remembered information about the various kingdoms from basic training, but the unfortunate reality was she hadn't used any of it over the last three years. It hadn't been relevant, so she hadn't retained it.

Carver stared at her as she tried to remember, and jumped in. "Calyndor is an extremely small, but wealthy, nation. They're regarded as frivolous people. Far more concerned with food or events than politics. They've never been a threat, and they don't hold any resources that other kingdoms have found valuable enough to plunder. Plus, the Calyndor typically squander their jewels in trades with other nations anyway."

Clara couldn't quite imagine a life without the threat of war. "If they're not training to fight or think about war, what are they doing on a day to day basis?"

Carver grinned as though it was something he would have greatly enjoyed. "They're living. They have adventures. They have fun. They visit different kingdoms and see the world."

"That sounds so pointless."

"You argue that this war has a point?"

Clara immediately stiffened at the implication. It felt like he was denigrating what so many people, including their fathers, had died for. "Survival?"

"Beyond survival though. If it was over, if we managed to end it, what then? Purpose shouldn't be tied up in a war."

"Isn't yours?"

Carver didn't respond immediately, and Clara knew he was taking her question seriously. Eventually he answered, "We're getting off topic." Blatantly ignoring her question he continued, "If you're a Calyndor girl you're going to have to smile."

"This won't work." She replied entirely monotone.

"Oh c'mon. I know you're capable of it." She glared at him, but he only laughed. "Besides, you have a beautiful smile when you choose to use it. With that smile and your wit, you could rob a man blind and he'd thank you for it. That's a skill we need on this assignment."

She almost gave him a hard time about calling her smile beautiful, but she enjoyed the compliment too much to want to punish him for giving it. Instead, she laughed. "See?" He pointed at her mouth, "That smile, right there. A real smile. That's what a Calyndor girl would have."

She kept the smile pasted on her mouth, and after a couple minutes it did feel genuine. "Okay, so I need to smile. What else?"

"Promise not to be offended?"

"Uh uh. I don't make promises like that. Spit it out."

"You're have to be…friendlier."

Clara slipped a knife out from a hidden pocket on her leg. She carefully flipped the blade as they walked, smiling mischievously. "Friendlier? Prey tell, what about me isn't friendly?"

Carver raised an eyebrow and shook his head. "Don't do this to me."

"Do what to you?"

"Act like you don't know what I'm talking about so that I have to spell it out. Then once I spell it out, you can pretend like it's all new information and get offended, even though you knew exactly what I was talking about from the beginning."

She put her knife away, losing the smile as well. She didn't like being called out so specifically. "Sounds like that's something you think I do often."

"Not often," he shrugged, "But it's been known to happen." It was a vague comment, one that hinted at their past. She hadn't done it to him on this trip, so it had to be something he was still holding onto from previous years. She started to think back, trying to recall any incidents like that. Their past wasn't something she wanted to ponder, so she quickly reigned in her thoughts. Remembering when she was his didn't benefit her. It was still too painful.

"Fine." Clara groaned the word, and raising her right hand continued, "I won't point knives at people. At least not people we're trying to befriend. I'll smile. I'll use less sarcasm. I won't glare at people. Anything I'm missing?"

Carver merely shook his head at her antics, but she saw the hint of a smile and felt satisfied. "You're also supposed to be my wife."

"Anything but that," she groaned again.

"Thanks." He responded shortly.

"I didn't mean it like that."

"I mean, technically, we just have the same last name. We could claim to be siblings instead. I know Command said husband and wife, but maybe we could take that as a suggestion instead of order."

She held up her arm only an inch from his. Her white skin now pink from the sun was dotted with freckles. His skin had tanned, and darkened to several shades beyond where hers could ever get. "Really. They'll believe we're siblings." Sarcasm dripped off every word, knowing that claiming to be siblings wouldn't be believed.

"It's either that or we're married."

She groaned again. "Fine. I guess we're married. Wait actually, for us to be married and from Calyndor, what would that look like?"

He grimaced, and she reconsidered the sibling idea. "They're known for their flirtation and PDA."

"Ugh." The sibling idea held even more appeal, but in her gut she knew it wouldn't work. The mission came first.

"Yeah. Not ideal."

"What if you were the adopted sibling?"

"Why do I have to be adopted?" He immediately shot back.

"Because, it was my idea?"

"I mean, I guess that could work," he thought about it, head tilting back and forth as he considered the possibilities. "Well, actually, I don't know that adoptions are big in Calyndor. It might raise suspicion."

"So we have to be married?" She hated the idea. The last thing she wanted to do was pretend to be his wife. She would rather stick needles under her fingernails than pretend to be his wife.

"It is breaking a rule. But technically the assignment comes first is our first rule. So we'd be breaking a rule to follow a higher rule?"

"Interesting logic," she muttered. It occurred to her how well he used logic to change the rules he had written. As much as it frustrated her, she didn't have a good response to shut it down.

"Do you have a better idea?" She could hear the annoyance in his words, and she hated to admit it, he was right.

"No." *The mission comes first. You're going to save Quorath,* she reminded herself.

"It's settled then. You're my wife. My fake wife." He quickly blurted, before mumbling, "But still."

24 CARVER

It's settled. You're my wife. My fake wife. But still. The second the words left his mouth Carver mentally kicked himself. He glanced at Clara, but she stared straight ahead, not daring to react to his careless words. His stupid, careless, *stupid* words.

He would benefit from running his words through his brain before letting them come out of his mouth. He didn't need to clarify what she was thinking. There was a point she would have been his wife. If *he* had chosen differently. If *she* had never tried to follow him. It was far too late now. History couldn't be changed, no matter how many times he attempted to rewrite the details in his mind.

The sun was high on the horizon when he felt a shift. They had left the forest behind a couple hours before, and the endless fields took on a more civilized air. Well trodden paths were coming into view, a ruined road visible among the wildflowers.

Most cars had been taken apart to use the electronics and pieces for other efforts, but a few vehicles still remained. Most of the roads were broken in too many places to be restored after the initial war. That was over 100 years ago, and many things were never rebuilt. While they had the knowledge to build most of it back up, roads were no longer practical.

The nations had formed into five individual kingdoms after that war. Firm boundaries were established, and the world outside the kingdoms ceased to exist. The radiation from the war was too great, and leaving the established boundaries or trade routes from the kingdoms was a death sentence.

Though most kingdoms were civil to each other, at least for the purpose of trade, Noxvalis and Quorath never restored that kind of relationship. So for the last 50 years, each tried to carefully sabotage the other. What they called a war, was at the surface quite petty. Noxvalis sent soldiers to Quorath; Quorath fought them off. Quorath attacked Noxvalis, and the cycle never ended. The war efforts had been going on for so long, no one could even remember why they started.

Truthfully, it felt like more of a feud than an actual war.

Carver justified it by knowing Quorath couldn't lay down its weapons. Noxvalis was bigger, and for some reason wanted to destroy them. Quorath would only survive if its people continued to fight back. So here he was.

They stayed to the side of the road, choosing to continue their journey on the softer ground rather than the broken concrete. Eventually they reached another dirt trodden road. This road was for more typical transportation. Foot traffic or animals.

The old concrete roads allowed people to travel too freely. Now, people stayed within their own kingdoms, seldom daring to travel beyond the safety of their borders. Concrete roads also dared militaries to provide more and more threatening transports. It simply wasn't worth it.

"Do you think we'll run into people soon?" It was the first time Clara spoke to him since his stupid slip up. He wondered how many times his words had replayed in her head. *Stupid.* The best word to describe him in every attempt to talk to her.

"I hope so. If we show up like this, we'll garner suspicion." A real response, the best he could do.

"Wouldn't want that."

"No," he kicked a rock and watched as it bounced along the grass, "We would not."

She fell into silence again, and desperate to bridge the void Carver said, "Was it hard spending so much time on in-house assignments instead of missions?"

She met his gaze, eyes wide. He almost smiled at her shocked expression, she looked so much younger again. But then her gaze hardened, "Trying to lord your greater number of missions over me?"

His heart dropped. How did he always manage to say the wrong thing? "No, Clara, no that wasn't what I was trying to do at all—" he would have continued justifying his comment but she started laughing.

"I know. I'm teasing. That's allowed." She quickly added as she continued to laugh at him, and as much as it jolted his pride, he enjoyed the sound of her laugh too much to stay offended.

"Maybe it should have been a rule," he muttered, giving her more to laugh at.

"To answer your question," she instantly sobered, all mirth gone from her tone. "It was. I wondered what else I needed to do to prove myself. At the same time, I had peace about it. I knew I was the best. I didn't need Command to prove that. Everyone knew I was the most dependable and the most valuable asset."

"And also humble."

She scowled at him, "You asked."

He nodded, smiling. "That I did, and I appreciate your honest response."

She nodded in return, and Carver felt the silence returning. He hated the silence. They used to laugh and banter the entire time they were together. They would discuss deep concepts, discuss every single thought they had. He pretended to be annoyed by how much she talked, but he loved every minute of it. He would trade so much to have it back.

Instead, the silence swelled around him, only broken by the occasional bird call or the wind brushing through the greenery. It felt so wrong, so wrong to be out here with her, like this. There was more he should say, some way he should assuage things between them so it would be easier to play their roles. It was a role that would possibly, probably, kill him to play. How could he pretend she was his wife while keeping professional boundaries? What constituted as a professional boundary anyway?

"Clara, we should think through how we're planning to be," he caught himself, "How we'll play our roles. Once we get there I think we should…" He trailed off as she held up a hand to stop him.

She examined the distance listening carefully. "I think I hear someone."

He stopped completely, straining to hear what had made her pause.

"We should change. You have the clothes we're supposed to wear into town, right?"

He nodded. She set her bag down and before he had a chance to respond, stripped her shirt off to switch them. She glanced up in time to see his jaw slacken, "Hey, eyes off me. Change." He swallowed hard but turned to his bag, unable to keep his eyes from straining back to her as she finished changing.

He changed quickly. The all black clothes were put back in their bags, and they both wore the softer colors of Calyndor. Clara looked significantly less intimidating. Pretty. While he was tempted to comment, he didn't want to receive another scowl and thought better of it.

He breathed in deeply, hating every single person at Command for what came next. He grabbed the box he hid in the bottom of his bag when he had found it that morning, and cleared his throat. "As you know, our roles were written before we were ever called to Command."

"You sound so serious. This isn't good, is it?" Her eyes were glued to him, and his heart started pounding.

He tried his best to keep his expression the same. "Just know this isn't from me. I tried to brainstorm another option."

He tossed her the velvet box, too annoyed by his role to even hand it to her, and as much as he wanted to catalogue her reaction, he couldn't keep his eyes on her. He scuffed his toes in the dirt, covering the light fabric of the shoes in a thin layer of dust. He couldn't believe that Command had forced this upon them. At the same time, why would they care how it affected them? They were soldiers and nothing more. With that in mind, he looked up.

Clara's mouth hung slightly open, and she gazed at the ring she'd placed on her finger. "I would've put it on you, but, well, the rules," he said, stumbling over his words in the way only she caused. "Wouldn't want to break them." Even though everything inside him longed to slip the ring over her finger just to feel her skin once more.

She swallowed hard. "This wasn't your idea." A statement, not a question. A reminder. She chewed on her bottom lip, her right hand twisting the bracelet on her left wrist as she stared.

"It wasn't my idea," he confirmed, though the admission killed a part of him. He always wanted to be the one to put a ring on her finger, the one to cause that look of amazement to cross her face. The ring he planned to put there was still in his drawer–a reminder. He loved her too much to keep her.

She swallowed again, seemingly coming back into herself. "Command sure has an interesting plan for the two of us." She met his eyes then, and he waited for the outburst or frustration he was sure would come. She just stared back, no emotions on display.

"It seems that way, yes." He continued to keep his words careful, waiting for another explosion from her. Waiting for her to scream or shout over the insensitivity.

"So, husband," she paused over the word, as if she was testing the feel of it. His heart swelled in a way that was definitely wrong. "How are we supposed to do this?"

He shrugged, shoving his ring finger into the thick silver band Command had provided to him. He flexed his fingers, the weight foreign and frustrating. "Follow the rules." He provided.

25 CLARA

The ring felt so wrong–so very wrong, and somehow so right.

Clara could hear people in the distance and knew they were fast approaching a caravan. That's where their act would begin. Calyndor was close enough most people came by horse and cart. Old fashioned, yes, but far easier and less expensive than navigating the ruined roads with a hard-to-find vehicle.

Her thumb traced over the band, and though she refused to look down again, every sense had become attuned to the ring.

It wasn't heavy, a thin silver band with a cluster of diamonds. She loved the ring. She'd never admit it to Carver, though. She couldn't have picked a better one for herself. It was beautiful, and small enough she could flip the diamonds to her palm and make it more discreet. It wouldn't attract too much attention, yet her new station was obvious. These were all logical reasons to love it. Everything had to be logical.

With the beauty of the ring, came the disappointment Carver hadn't been man enough to slip it onto her finger. She understood, of course, the rules and all of that. Goodness knows, she was an avid enforcer of every small detail. But still. The one man she'd loved, and she had to put the ring on her own finger. There was more than a touch of irony in that.

"We're almost there." Carver interrupted her thoughts, and she stopped twisting her ring as though caught. He glanced at her nervously. It was a new expression on him. She'd never seen his confidence waver.

"Are you okay?" She asked.

"I was wondering about you. Are you going to be okay with this role we're playing?" His words were careful, his intent clear. He was truly worried about her. Ha.

"Do we have a choice?" She provided the answer she thought he needed to hear. She wouldn't tell him how her heart constricted when she put the ring on her finger. She wouldn't tell him that she kept glancing at his profile and thinking how much she wanted to be his again. No, she would keep to the assignment. She was an assassin. She was strong enough for this.

"There's always a choice."

She rolled her eyes. "Carver, I've killed countless people. This will be a breeze." Her tone sounded far lighter than she felt, and she was proud of how well she was already acting. She could do this.

His cheeks flushed, but he nodded. When they were close enough to hear the individual voices, he reached out and took her hand. For a second, his touch froze her blood and she wanted to rip her hand away and punch him. Hard. *It's not his fault.* She reminded herself as she took a deep breath in and forced a smile to her face. It was difficult at first, but after a couple minutes her smile felt almost natural.

Every brush of his skin across hers as they held hands and walked was a beautiful agony. His hands were more calloused than they were before…before her world fell apart, before they ended up here. Before.

"We don't have to do this," Carver whispered as they saw the group of people.

"You know that's not true," she whispered back, keeping the smile pasted on her face.

"Maybe smile a little less." He murmured casually, "You look like you're trying not to let people know you have something stuck up your butt."

Clara laughed, the smile becoming real at his absurdity. "What?"

He shrugged. "Hey, it worked." She didn't need anything to prove that his smile was real. She'd seen it a hundred times before, and like always, it did something to her insides that wasn't an altogether unpleasant sensation. Unwanted, absolutely. Unpleasant, not entirely.

"Here goes nothing." Carver tugged on her hand gently, never loosening his grip. Her stomach flipped. If only she didn't find him attractive, this would be fine.

"Only it's everything," she muttered back, grateful for his tether as they approached the group.

"Mind if we join you?" He called out.

A couple of the people paused to assess them, but most of the group kept walking. There were close to 20 people, more with the children running around the carts and in between everyone. A few people were in the carts, but the majority were walking, carrying casual conversation with other members of the group. It was an interesting display. Clara stepped closer to Carver, and he dropped his hand to pull his arm around her shoulder.

His warmth and closeness were entirely unexpected and she leaned into his embrace, forgetting momentarily this was only a role. "My wife and I are headed to the festival. I'm assuming that's your destination as well?"

She placed her hand over his, keeping his hand on her shoulder. He laced his fingers with hers, and the smile she wore as they approached the group was entirely real.

One of the women who was assessing them walked over. A hint of suspicion remained in her eyes, but her smile and posture were friendly. "Of course. You're welcome to join our group."

"That's wonderful to hear," Carver exhaled, "I'm sure it will make the journey feel that much shorter."

"Yes. We're only a day's walk out, and you'll be safer at night sleeping with our group anyway." She looked curiously at Clara who still had not spoken. Clara was terrified. Everything Carver said about being undercover rushed through her mind until it was nothing more than a muddled mess. How was she supposed to do this?

"I'm Julia." The woman introduced herself.

"Carver," he shook Julia's hand, and they began walking with the group. "This is my wife, Clara."

"Hi," Clara finally piped in, hating herself the entire time. Why couldn't she seem calm and relaxed like Carver?

"Have you been married long?" Julia asked.

Clara inwardly panicked. They didn't get this far into their story. "About a year." Carver answered like it was the most natural thing in the world. Relief flooded Clara's chest, and she squeezed his hand on her shoulder gently in gratitude before realizing that was against the rules. "We actually honeymooned at the beach west of Noxvalis, so we've been out this direction before."

Clara focused on maintaining a neutral expression, not letting her jaw drop at how seamlessly Carver lied. He didn't think about it. Even knowing him as well and as long as she had, he could have convinced her with that lie. She knew she needed to chime in at some point. She was supposed to be girly and fun.

She forced a light giggle, "It was an amazing honeymoon," and raised her eyebrows at him suggestively. *Yes, make everyone uncomfortable by referencing sex. Pretend you aren't insanely uncomfortable.* Her inner monologue chided.

"That it was my dear," he reached across to grab her free hand and raised it to his lips pressing a kiss across her knuckles. Clara kept her perfect smile. Truly, she wanted to slap him across the face but that wouldn't go well. It was only fair in a way. She squeezed his hand; he kissed the back of hers. They were both tormenting the other and shredding the laws they created. It was all for a greater purpose. Justified.

Julia smiled at them, clearly enjoying their flirtation. "Ah, to be young again. My husband and I had the time of our lives in our 20s. Kids change everything, you know."

Clara didn't know, but she nodded as if she sympathized. Maybe she was capable of pulling this off. "So I've heard. We decided not to try during our first year of marriage."

"Smart move–gives you plenty of time to practice." Julia's dark eyes sparkled with her suggestion. She continued to smile at them, and Clara couldn't help but think she had the most perfect lips. Naturally pink. Even though she was older than her and Carver by at least a decade, Clara thought she was still gorgeous.

At her suggestion though, Clara began to inwardly panic as images of the future she almost had with Carver flooded her mind. His arm around her felt far too warm and heavy, and she wished to all the gods she could be anywhere but here. Give her a battle to fight, something productive to do. Don't make her finish out this conversation.

Outwardly, she laughed airily, and Carver joined in. "Yes ma'am.

That's our plan." He looked down at her, his eyes too probing for her to cope with so she looked away.

One of the children screamed and yelled at another child. Julia sighed deeply. "It was very nice to meet you both and we're glad to have you among us. I have to deal with my children, but perhaps tonight you can meet my husband and we can get to know each other a little better."

"We'd like that very much." Carver confirmed.

Clara's turn to complete her act, "It was so nice to meet you."

Julia walked away and when she was on the other side of the cart, Clara let her smile drop. Carver removed his arm from her shoulder as he stretched, and instead lightly grabbed her hand. If anyone looked over, they kept the appearance of being a couple and so in love, but it was easier for them to maintain their real boundaries when they weren't pressed against each other.

"You okay?" Carver whispered.

She peered up into his dark brown eyes, and immediately wished she hadn't looked at him. He was way too attractive. With her hand in his, her heart was beating too quickly, and there was a traitorous part of her wishing this wasn't an act.

She didn't know how to answer him. Did she tell the truth? Did she admit that already this act was destroying the walls she had built and she would quite possibly never be okay again? Or did she play her role? Strong, uncaring, ready to deal with anything and everything that came her way. His eyes urged her for an answer, and as much as she wanted to lie, the words wouldn't come. She was living too much of a lie as her hand tightened around his. He squeezed her hand back and the words tumbled out before she could stop them.

"I don't think I'll be okay again after this assignment."

26 CARVER

Carver stroked his thumb across her fingers–aware the action worsened the situation, but still feeling the need to offer some form of comfort. What else could he do? There were only dumb platitudes that didn't actually mean anything, and he wouldn't disrespect her by quoting those. *It'll all be okay. Everything works out for good. This is all just a test. Just think, we're saving our kingdom.*

He cringed inside even as he thought through these. No way he would say any of those to her.

"I never wanted you to end up here." He whispered. Nothing else felt like a good answer. Everything else was far too flat and fake.

Her brow furrowed and she leaned closer to him. "What do you mean by that?"

He sighed deeply, swinging their clasped hands in the space between them. To everyone watching, they appeared happy enough, as if they were simply having a mundane conversation. "I tried to protect you."

"Protect me?"

He shook his head. "It doesn't matter. It clearly didn't work."

Her hand fell slack in his, and he met her gaze. "It does matter. Explain." Her voice remained quiet so as not to attract attention, but he could hear the sharpness of her tone–sharp as a knife.

He was overly aware of his heartbeat as adrenaline flooded his veins with the realization of what he was walking into. He was dangerously close to admitting something he couldn't take back. "I didn't mean anything by it." He tried to brush it off, "You can't blame me for wanting to protect you."

"No, Carver, you did mean something by it. Don't pretend I can't read you. Answer the question." Dang. She still knew him a little too well.

Carver bit his lip, contemplating how much of the truth he could share, or if a version of truth sufficed. "I'm not sure you want to know the answer."

"I wouldn't have asked if I didn't want to know." He heard his own words reiterated in that statement.

He waited to respond, hoping that someone or something would interrupt them so that he wouldn't have to answer. She'd never forgive him if he admitted the truth. The rest of this mission would be more than miserable. Would she even be willing to continue? Maybe she would quit and that would be that. She wouldn't die on this mission, instead she would die at the same time as everyone else when Noxvalis unleashed the biological weapon. What a thrilling thought.

"Carver, answer the question." She tugged on his hand, desperate for the truth.

He immediately regretted looking into her blue eyes as everything he felt about her rushed to the surface. "I was only trying to protect you." He whispered.

"Yes, you said that."

"I didn't think you would survive as a Viper." He flinched as the words left his mouth. It was far too late to recall them. He dug his own grave.

"What?" She yanked her hand away from him, but after glancing around nervously, returned her hand to his. She very much looked like she was considering all the ways she could murder him. He couldn't blame her. "You didn't think I would survive."

He shook his head, staring at his feet as they trod over the red dirt road. It wasn't as dark as blood, but as thoughts ran through his head he wondered if it had been tinted by the war and faded over time. "I wanted to protect you. I promised I would."

"A promise to whom?"

Your father. Before he died. "That's not important."

"It is to me." Frustration bled over every word, but this was the one answer he couldn't give her.

"I can't tell you that." He looked up at her, begging her to understand there were things he couldn't answer. "Ask me something else."

She gnawed on her lip, eyes angrier than he'd ever seen. All her fury was directed at him. "What's the point? You're a brilliant liar. You won't give me the truth anyways."

Ouch. He felt the dagger to his heart, the pain hitting deeper because he knew it was well deserved. "Clara," he kept his voice soft, "I'll give you as much of the truth as I can."

"And I won't pretend to believe you." She pasted her smile back on her face, looking every bit the part he told her she would play. His heart broke at the falseness she stepped into.

She directed her gaze away from him, watching the other people in the caravan. How could he make this better? She had to trust him at least a little for him to keep her alive. That may be out of his control already.

"I told them to put you in the Vipers because I figured after a few weeks you would either give up or be cut, and you'd be able to go home." He let the admission slip, regretting the second the words were past his lips. Apparently, today he was not only digging his grave, he was going the extra mile so his body would never be found.

"What?!" She shouted, and Carver gave her a look as he glanced around. She laughed loudly as though she was reacting to something he had said, and he was relieved she was able to pull it off. She tugged him closer to her, crossing her arm to grab his wrist. Her grip was harsh and he resisted the urge to grit his teeth as she dug her nails into his skin.

She kept her smile pasted, the perfect facade to anyone watching. He hadn't expected her to be this good. He wouldn't lie. He was impressed with her performance.

"You did what?" She hissed through her teeth, lips still curved in a vicious smile.

He knew he had admitted too much already, but now that part of it was out in the open, it felt less harmful to admit to all of it. "I wanted to protect you. You wouldn't have been safe as an operative. I thought you'd come to your senses and go back to your normal life."

She laughed again, but he could hear the anger in the noise. "I didn't want to go back to my own life. I joined the army because I wanted my life to be worth something more."

He rolled his eyes, "Oh be honest, Clara, you joined because you followed me."

Her lips lifted. "So full of yourself. Is that what you've told yourself the last five years?" She chuckled darkly, "That I followed you? Oh my word, *you're so amazing.*" She gushed, every word overly exaggerated, "I just *couldn't live* without you. So I followed you to the army. Pushed through two years of basic training, became one of the best soldiers, actually, all because I couldn't stand not seeing your face."

He grimaced; she continued, "You're so full of it. Did you ever think *maybe* I joined because I wanted to do something for our kingdom? *Maybe* I joined to take up my father's legacy? Do something that was actually worth something?"

Her eyes flamed again, and *dang she looks hot*. Not a helpful thought. But it was true. His eyes shifted to her lips momentarily before he caught himself, and was thankful she didn't notice.

"I was elected as an operative. I worked hard for that. And I was put in the Vipers. Didn't it ever occur to you that I was placed there because I was capable of surviving it?"

"But you weren't placed there because of you." *Idiot.* Those were the worst words he could have possibly said. It was a fatal mistake for him, even more egregious than starting this conversation. She might have moved past everything that had already been revealed. Now, it was too late to ever get out of this grave.

"What?" She gritted out.

"We're breaking rule number 4." He whispered against her hair, trying to keep up their pretense. He used the opportunity to look around, and no one was paying them any undue attention. He kissed the top of her head before he pulled back.

"I don't care. You started this, please, finish it." She tugged his wrist, nails biting once again, "And don't. Kiss. My. Head."

"Fine." He was past the point of return, and no matter how much he would regret his next words, there wasn't a true way out of it. She wouldn't let it go. Plus, she'd be safer away from him, and maybe this would create the distance he knew they had to keep. "My father was close friends with one of the Command leaders."

"Fine, so?"

"So, when we graduated basic I pulled a couple strings and

convinced them to draft you into Vipers. It was the most physically intense sector, and, like I said, I assumed you would either quit or be cut within a few weeks."

His admission stunned her into silence, and that scared him far more than her fury had. He could only imagine what she was thinking. He didn't have to imagine for long.

"You never did think very highly of me." She shook her head, "Glad to know I wasn't crazy in believing that." Her eyes glazed, but she blinked hard and the look was gone.

"Clara, that's not fair or true. I did think highly of you, do," he corrected himself, "think highly of you. I just wanted you to be safe."

She stared out across the caravan, and he stared at her. At the dark hair brushing across her cheeks, at the intense look still burning in her eyes, at the tilt to her chin he knew was evidence of her extremely restrained anger.

"No, Carver, you didn't think I had what it took. You assumed I followed you. The folly of a rich girl who isn't capable of actually doing anything. Well guess what, you were wrong. I'm on the same level as you now. It's refreshing, actually, to know exactly what you've believed about me." Her voice was calm and controlled, every word calculated.

"That's not fair."

"You don't get to tell me what's fair. Your powers of manipulation only work so far." There was no anger left in her tone. Nothing but a factual statement. Cold. Uncaring. Perfect.

"I've never manipulated you."

"Not directly, maybe. But you've manipulated events around me in an attempt to control my life. I don't appreciate that. It's not your job to protect me."

"It is my *honor* to protect you." He tried to explain. But he couldn't find the words to placate her. He couldn't tell her how much he had loved her. How much he still loved her. How yes, it wasn't what he should have done, but it was truly a selfish move on his part. His desire to keep her alive was so he didn't have to live without her.

"Don't protect me anymore. We've already broken enough rules."

27 CLARA

The caravan stopped to make camp shortly after the sun set. Everyone was full of laughter and energy. They built a couple small campfires, and one of the men brought out a fiddle and played for them.

Clara clapped to the beat, smiling as the children danced and ran in circles around the flames. A couple of the adults stood and danced in a beautiful pattern. She focused on the flames, the laughter, the music–not Carver's arm around her. She tried to disassociate from that, because every time she thought about his presence next to her she wanted to scream.

She wanted to beat the hell out of him, show him exactly how capable and strong she was. She would prove to him she didn't need his protection; he needed to be protected from her. But she couldn't. Her assignment rested on her pretending to be his wife. Her assignments came before her emotions. Always. This was no different.

She wasn't sure what she had done to deserve this kind of torture, but perhaps the gods were real and she had managed to piss off one of them. Or, every single one of them to have warranted this kind of sentence. The fate of a kingdom rested on their ability to play a role they discarded years before.

Carver tried to apologize at least five times before they made camp. She smiled at him, conveying to everyone around them how in love she was. But she stopped responding to him. The puppy dog look he kept giving her told her he knew exactly how she felt about him right now. Good. He deserved all of her hatred and more. He should know every smile was an act.

"Wanna dance?" He whispered, breath tickling her ear. She stilled, and breathed in through her nose, out through her mouth, to keep from jerking away from his nearness. Her skin crawled, and she almost shivered.

"No." She didn't wish to elaborate. His arm around her was hard enough. But his body pressed against hers? A smile pasted on her face as they swayed to the music? That was more than she could take.

"Oh c'mon. It'll be a good show for everyone. We're supposed to be newlyweds, and I don't think we've done a very good job of convincing everyone we're completely in love." He continued whispering in her ear, breath hot on her face. She swallowed, eyes glued to the fire.

"Well, maybe that's because we're not."

"Rule number one." He cited, moving away. She turned to glare at him, annoyed how his dark eyes reflected the light of the flames and caused his entire face to glow with warmth.

"After breaking the rules all day you're citing them to me now?"

"We agreed the rules were written in order of importance, right? So we need to make sure number one stays the top priority. Besides, just because we broke one once, doesn't mean we should continue to break it."

"Doesn't mean we should continue to break it?" She gritted out, "Then why are you asking me to continue touching you?"

He closed his eyes and inhaled deeply. "You know what, Clara? Forget I asked."

He leaned back, his face devoid of emotion as he laid on the grass.

Julia stumbled over, a drink in her hand and her eyes bright from whatever was in the jar. "Aren't you two lovebirds going to dance with us?" She laughed loudly, and Clara smiled agreeably. "Wait, you need to meet my husband Mark!" She called out for him to come over.

"Carver isn't feeling well. We'll sit this one out." Clara explained, stroking Carver's arm gently. The picture perfect wife.

Carver sat up, and Clara's hand fell to the ground. "Actually, I'm feeling much better now and think we should go out."

Despicable human. She couldn't reject him in front of Julia. "Oh, hon," she laid it on thick, hoping Julia's slightly dazed state made it more believable, "It was a long day. I don't want you to push yourself too hard."

He stood up and brushed the dirt off his pants. "You know, I think it'll help me feel better." He smiled at her, but she could see the smugness behind his look. Another deep breath through her nose, out through her mouth, and she resisted the urge to pull him down next to her as she took his hand. The good Calyndor girl would never do that. So she couldn't do it, no matter how much she wanted to.

A man she could only assume was Mark, reached Julia's side and wrapped his arm around her waist. "Julia's told me a bit about you two," he smiled. His eyes crinkled at the corners, and he looked at least ten years Julia's senior. Julia gazed up at him, love struck eyes making Clara feel both envious and sick to her stomach.

"We're always happy to have new people join our caravan. What part of Calyndor do you hail from?" He was far more sober than Julia, and Clara knew she couldn't smile her way out of this one.

Before she could panic, Carver jumped in, "The south. Our family owns a couple shops in that area. It isn't often we get away. But we couldn't resist traveling for the festival. I've heard it will be...enlightening."

Mark nodded, accepting Carver's answer without hesitation. "There was a rumor they're unleashing some of the...*projects* they've been working on."

"Projects?" Clara couldn't help questioning. She looked up at Carver to see if he understood the implication.

Julia laughed loudly, "Mark just likes to be confusing." She smacked him on the arm lightly, and he softened, relaxing under her touch. "You're both dancing with us, right?" Carver spun Clara in a circle she was completely unprepared for; she almost tripped and he caught her haphazardly as he pulled her back, his hand resting on her low back. Clara sucked in a breath. Julia clapped her hands excitedly. "This is my favorite part of trips. It's so much fun and it's never the same when we're home." Julia gazed up at Mark again, "The dancing, the music, the drinks," she giggled turning back to Clara, "The time with loved ones that feels more..." her voice trailed off momentarily as she searched for the word, "Intentional, than the day to day routine."

Clara smiled back at Julia, "I understand," she lied.

Carver tugged on her hand, pulling her onto the dance floor. The second Clara turned her back on the happy couple, she dropped the pleasant expression and glared at him. He ignored it entirely, not deigning to even raise an eyebrow at her anger. He spun her away from him, gracefully pulling her back against him as he led them into the dance circle.

She would have stumbled, but her feet stayed sure and his confidence in the movements kept her own responses smooth. He tightened his arm around her waist and she felt the air leave her lungs. "I hate you." She whispered, attempting to ignore the feel of his arms around her body. It wasn't fair. He stepped precisely, leading her through the moves of the dance.

"No you don't." He whispered back. He rested his chin on her hair, cocooning her in his warmth as the cool night air blew throughout the camp.

"Projects?" She asked him quietly. If she could keep the conversation work related, maybe she could convince herself she wasn't enjoying this. Enjoying him. Maybe she could ignore how safe she felt in his embrace, ignore how his slight beard tickled her cheek when she leaned in to ask him a question.

He glanced around, "Maybe more scientific developments?"

"Maybe."

She balled her hands into fists, refusing to touch him more than she was forced to. When he spun her out and back into him, he twirled her so her back was against his chest. "You know, you're allowed to have fun in moments like this."

His breath on her ear caused her to shiver, and his arms brought her even closer. Her heart pounded under his touch, and she couldn't ignore the fact she wanted more. She wanted his hands on her. She wanted him to feel just as tortured as she felt.

He spun her so she was facing him, pulling her waist against him as they swayed. His thumb traced across the line of skin where her t-shirt had lifted. She reached one hand up and wound her fingers through the curls forming at the nape of his neck. He closed his eyes and leaned back ever so slightly into her touch.

The music grew softer, and his arm around her waist tightened as he looked down at her. His face was only inches from hers, and he started to lean down, closing the gap between their lips as his eyes flicked across her face.

Terror filled her mind. She couldn't let him kiss her. If he did, she would fall again, right back into his orbit. A moth to a brutal flame. He wouldn't even see the damage he caused, but she would be irreparable. Burns heal, but they always scar. "Don't do this to me," she managed to whisper right before his lips touched hers. Somehow, mercifully, those almost silent words caused him to release her.

"You know what, I am pretty tired. We should crash." He said loud enough to explain their departure. He kept a loose grip on her hand, all for show of course. Relief, and disappointment if she was honest, flooded her chest as they left the flames and dancers.

They grabbed their bags from their previous spot, and walked far enough from the group they could barely hear the shouts and excitement.

Clara enjoyed the momentary silence, but knew questions from Carver were quickly coming. "What," he inhaled, and she could hear the tension in his breath, "Exactly am *I* doing to you, Clara?"

She wished he hadn't said her name. Wished that single moment hadn't taken her back to when she was his. Her name sounded so wrong on his lips now, and she wanted him to take it back. Foolish.

"Everything." She whispered as she unpacked her blanket. She was determined not to lose her composure, determined to keep her focus and complete this mission. Carver wouldn't be the death of her. He wouldn't stop her from fulfilling this. She could do it. She could and she would. She wouldn't let petty emotions rule her actions.

"Everything?" He questioned.

"Just drop it, Carver, okay? This isn't a conversation I want to have right now."

"What is a conversation you want to have right now?"

"We're really bad at following the rules." She spit out, trying not to cry. Tears filled her eyes anyway, and she paused to take a deep breath and compose herself. She was grateful for the dark, grateful he couldn't see the anguish consuming her face.

"Is that even relevant anymore?" His voice remained perfectly calm, sterile, almost. He was logical with the mission as the only thing of concern. Because, of course, she wasn't his concern. She never was.

"Yes, Carver, yes! It's all relevant." A tear fell but she swiped it away before he commented, "You want me to trust you for this mission. You want me to trust you to have my back. But how can I? How can I trust you with anything? You never follow through on your word. This time around is no different." She closed her eyes, blocking out the sight of him. She couldn't stand the hurt look on his face. It wasn't fair her words could hurt him in that way. Not when he hurt her the way he did.

"And I," she paused, attempting to maintain some semblance of composure as her voice broke, "I fall for it every time. No matter how strong I am, how strong I become, I still see you as this knight in shining armor. And you're not. You've hurt me more than anyone else ever has. You didn't save me. You're not the hero. You may not be the villain, but you made me who I am. Do you understand that?"

He shook his head as she continued. "Weapons are forged. I'm no different. The fire that pushed me to become this was your betrayal. Don't expect me to forget and just trust you like everything is okay. It's not okay. None of it is okay."

"Okay."

"That's it?" She raised her voice, and could feel the hysteria building. "I say all of that and the only response you have is 'okay'?"

"What response do you want me to have?" His voice was rougher than she had heard it before, and she took a step back awaiting an outburst from him. "Do you want me to say that you're right? That I'm a horrible person and all I'm capable of is hurting you? I know it's true! I know, okay? And I'm trying to do the right thing and protect you now, but it's never enough, is it? All I've ever done is try to protect you."

"Maybe you shouldn't." All of her aggression flew out in that one statement.

"Yeah, I'm getting that." He ran a hand through his hair, the defeat clear on his face.

He laid out his blanket, and folded himself into it facing away from her.

Another tear trickled down her cheek as she watched his form inhale and exhale. She didn't bother to wipe it away as she laid out her own blanket and curled into herself.

28 CARVER

It was lovely to know everything he had done was worth absolutely nothing. He had only ever tried to protect Clara. And she blamed him for it. She wished he hadn't tried to protect her. She blamed him for the villain she now saw herself as. Maybe it was his fault.

He wrapped his arms across his chest, trying to fall asleep, but all he could think was how much he had screwed this up. He knew it was his fault. If only. If only what? If only he had married her? If only he hadn't intervened and had let her get assigned to the army or wherever else they would have put her? If only he hadn't been put on this assignment?

So many options, but none of them fixed this current problem. In fact, most of them only exacerbated it. There was no use daydreaming about things he couldn't fix. He wished he could fix them. Desperately. But he couldn't.

He tossed and turned, watching the clouds roll across the sky in the moonlight and praying it wouldn't rain. If this assignment got any more complicated he might just lose it. He was supposed to be the strong one. From all his training, he knew how to minimize and destroy his emotions. Yet somehow, he couldn't build enough walls against her. She knew just where to push. Just what to say for all of his defenses to be rendered useless.

"Carver?" She whispered, and against his better judgment, he sat up to face her. He didn't say anything. She sat, pulling her knees against her body and wrapping her arms around them. "I'm sorry."

"You don't have to be sorry." He still sounded angry, but to hell with her apology. She didn't have anything she needed to be sorry for. He was the one constantly messing things up. If only he had just—

"But I am. It wasn't fair to say those things."

"Clara, everything you said was true. I wouldn't trust me either." His words rang true, even so, he wished they weren't. He wanted to be trustworthy for her. He wanted to be her friend, her protector. He wanted her. *You can't have her*. He reminded himself. He would have to continue reminding himself.

She shifted in her blanket, trying to draw it further around herself without pulling it off the ground. "I do trust you."

Her admission sat in the space between them, removing a burden while adding a new one. If she trusted him, then maybe he did have a chance at protecting her as they went into the city. If she trusted him, he would hurt her again.

"I'm only trying to protect you."

She shook her head, hair flying across her face. He wanted to tuck it back behind her ear, but he resisted. He didn't need to get in more trouble. "Don't try to protect me. Trust me in the same way I trust you. To protect ourselves and watch each other's backs. Neither of us actually needs protection."

He disagreed, strongly, but he wasn't willing to ignore the olive branch she was extending. "You know, if any of the caravan walks this way, they'll question why newly weds are shivering in the cold air feet apart from each other."

He swore she rolled her eyes, even though it was too dark to tell for sure, but she laughed and he smiled. He could do this. They would be okay. "Is that your way of inviting me into your bed?" Her implication caused his own laugh.

"Not like that." She smiled. *Though if you insist…*He quickly shut that line of thinking down. *You can't have her.* It became a chant in his mind.

She stood up, and he spread his blanket out flat so it was big enough for the both of them. Again, they slept next to each other. Still not touching, though closer than the night before. "Do you ever wonder about the what ifs?" She whispered right as he was about to doze off.

"Of course." He mumbled back.

"Sometimes, I wonder where we would be if there was no war. When I was younger, I always thought that the war was what pushed us apart. If we hadn't signed up for basic, if we hadn't become operatives, if that hadn't been our goal we could have stayed together."

Now he was awake, and as much as he wanted to remind her of the rule she was breaking, he wanted to hear the rest of what she had to say more.

"But then, I realized that without the war, we never would have met. Our fathers wouldn't have been friends, you wouldn't have moved into the house on our property, my father wouldn't have died, and, in a way, drove us together. So the war separated us, but it is also what initiated everything for us."

"Yeah," he agreed.

"I've wondered, are we blessed or cursed for meeting? Was the war the issue and we never should have met? Never ended up in a position to hurt the other? Or, was the war a driving marker of fate, to give us the time we did have?"

"Clara, I'm too tired for this." His heart couldn't stand the direction this was headed. The implication their love and eventual break up was all connected to the war and fate. He didn't want to think about it. He believed that everyone was in charge of making their own decisions, and it was up to them to live by it. That's what he had done.

"Sorry."

She turned her back to him, curling in on herself. He wouldn't apologize this time, though. He was already doing everything in his power to not wrap his arms around her and tell her that it was all fate. That this assignment had driven them back together and he would never let go of her again.

It wasn't true and he couldn't live with himself if he lied to her like that. He was a soldier. He would do whatever was required of him. She wouldn't be safe if they were back together. So he laid his arms next to his sides and tried to find some form of sleep. He needed his rest if he was going to protect her. It didn't come easily, but eventually he drifted off.

He squinted awake, the sun already bright on the horizon. Clara wasn't next to him, but he didn't think much of it. She had most likely gone to the bathroom or something. He chuckled to himself about her panic the day before when he had been the one who had left before she woke up. She definitely worried more than he did.

She trekked back over a few minutes later, the rising sun framing her silhouette. *Wow.* She was beautiful.

"Why are you staring like you've seen a ghost or something?" Her tone, however, was not beautiful.

"Nice scenery." He muttered.

She shook her head and bent over to pack her bag. That certainly didn't help, and he pulled his eyes away before she could stand up and accuse him of staring again. He had to get his mind straight.

"Sleep okay?" He asked.

"Since when do we make casual conversation?"

"I'm gonna go with no. Or are you just hormonal?" He winked when she glared at him.

"I'd slap you if you weren't my partner." She paused, straightening with her bag in one hand as she pondered, "Actually, I'd slap you anyway."

He came up behind her, and though he knew it was a bad idea, wrapped his arms around her waist. She instantly struggled against him until he hissed, "Look."

She relaxed against him as she waved at Julia. Carver knew her smile was only for Julia and that Clara still wanted to hurt him, but for a moment he could pretend all was right in his world. He could pretend he wasn't memorizing the scent of her hair. He could pretend the curves of her body didn't feel like home. He could pretend all of this wasn't just pretend.

29 CLARA

The rest of the trip to Noxvalis was miserable. The sun burned hot overhead, and Clara dreaded the sensation of Carver against her skin. She couldn't get mad at him. He was just playing his role. The doting husband. Far more perfect in this play act than he was capable of in real life.

She had loved dating him, had loved being his. But even when they had been together, he never acted like this. Her heart ached; now she knew even when she had him, she never had the best parts of him. She supposed the fault lay within herself. He had assured her, over and over, that he truly liked her. Was truly in love with her. But she had always suspected he wasn't fully sincere. It sucked to have her worst fears come true. At least she had been proven right.

Confusion ran rampant in her mind as it bounced between his intentions, her feelings, and the reality of the situation. He claimed he only wanted to protect her, but she knew he had thought her weak. Presumably still did. That was the reason he wanted to protect her. And that wasn't a very good reason. She was highly capable, and constantly proved that, thank you very much. Maybe his intentions weren't all that complicated.

Her feelings though, *dang*. There were moments when he grabbed her hand or spun her around and everything inside her felt *alive* again. She felt like the girl she was before. Before they broke up, before she became the monster she felt beneath her skin.

Julia walked with them for a little while, and kept a steady stream of chatter with Clara. Most of it was about her husband and her three boys, "They're 9, 12, and 15 now. It feels like time has just flown. I don't know what I'll do when Ezra, that's the oldest, you know, moves out in a couple years. I think it might just break me." Clara resisted the urge to roll her eyes at the emotion in the woman's voice. It was sweet, she supposed, that this woman was able to care so much about something so menial–a child leaving for school, or to work a job locally.

She wasn't losing a child to the war, or being threatened with the extinction of her kingdom. Yet she was far more emotional than Clara would ever be. Instead of voicing this, Clara smiled and said, "I suppose that's a sentiment I'll understand better once we have children."

She felt Carver's hand tighten over hers, and she was proud she managed to catch him off guard. He wasn't the only one capable of brilliant flirtation, regardless of what he said about her people skills. "In fact," she pulled herself closer to Carver, tucking herself behind his arm. She had Julia's full attention now as she whispered conspiratorially, "We're hoping that it won't be long until we have an announcement to make."

Julia exclaimed in surprise, "You're pregnant?" Clara was shocked that Julia could be so excited for someone that was a stranger to her. For the first time in a while, Clara felt human again. She felt less like an assassin, and more like her. It warmed something inside of her to see the care in Julia's eyes, even if it was only because of a lie.

"Not yet, but we are going to try now." She wiggled her eyebrows and Julia burst out laughing.

"Well, have fun in the process." Julia winked, and Clara could feel the muscles in Carver's arm tense. She squeezed tighter. "Though, as beautiful as the two of you are, I imagine you are having fun."

"Oh, absolutely." Clara gushed, "No one told me that marriage could be this much fun." She laid it on thick, inwardly gagging at every word she said. But it would be worth it if Carver was uncomfortable.

He chuckled next to her, "Okay, Clara, I think that's enough."

"What?" She laughed, "You don't like me telling people you're good in bed? I thought that was a marker of admiration." Carver flushed, and ducked his head.

"And he's modest too?" Julia inserted, "Wow, you lucked out."

"I really did," Clara confirmed, now ready for the conversation to end. She succeeded in making Carver uncomfortable, and now she wanted to back out. As if noticing the change, Julia excused herself to check on the boys, claiming to have heard screams.

"I didn't appreciate that." Carver said quietly once they were walking by themselves again.

"No? There's a lot I don't appreciate either." She responded curtly, keeping her eyes on the path ahead.

"That wasn't part of the act though."

"Really? I don't think Julia will ever question whether or not we're actually married." She looked at Carver pointedly, "And if Julia doesn't question it, no one else here will either. Don't tell me it wasn't part of the act. You're just mad I figured out how to play my role so well so quickly."

"I'm not mad." His jaw clenched, tight enough she was surprised she couldn't hear his teeth grind.

"No? You sound pissed." Her voice stayed light, and she hoped her levity would fuel his anger.

"I'm not. I'm frustrated, but I'm not mad." His voice remained perfectly calm, not a hint of the anger she was trying to incite.

"Why are you frustrated?" It was a question she knew she shouldn't ask. A question designed to take the two of them down a non-useful path.

"This role." He didn't explain the statement, and Clara let the silence reign between them, debating pressing him or allowing him to expand it on his own.

After what felt like an eternity he continued, "Do you know how much I had thought about…us?"

Clara felt her face heating now, and her stomach twisted painfully as she answered, "There is no 'us' Carver."

"Not now."

"Not ever. I think this role is playing tricks on you. You've made it very clear, *very* clear, there can't be an us."

"I know." He answered softly. "It frustrates me when you act like that because it makes what we could have had feel too *real*."

"That sounds like something you have to get over." Her tone was harsh, but he needed to understand. She couldn't keep running circles around the idea of them. "You told me to get in character. You told me to be convincing. I have done everything you suggested, and I've done it damn well. You can't get mad at me for following the instructions you laid out before me.

You think I wanted this? You think I wanted to trek across the country with my ex-boyfriend to save the nation? Yeah, absolutely not. But here I am. So get your *feelings*," she spat the word like a curse, "together Carver, cuz we aren't failing this mission. If I'm not allowed to be emotional, you certainly can't be."

He didn't respond for a long time. Clara refused to apologize or feel bad about what she said. It was fair. He deserved every word and more. His decision split them apart, now he didn't get to play around with the idea of bringing them back together. It wasn't an option. No matter how traitorous her heart wanted to be.

30 CARVER

Julia pulled Clara to the side, encouraging her with some motherly advice or something–Carver wasn't quite sure. He only knew that for the next hour, he was stuck walking next to Mark. How thrilling. While Julia accepted everything Carver and Clara told her without hesitation, Mark was far more inquisitive. Every response provided an opportunity for another question, and similarly to Julia, no topic was taboo. In fact, Mark had a tendency to question everything. Even the most minute details of their conversation.

How long had they lived in the south? What kind of factories and shops? They had honeymooned on which beach exactly? The questions went on and on, but Carver refused to be frustrated, instead he focused on the much needed break from Clara. All the emotions he had fought when he ended things with her were rushing back, and he was still refusing to give them any ground. His reasons for their break up were still valid, and holding her hand or a picture of them in bed wouldn't change that.

"Is your wife aware of the projects that will be on display in

Noxvalis?" It was the first time Mark addressed the future as opposed to prying.

"Projects?" Carver asked, a flash of paper with the word "creature" written on it coming to mind. Was this what Command was trying to hide?

Mark glanced over his shoulder to make sure Julia wasn't close. "Noxvalis is the most scientifically advanced nation."

"Yes." That wasn't a sinister secret.

"People with that kind of knowledge rarely use it for only good. They usually use it to gain more power."

Again Carver said, "Yes." Did Mark have a point with this?

"Noxvalis created biological weapons." Carver forced his expression into surprise. "Not only that, but they have been experimenting with genetic modification." Carver also knew this, but continued to feign utter shock. "The festival is a fun cover for them to show off the...creatures they have created with this modification."

This was confirmation for him. Command hadn't mentioned anything about this, and he didn't have to fake his surprise. "Creatures? They've created creatures?"

"The rumor is they have mixed DNA from various animals and spliced it into the DNA of human embryos."

"But you believe it's not a rumor?"

Mark lifted a shoulder. "I can't be sure. I'm not sure if Julia told you, but I'm on the counsel board at Calyndor. I serve the queen. We hear all kinds of reports. Most of them go in one ear and out the other. People make stuff up all of the time for attention."

Concern bubbled in Carver–they were journeying with a government official from their supposed kingdom, but if they hadn't been found out by now, they should be fine. It was just their luck this was the group they joined. "So why did you believe this report?"

"I didn't say that I do." Mark carefully evaded the direct question, "For sure, at least. But this is one of the few reports that has come in from several different officials of various nations, and several Calyndor citizens who had returned from a trip to Noxvalis."

"I see. Why are you telling me this? Isn't it sensitive information?" Carver tried not to sound too untrusting, but it was a valid question.

"Your wife is very innocent." Mark smiled softly, like a father talking about his daughter, "I just want you to be prepared for how this could affect her if the rumors are true."

Carver almost laughed. *Innocent, ha.* Clara would be so proud to know just how well she had completed her cover. "I appreciate that, Mark."

Mark nodded. "We all have to look out for each other. It's a crazy world we live in."

"That's for sure." No one talked about how things had changed after the last world war around a hundred years ago. The consequences and division had devastated everyone. Not a single area had been left untouched. Many areas no longer existed.

Though it wasn't discussed, underlying comments were used as a reminder that the war was recognized. On the brink of such destruction, humankind did what humankind did. They survived, and they found a way to get past the horror and look out for each other.

"Life takes on such a different perspective after you get married. And don't even get me started on when you have kids. Suddenly you see the threats in everything. The youthful invincibility fades away and the reality that you have been gifted people this important and it's your job to protect them sets in."

The words hit Carver hard. He hadn't married her, but he knew exactly what Mark was saying. *Did I break up with her because I was afraid to protect her for the rest of my life? Was leaving her actually an act of self protection?* "I know exactly what you mean." It was a road of thought he didn't want to travel. He believed himself the protector; he had done what was right for her, to hell with himself and his feelings. He couldn't stand the thought that Clara had been right all along and he hurt her, irreparably, in a vain attempt to protect himself.

He turned to look at her walking with Julia. Julia had linked her arm through Clara's, and Clara walked with the ease of someone who had never gone through anything difficult. He could see the innocence Mark was so concerned about. It was like she was the girl he met at 14 again. Before the world had jilted her in every way possible.

He supposed it was true that no one died a virgin. Life did, in fact, have a way of screwing everyone. Mark bumped Carver with his shoulder. "You should steal your wife back from Julia. We're not far from the city walls, and you'll want to see her reaction as we approach them."

"I appreciate your advice and warning, Mark."

They shook hands and Mark responded, "Not a problem. You seem like a good man, Carver, and I wish you and Clara all the best."

Carver sauntered over to Clara, and couldn't miss the slight shift in Clara's eyes as he approached. Her smile didn't falter, but it didn't overcome her features the way it had a moment before. She used to light up when she saw him. "Julia, I need to steal my wife back from you."

Julia smiled brightly, "Of course." She patted Clara's hand warmly, "It was so nice getting to know you better, dear."

"You as well."

Clara slipped her hand behind Carver's arm, leaning against his shoulder as Julia waved back at them when she caught up with Mark. As soon as Julia faced away from them, Clara returned to a normal standing position, keeping her hand behind his arm but not letting any other part of her body come in contact with him.

"Mark gave me more information about the projects he referenced." Carver whispered, ignoring the way his heart plummeted when she put the distance between them.

"Oh?" The innocent look stayed on her face, but her eyes scanned his, desperate for the information he was currently withholding. He considered toying with her, but decided against it. They needed to be on the same side as they approached Noxvalis.

"Apparently, Noxvalis has been experimenting with genetic modification as well as biological weapons."

"We knew they were messing with genetics."

He nodded, forcing himself to look calm, and she did the same. "We didn't know they had started mixing animal DNA into human embryos and creating...creatures."

Clara gasped, but quickly released the surprise as she looked around checking no one had noticed. "That's what Mark told you?"

"Apparently he's on the counsel board in Calyndor. He reports directly to the queen."

Clara's calm expression faltered yet again, "You didn't say anything that could cause us to be found out, right?"

"Of course not, I'm not the newbie here." He grinned, and she shoved him.

He caught her hand and tucked it back in the crook of his elbow. "Careful. Wouldn't want them to think we hate each other too much."

She rolled her eyes, a smile across her face. The sun shone on her face, her cheeks and nose pink. She looked adorable, and Carver almost forgot where they were. Momentarily, he felt like he was back in time. Her voice, graciously, shattered that impression, "Does this information change anything for us?"

"It shouldn't. There's nothing we can do about it right now. We have to fulfill our assignment. That's the only important thing right now. We can't help anyone if our kingdom is obliterated." He stared straight ahead, unable to watch her any longer. She was too good at her role. She was too much the girl he had loved instead of the lethal assassin he needed her to be. He had to distance himself emotionally if he wanted to follow the rules.

"I love how you manage to say 'if our kingdom gets obliterated' while keeping a smile on for the sake of everyone around us." She quipped lightly.

"What can I say?" His lip quirked up, "I'm just that good."

"You're an ass."

"Oh, absolutely."

31 CLARA

The walls of Noxvalis were bigger than Clara ever imagined. Her jaw dropped as they approached them, and though slightly embarrassed, she kept the expression deciding it fit her character well. "Woah," she whispered as they approached the gate.

The walls towered over them, guards stationed along the edges with rifles strapped across their chests. Their armor glinted in the sunlight, and she squinted as she tried to take in the size of everything. "Very impressive." Carver murmured.

He slung his bag to the front of his body, rooting around for his paperwork. Once Clara's amazement faded enough for her to focus, she did the same. She resisted the urge to scrunch her face at the paper. These written words, her name, birth date, place of origin. This piece of paper, this assigned identity, had caused so many issues between her and Carver already. She could only imagine how many more it would cause once they were within the city.

"Getting out will suck." Clara whispered. The gates looked heavy, and once they closed the only exit was over the wall, or through one of the smaller doors which were sure to be guarded.

"Just think of it as an exciting challenge." Carver's voice remained positive, causing her anxiety to flare within her even more. She twisted the bracelet around her wrist, eyes darting as she tried to map out all of their surroundings.

"Ever the optimist."

"Well, of course." He took her hand as they got into the line following the caravan. She almost snatched it back, more uncomfortable now that she couldn't continue twisting her bracelet.

Julia and Mark waved at them from the front, and Clara smiled in response when Julia blew her a kiss. They wouldn't see them again, and though Julia's effervescence annoyed her at first, Clara found she was sad to separate from them. She missed her mom in a way she wouldn't admit. Not the shell her mom became after her dad passed, but the bubbly, excitable, borderline insane woman she had been before.

The line moved quickly, and Clara noted the soldiers weren't exactly being thorough. Though there were hundreds and hundreds of people, the guards stationed felt almost as numerous. Some moved definitively through the masses while others manned their stations, stoically eyeing the crowds. Carver dropped her hand as he changed the position of his bag, and Clara immediately missed the tether he had provided.

She chewed on the edge of her cuticle, feeling the noise surrounding her. She was struck with the need to shrink inside something and block everything out. Everything was far too overwhelming, far too out of her control. Why did she think she could do this?

Carver pulled her hand away from her mouth, lacing his fingers with hers. Her heartbeat raced, but before she had the chance to say anything he shrugged and said, "You're supposed to be Calyndor. Be happy and flirty." His eyes glinted mischievously.

"Don't tell me what to do." She answered, but with a smile.

He bumped her with his shoulder. "There we go."

"What?"

"You look happier already."

She rolled her eyes, but for once she didn't have to force a smile. Carver leaned over, his breath on her neck making her hair tickle her ear, "Do you think if I kiss you, the PDA would make the guards uncomfortable and we'd avoid any closer scrutiny?"

She jerked back from him, but didn't let the shock stay as they moved closer. "You'd make *me* uncomfortable."

"So was that a yes or a no?" He finished the question with a light kiss against her neck, and she clenched her teeth to keep from lashing out at him, even as electricity raced down her body. It wasn't fair. *He shouldn't be doing this to me.*

Clara turned to him, smile pasted on her face, her voice artificially sweet and said, "It's definitely a no." Then to get back at him for kissing her neck, she leaned into him and whispered in his ear, "But maybe if you're sweet to me *I'll* kiss *you* a little later."

The tips of his ears grew pink, and she grinned, knowing that all he could think about for the moment was kissing her. She appreciated that she still held some level of control over him.

They held their identification papers out to the guard, and he glanced at the papers, their arms wrapped around each other, and the single bag they had on their backs. He pushed them through without a question, handing both of their papers back to Carver.

"Well, that was easy." Clara exhaled heavily. She knew getting in was the easy part, but it was still a relief to be within the walls. It didn't feel stifling at all. There definitely weren't too many people in the street, and it definitely didn't feel like the walls were looming over her, threatening her with death. No, she wasn't concerned at all.

"Now, the fun part." Carver tugged her hand, winding them through the busy populace. She took a deep breath, shaking off the anxiety that was attempting to suffocate her. This was a mission. She was good at those. She was good at this.

As Carver pulled her down the street, Clara couldn't help her amazement. "Hey, slow down." Every building was skillfully designed, stone carvings in many of the older ones. Music came from the center of the city, loud enough to be heard even from the outer roads they walked on.

"Why?" He asked, even as he came to a stop next to her.

She let go of his hand and looked around, unable to pull herself into character as she took it all in. "Have you ever seen anything like this?"

Carver looked around, but his face remained impassive as he shrugged, "What's the big deal?"

"Carver, it's beautiful! The wealth, the detail, the music, the smell. Man, I'm starving."

"Okayyyy," he drew the word out, unimpressed by her rambling. "Let's find our contact and then I'll take you to explore the city for a bit and get food. How's that sound?"

Amazing. Her stomach growled in response and she laughed, "That works." Excitement bubbled in her chest with the adventure. When was the last time she felt like this? Certainly it was before becoming an operative. Had she even felt this during basic training? No, she was too concerned with proving herself.

He glanced between the buildings, taking a second to orient himself. She wasn't focused enough to do the same, but trusted he would get them to the location they needed to be.

Trust. It was an interesting concept between the two of them. A fragile thread. Barely enough to keep them together and focused on this assignment.

Carver took her hand, clasping it tightly, and pulled her along with him. He wove them in between the buildings, pausing only to reassess landmarks, and after a few minutes stopped in front of a dark purple door. The sign above the door read "The Midnight Quill," in bold black letters, outlined in metallic ink. Clara recognized the name from their debrief.

"Should we knock?" It was the first time he'd hesitated since they had reached the city, and Clara felt herself step back into the position of control.

"No. It's a public bookstore. Knocking would be weird."

Clara opened the door and stepped inside, pausing for a moment to let her eyes adjust as Carver followed her in. A small water feature trickled on the counter, and the lights flickered almost like candles. The shelves were crammed with books. Most of the spines were facing outward so it was easy to browse, but some were so full they were jammed in however they would fit.

Clara reached out to trace the spine of one of the books but startled when a woman said, "May I help you?"

"Ah, yes." Carver cleared his throat as they both turned to face the friendly voice. She was beautiful. That was the first thing Clara noticed. Dark auburn hair curled gently around her shoulders. Her eyes were a muted green, but in a way they made you look twice to see the hints of gold.

Carver straightened, and Clara felt both amusement and a hint of jealousy, but she ignored both. He looked awkwardly at her and after she looked around to ensure no one else was in the store she said, "Is it better to trash or burn books?"

"Neither, information should be preserved." The woman replied softly, a questioning look in her eyes.

Carver jumped in with the second response, "Yes, but some information is too dangerous for that."

The woman smiled. "So you're who they sent." Her voice remained soft, every word finding its own melody.

"That we are." Carver confirmed, still observing the woman.

Clara wanted to smack him, if only to make him unglue his eyes from her.

"I'm Marsh."

"Marsh," Carver repeated, taking her outstretched hand and gently shaking it, "Carver, and it's a pleasure to meet you."

"I'm so freaking sure it is." Clara muttered under her breath, amusing herself with the aggression in her tone and Carver's eye roll as he dropped Marsh's hand.

He shook his head, "And this is my clearly *friendly* partner, Clara."

Clara dropped her tone, "It's a pleasure to meet you."

Before Carver had a chance to respond, Marsh jumped in. "Okay. You guys have been traveling for awhile, neither of your auras are happy, and I'm definitely picking up on some kind of unsettled vibe."

"Auras? What are you some kind of psychic?" Clara cut herself off before she added freak to the end of her statement like she wanted.

Marsh's polite smile didn't falter, and Carver gaped at her for her rudeness. "Clara—" but once again Marsh jumped in.

"It's been a long journey for both of you," she reiterated, "I have a room ready for you to stay in. Let me escort you there, and perhaps we can have a more civil conversation in the morning after you both get some food and sleep."

32 CARVER

"You didn't have to be so rude." The statement had resounded in his head since Clara's comments to Marsh. Now that they were shown to their room, the door securely closed behind him, he could call her on it.

Marsh gave them some jerky, and though it wasn't a meal, sleep suddenly felt more important. She had led them to the third floor, and their small room felt more like an attic than a bedroom. The bathroom was just as tiny, but it would suffice. He could practically feel the energy radiating off Clara as she moved around the room. There would be no personal space here.

It would be fine. As long as they were smart and followed the rules.

Clara sighed heavily. Setting down her bag and stretching out her shoulders before she deigned to respond, "You actually want to get into this."

"Yeah, I do. You don't always have to be a bitch."

She grinned and Carver almost took a step back at the look in her eyes, "You're right. I don't have to be a bitch. I get to be."

She started to unbraid her hair, winding pieces around her fingers. He stood there, exhaustion setting in, mesmerized by the simple act of her undoing her hair. He shook off the distraction and brought himself back to the conversation. "You can be a bitch to me." He exhaled, forcing himself to keep his tone calm. He didn't want to fight. "But you should try to be nicer to other people."

She stopped messing with her hair, "Why?"

He couldn't do it anymore. She was infuriating. "Because if you learned to be nicer you might actually have friends! Might actually have a relationship! You might enjoy your life instead of waiting for things to implode all the time."

"Excuse me?" He should have taken that as a warning. Should have backed off. He knew it, but he didn't care.

"You made it your mission to make our trip as miserable as possible. Even dancing. Man, Clara. I was having fun. But you had to ruin it. You're incapable of smiling unless it's forced for an act."

Clara crossed her arms over her chest, "Let's talk about ruining things, shall we?"

"Uh uh," he shook his finger at her, "The rules."

"The rules are in shambles, Carver, or have you not noticed? I was happy. Do you get that? I was in love with you. I trusted you. More than anyone in the entire world. Do you understand what it feels like to have an entire future planned, an entire future promised and then have it ripped away? Without an explanation?"

He opened his mouth to rebut her, but she held up a hand and continued, "Of course, I'm not happy. My hands are perpetually stained with blood. The only thing I've seen in the last three years is the pain *I* am capable of inflicting. You don't get to come in and tell me to be happy. Everything inside of me is so close to breaking. If I start to feel anything, most of all happiness, it will destroy every wall I've put up to survive. So excuse me if I've become a bit frosty. I'm only the person you forced me to become."

She took a deep breath, but Carver was too stunned by her confession to respond. "Now Marsh was right. I'm completely exhausted. And I don't want to talk this through. I want to take a shower in the bathroom, and climb into bed for the next six hours. Minimum."

She pulled a change of clothes out of her bag, and locked herself in the bathroom without another word.

Carver's heart ached. He heard the water turn on, and did his best not to picture her unclothed as he focused on unpacking the weight of her words.

She was right. He had put them here. It wasn't intentional, but it was his decisions nonetheless. He couldn't go back in time and fix them. He would do anything to save her from this pain, but he couldn't see that the alternative would have been better for her. So what now?

She walked out, rubbing a towel through her hair, dark circles prominent under her eyes. "Take the bed. I'll crash on the floor." The best he could offer her without continuing their earlier conversation.

She looked ready to protest but he jumped in, "I still need to shower. Go ahead and crash."

He didn't wait to see if she obeyed his order, already locked in the bathroom. They needed to go back to their rules of engagement, because this was not going well for him. He couldn't focus on the assignment. He couldn't focus on anything. Anything except how deeply he had failed in the only thing that mattered. He hadn't protected her. Not enough, anyway.

He slumped onto the floor, completely drained and over-whelmed. His pulse thundered in his ears, and his mind felt foggy. Some part of him had known it would come to this. The only competition to his devotion for kingdom was his desire to keep her safe. The only thing able to deter him from keeping her safe was his loyalty to his kingdom.

Would they be at odds with each other?

He didn't wait for the water to get warm before stepping in and letting the drops parade across his face.

The tiredness hit him like a weight, and he stumbled out of the bathroom, careful not to wake her. Though tempted to crawl in beside her, he instead took two blankets from the chair and laid them on the ground. He was asleep within moments of his head hitting the pillow.

His anxiety faded into the dream world. He was too exhausted to do anything but surrender to the images.

33 CLARA

The world was completely dark when Clara awoke. She blinked slowly, orienting herself to her surroundings. Between the bed, their bags, and Carver stretched out across the floor, there was almost nowhere to walk. The two of them fully consumed the room and it was stifling. Carver's shallow breaths were loud in the silence, grating across her skin. How much longer could she be this close to him and not break?

She inched out from under the covers, bare feet hitting the uneven wood flooring. She carefully stepped over Carver and to the window. Tugging on the blinds gently, she managed to move the slats enough to see out without opening them entirely.

Carver stirred behind her and she froze, not wanting to wake him. He didn't open his eyes, still dead asleep.

The outside world was still abuzz with life, and she was amazed at the energy that pulsed up from the street. Bright lights shone from various buildings. Men stumbled down roads and alleys, some with bottles still in their hands. Even from her perch on the third floor, she could hear the sounds of music from one of the establishments.

Girls clothed in almost nothing beyond feathers and beads called out to the men, waiting on corners for their opportunities. With the number of drunken bodies and celebratory attitude, most found someone. She watched for a few minutes before letting the slat fall back.

She allowed her eyes to readjust to the darkness so she didn't trip over Carver. Once she could make out his form again, she stepped over him, grabbed her bag and slipped out. There was too much chaos in the streets for her to stay inside. She wasn't sure how long she had slept, but she felt refreshed enough. Drunk men were the perfect way to learn more about the city and what she needed.

In the hallway, she pulled out one of the other outfits Command had sent befitting a Calyndor girl. A flouncy skirt red, *please kill me now*, and a tight black tank. At least she liked the tank.

Only one street over from their building, she found a popular bar. At least she assumed it was popular. People were continuing to pack inside, even as patrons who had enough found their way back into the street. Or were tossed into the street–depending on their sobriety and attitude.

She slipped inside, remaining unnoticed against the wall as she observed. A couple poker tables were surrounded by men thoroughly engrossed in the game, or the girl in their lap. One man in particular stood out to her.

His coat was a little too nice in comparison to those around him, but he had intentionally ripped a sleeve to make it look older. The line was a little too straight. His shoes were purposefully covered in dirt, not a single scuff present underneath the thin layer. His eyes stayed alert as he watched the other players. She wasn't sure who he was in the city, but he was someone with money and a position. He held himself with far too much confidence not to have a role that fit that. He was her best bet.

She waited until he excused himself from the tables, and once he ordered a drink, she moved towards the bar. A spot opened near him, and she gracefully sat, crossing her ankles together even as her skirt shifted to lay across her mid thighs. He glanced at her out of the corner of his eye, but she pretended not to notice.

When the bartender reached her, she motioned to the man's drink and said, "I'll have one of whatever he's having."

"That's a stout drink, girl, are you sure?" The man asked, now looking at her with open curiosity.

She smiled at him, attempting to charm him in a way she wasn't sure she was capable of. She shrugged as delicately as she could. "I think I'd like to try it."

"Suit yourself." He went back to his drink, and she kicked herself for losing his attention.

Unfortunately, all of her training had to do with forcefully making men talk, or leaving them where they could never talk again. Neither option worked here. She needed to *charm* him into talking. How on earth did one do that? Carver was great at charming people. She could figure it out.

When her drink was placed in front of her, she took a sip and managed to avoid a grimace. It wasn't good. But she wouldn't let anyone else know that. With another sip, she asked, "You in town for the festival?" Keeping her tone as bouncy as she possibly could. Bouncy was the best word she could think of for how Reese managed her conquests. It didn't come easily to Clara.

He turned towards her, and she congratulated herself for having gained his full attention. His eyes roved over her, and she couldn't stop the flare in her chest that insisted she should stab his eyes out. "I'm one of the organizers of the festival." He said, practically puffing his chest out as he continued to stare at her.

"No," she gaped at him, channeling whatever stupid inner school girl she could find. "That's amazing. Then I bet you know where all the best spots are."

He took another sip of his drink, eyes never leaving her body. "It's my job to create the best spots."

"What's your proudest creation?" She concluded the question with another sip of the terrible liquid she held. It took everything inside of her not to gag, but she was where she needed to be.

He leaned over, intruding into her space to whisper the answer. "The creatures we've created. I'm sure you've heard the rumors."

She let her jaw drop as though she was insanely impressed. "Those aren't just rumors?"

He shook his head, a smile settling on his face. She felt a chill run down her spine and didn't want to know what he had created. It couldn't be good. "I could give you a special tour if you want." His voice was still low, words murmured directly in her ear. His sticky breath made the bar feel smaller and more overwhelming. She reminded herself it was a game, and he was giving her exactly what she wanted.

She took another sip of her drink as his hand reached out to stroke lightly across her thigh. Her skin crawled. She could stab him. She was all too aware of the daggers she had strapped high under her skirt, and the small one she kept against her side. She couldn't do that. She knew that. As much as she wanted to, she couldn't. She wouldn't. "What exactly," she dropped her voice, now leaning closer to him, "Does a special tour entail?"

"They're in their cages for the night. I could take you and explain to you every single one."

She breathed out as though heavily impressed, "That would be incredible."

His hand moved a little higher, his thumb rubbing her skin. If there wasn't a purpose she would have decked him. If she hadn't needed to see the labs she would put a knife in him right now. But she knew what was at stake.

"Why don't we finish our drinks and then we can go?" He looked at her like he was winning a prize. It would be fun to let him know he was, in fact, not that charming. She could go with him, get the information she needed, and then leave him in an alley somewhere. No witnesses, no one to miss him. She doubted he had anyone who would truly miss him anyway.

34 CARVER

Carver woke in time to see the door closing. He changed quickly, counting to ten in his head, before he opened the door to follow her out. Hopefully, she wasn't stupid enough to try and explore the city on her own. But knowing Clara, he couldn't guarantee that would be the case.

Sure enough, she slipped out of the building, walking down a couple alleyways as she surveyed her surroundings. He stayed far enough back that she wouldn't notice him, blending into the shadows and avoiding the very drunk men that almost stumbled into him.

He watched as she stood outside of a massive bar. Loud music and bright lights flared inside. She didn't hesitate for long before she was inside. He didn't want to follow her in directly. That would be too obvious. He needed to protect her without further infuriating her. Dealing with another bout of her anger was more than he could take tonight. He might be tempted to do something stupid like tell her why he was trying so hard to protect her.

He waited for a few minutes, apparently long enough for one of the girls to notice him standing there. She draped her arm over his shoulder, "You look like you could use some company." Her voice was sickeningly sweet.

He carefully removed her arm, "Actually, I'm good, but thank you."

She pouted at him, "Not up for a little bit of fun?" The beads across her cropped top swished as she reached out to touch him again.

He caught her wrist, pulling her arm down before she could reach him. "Not tonight."

"Are you sure? I'll make it well worth your while." She didn't bother disguising her meaning as she angled her body towards him.

"I'm sure you would. I'm actually meeting someone inside. Thank you." He quickly walked into the bar before she had a chance to recover and try a different tactic.

Inside, the noise was overwhelming. Most of the occupants were drunk. Shouting, spilling drinks halfway to their mouth, threatening each other, stumbling with every step they took. He was surprised more of them hadn't been kicked out yet. It took a minute but he spotted Clara at the bar.

He was relieved at first, until he saw the man next to her who was grabbing her thigh and leaning into her. How dare he. Carver didn't have a chance to think through the anger before he reached them. His fist collided with the man's face, as though of its own volition. He didn't even feel the collision.

Clara shrieked, and he couldn't tell if it was part of her act or if it was real shock. The man clutched his bruised cheek, but before Carver could say anything else, two men grabbed his arms and were pulling him towards the door. "Don't come back!" They yelled at him as they pushed him into the street.

He stumbled, regaining his footing after a few steps. Stunned, he stood there not even sure what had happened. Had he hit that man? That wasn't a usual response for him. As the adrenaline faded, his knuckles smarted, and he realized that he had, in fact, decked someone. In an attempt to protect Clara. Crap. This wouldn't end well for him. So much for avoiding a fight with Clara. He groaned.

A few minutes later, Clara found him. "What the hell were you thinking?"

"I wasn't. I thought that would have been apparent. I was trying to protect you."

"We've been over this. I don't need your protection. Why can't you get that into your stupid ass head?"

"That man was touching you!" He defended himself, motioning towards the bar.

Clara looked around, noticing the people filing back and forth and grabbed his arm. She hauled him into a nearby alley. "That man was giving me exactly what I wanted." He raised his eyebrows, anger flaring even deeper, "Not like that!" She sputtered, "I was getting information for our assignment. He was about to take me to the labs and show me the creatures they've created. A personal tour, with information on how they created the creatures. Do you know how much that would have helped with our plotting?" She hissed, seething at him as she stood way too close.

His heart dropped, "I didn't know," he whispered.

"I didn't like him touching me, but I was putting up with it for the sake of information. The assignment comes first, that's all it was. You ruined our chance of getting access to the labs in a non forceful way. All because of your stupid, *stupid* jealousy."

"I'm not jealous." She shoved him into the wall, and he grunted even though it didn't hurt.

"Sure. You decked him because you're not jealous. Don't lie to me, Carver. You preach about how we need to trust each other. Assignment first. Follow the rules. But you break them at every turn." The street light behind her provided an almost halo. Her silhouette forceful and perfect as she continued to glare at him.

"I didn't mean to." He had nothing real to say. No apology could fix this.

"That makes it even worse."

She was breathing hard, the argument having worked her up. "Okay," Carver exhaled, trying to figure out how to put all of the pieces back together. "None of this changes what our assignment is."

"Just makes it more difficult to complete the assignment," she muttered, but didn't continue when he glared at her.

"We need to come back to the assignment." He inhaled deeply, letting his breath out all at once. "We've gotten off track. We have to go back to following the rules."

"We never should have left them to begin with," anger still coated her voice but he chose to ignore it.

"We have to act like a couple for the sake of the assignment, but when we're not in front of people we go back to our usual cold exteriors. Agreed?"

She rolled her eyes, crossing her arms over her chest. "Agreed."

"I'm sorry," he forced out. He knew he owed her the words, but he didn't want to offer them.

"Okay." The venom was gone from her tone, and he allowed himself a slight smile.

"Should we go back then? Maybe eat something and see if we can come up with a plan since you destroyed mine?" She kept her tone light, but he felt the accusation all the same. She hadn't truly forgiven him, and he couldn't expect her to.

He ignored the burning desire to defend himself, knowing it wouldn't matter. "Marsh might have some better insights on the city anyway." He agreed.

"I'm sure she does."

He heard all of the sarcasm in her tone. "Why do you dislike her so much?"

"Who said I dislike her?" Clara asked as they reached the door to the bookstore.

Carver folded his arms, refusing to go inside until this was resolved. "Your tone suggested a great dislike for her."

"I don't dislike her." Carver raised his eyebrows, waiting for her to continue, "I just have a suspicion that she will be more of a distraction for you than a help for our mission."

"So you're jealous. After accusing me of jealousy."

"I'm not jealous!" She defended.

"You totally are." He smirked as he opened the door and walked into the bookstore. Clara followed behind still justifying why she was concerned and how she was absolutely NOT jealous.

"You know, it's nice to be cared about."

She rolled her eyes, "I don't care. Can you stop being an ass so we can focus on figuring out a plan to get into the labs?"

"Can you keep your jealousy from getting in the way so we can plan?"

"I'm gonna murder you."

He tsked at her, "The assignment comes first. You can't murder me."

"Oh, I'll wait until after it's over. I'll slip into your sector and slit your throat." She hissed at him, and he almost believed her capable of it.

He gasped, grabbing his throat with a smile on his face. "You wouldn't dare."

"I—"

She was cut off as Marsh entered the kitchen, rubbing her eyes. "Ugh, do you two always argue like this? How do you ever get anything done?"

Carver and Clara exchanged glances. Though Clara was still

glaring at him, he felt like a berated child as Marsh brewed a pot of coffee. "Sorry to disturb you."

"I'm a light sleeper." Marsh explained. She tied the front of her robe together and leaned against the counter. "My question still stands. Do you two always argue like this?"

He didn't like the look of concern on Marsh's face, and wanted to prove all was well. "It's all in good fun."

"Don't lie to me." She deadpanned, the sweetness from her tone earlier in the day no longer present. "I don't know what this is between the two of you, but I do know that if you don't get it together, you will be the end of our kingdom."

She poured three cups of coffee and joined them at the small table. "I know you were sent here by Command. I know you have a limited number of days to get in and out. So, let's figure out a plan, and stop picking at each other."

Thoroughly silenced, Carver took a sip of his coffee. He grimaced at the bitterness, but didn't comment.

"I'm assuming the weapon is in the same labs they keep the creatures."

Marsh shook her head, "The creatures are kept in a surface level lab. They're close enough to the festival to be displayed on a daily basis. The weapons lab is under the edge of the palace."

Carver looked pointedly at Clara, "See?" He mouthed at her. A justification of sorts for having messed up her plans.

She stuck out her tongue, and Marsh sighed, "Of course. I got stuck with two extremely immature people."

"Immature is an unfair assessment." Carver responded, leaning back in his chair with what he hoped was elegance.

"I disagree." Marsh shook her head, "Moving on. The lab is under the edge of the palace. It's heavily guarded. The only entrance from the outside is in the forest, and is usually surrounded by 4 guards. However, the guard change occurs every 3 hours during the festival. It is left unguarded for exactly four minutes and twenty-two seconds during that time. Ideally, you would go in during the height of the festival, and be prepared to leave exactly three hours later."

Clara chewed on the edge of her lip, and Carver thought about bumping her to make her stop, but didn't want to receive another warning from Marsh. "In the morning, you both should explore the festival. We're still in the opening ceremonies. Learn whatever you can to take back to Quorath. Everything they can show off is on display. Creatures, weaponry, technology." She paused to take a sip of coffee, "Noxvalis is far more advanced than Quorath. We need to figure out how to recreate this technology if Quorath is ever going to stand on its own."

"Understood." Clara responded, wrapping her hands around her mug. "What equipment do you have for us to complete the assignment?"

"Only what I could get without being noticed. Knives, a taser, guns, though those aren't ideal for the lab with the oxygen content and machinery, and all the clothing you need to continue masquerading as Calyndor. Weapons aren't easy to come by here, and I couldn't get more without awakening suspicion."

"Any suggestions for how to get out of the city once we get the biological weapon?"

Marsh stood up, and grabbed a book off one of the shelves. She opened it and withdrew a hand drawn map. She pointed to the lab and traced her finger across to the wall. "Your best bet will be going out through the small door here. There's usually two guards, so you'll have to handle them. There's a forest on the other side of the wall, and if you can get past the initial guards on top, you can avoid the arrows because of the trees. I haven't explored much beyond that though. Once you're out of the city, you're on your own."

"Doesn't sound too bad." Carver said casually. He was feeling more and more confident about their plan.

"Ha." Marsh exhaled, "Let me spell it out for you. The guards all have brutal weapons. The lab has a security system inside that requires a password I don't know how to get. Once inside you have to avoid all of the scientists that aren't at the festival to find their most secret compartments and retrieve the biological weapon. I'm not sure if you were given knowledge of the weapon you're supposed to find, but it's small. It's a perfected formula. 10 vials. All it takes to wipe out a kingdom."

Only 10 vials. An entire kingdom could be killed with 10 vials. What was this weapon they were retrieving? His mind churned through the possibilities, and everything strange that had happened thus far.

"Marsh?" Both women looked at him. "Have you heard any reports on Hillcrest and Westmere? Both cities were abandoned when we reached them."

Marsh shook her head, confusion clouding her eyes. "I can't think of any reason for them to be abandoned."

35 CLARA

Morning came without any enthusiasm. Clara was refusing to talk to Carver whenever Marsh wasn't present, and Carver obviously didn't care enough to try and bridge the gap. Sure, her plan at the bar may not have been foolproof. But it would have been something. She was doing so well at manipulating that man, she would have convinced him to take her to the weapons lab after they saw the creatures.

At least, that's what she kept telling herself to justify her anger with Carver. Anger wasn't the only emotion flaring in her veins. As she repeated why she was angry at him, she couldn't help the additional flare of heat from how he defended her.

Carver was already downstairs, likely flirting with Marsh. He had given the excuse she would have more space to get ready for the festival if he went ahead and left the room. She hadn't objected. A few minutes without the constricting presence of her self-decided bodyguard? Yes please.

She took her time in the shower, enjoying the warm water running down her back. Carefully braiding her hair as she dried off, she chose one of the nicer outfits Marsh had presented to her. She almost didn't recognize herself in the mirror.

The colors were too bright. The skirt too frilly, the top too emphasizing of what little curve she did have left after all her training. The neck of the light blue tank was ruffled and scooped into a low V, tucked into her skirt that flared as she moved. The skirt was a pastel yellow, dotted with flowers in the same shade as the tank. She twisted and turned in the mirror, biting her lip as she stared at her reflection. She almost looked…pretty.

It wasn't a word she had associated with herself in years. It felt too gentle, too calm. It covered all the fractured pieces she had become. But for today? She was pretty.

Having reached this conclusion, she smiled at her reflection and smoothed the top of her hair one last time. Instead of a braid, she twisted a piece of hair on either side and pinned them, creating a crown like adornment. The shoes Marsh left for her were sandals, and though she was entirely opposed to open toed shoes, it did go well with her outfit.

She walked down the flights of stairs, wondering what she would find. With all of the rules they had broken, would Carver be hitting it up with Marsh? She couldn't blame him. She was attractive. And from the way Marsh looked at Carver, she was attracted *to* him. Clara wouldn't voice these thoughts. Heaven forbid Carver have a legitimate reason to tell her she was jealous. She wouldn't give him that kind of satisfaction.

Nevertheless, she was relieved to reach the kitchen and see Carver sitting there alone. His chin rested on his palm as he stared lazily out the window. He didn't look at her, and she wondered if he had noticed her arrival. Growing impatient, she cleared her throat.

"I knew you were standing there." His tone was light, forced.

"Sure. That's why you waited to comment until I cleared my throat."

His gaze snapped to her and paused, taking in the outfit. "I paused because I was thinking." His eyes roved over her body, making her flush.

"That's a new action for you." She answered teasingly.

"Disagree." He hadn't stopped staring at her, and Clara could feel her face flush.

"Would you stop?"

"Stop what?" He asked, carefully meeting her eyes.

"Stop looking at me like that."

"Like what, Clara?" His voice softened as he said her name, and a rebellious part of her heart started to melt towards him.

"I don't know. However you were looking at me a second ago. Don't look at me like that."

"How can I not look at you like that if I don't even know how I was looking at you?"

"You're confusing me."

He laughed, "You're confusing *me*." He took a deep breath in, "You look great, Clara."

She twirled in a circle, feeling more and more like the role she was playing. "Thanks, Carver."

He stood, stretching his arms over his head as he yawned. His shirt came up just high enough to see the outline of his lower abdomen, and she glanced away before she had a chance to do or say something stupid.

"You look great too." She didn't sound as confident as he had with his statement, but it was true. He wore a bright blue shirt that stood out against his tan skin, and was fitted across his chest. His khaki pants clung to his body and accentuated the fact he had more curves now than she did. Complete with a pair of sandals that almost matched hers. They certainly looked together.

"Thanks, babe."

"Don't push it. I'll still punch you." She responded, but there was no malice left in her tone.

"What? You don't like that nickname? I thought it could work as a term of endearment while we're in public."

"Find a different one."

"So hard to please, my dear."

"Better, but keep trying."

"Oh. My. Word." Marsh groaned stepping into the room, "You two never stop, do you? Why don't you just have sex and move on?"

Neither of them responded, both staring directly at Marsh. "What? It's not like you two aren't aware of the sexual tension in the room. You've been working together too long. Sometimes you just need to get it out of your system."

Clara laughed awkwardly, trying to clear the stifling air she suddenly felt. "That's not the case with us."

Marsh crossed her arms, "You can deny if you want. But I know what I'm seeing. Do us all a favor. Get it out of your system, and move on with the assignment. Your bickering is a waste of time, and a frustration to anyone who happens to be in the vicinity. Which currently, is me."

She set a kettle on the stove, and turned it on.

Carver cleared his throat, "We're heading out to explore the festival."

"Good. You two should talk about what I said. Might save me a headache over the next few days."

With that parting, Clara followed Carver out the door, very much wishing the earth would open up and swallow her. It was bad that Marsh had called them out on their attraction, but worse, she wondered if Marsh was right. Was it more of a sexual tension than a lingering attraction from their past?

She wouldn't sleep with him. Of course she wouldn't. She

wouldn't while they were dating, and she wouldn't now. She'd always been a little too logical. She wanted to sleep with him of course, and they'd messed around, but when it came down to it, she was glad she hadn't. Far too many risks associated with that, and none were things she was willing to contend with.

"Soooooo," Carver reached out his hand to take hers as they walked down the street. "That was interesting."

"You're not getting in my pants." The tips of his ears flared red and he wouldn't look at her. She felt a surge of pride for making him uncomfortable.

"What? I, uh, I wasn't asking to." He sputtered.

"Good. Because it's not happening. This isn't sexual tension."

He rubbed his thumb across the back of her hand and she had to resist pulling away from him. "It's not? Then what, my dear, would you say it is?"

"Unresolved emotional trauma."

"Ha. What textbook did you pull that out of?"

"It makes a lot more sense." She insisted.

"Not really."

"Um, are you admitting you do want to screw me?"

His ears had finally toned down, only to flare red again. "Not at all."

"But you just admitted that sexual tension makes the most sense. If you think it makes sense, you must feel sexual tension towards me, ergo you want to screw me."

"You know what?"

"What?" She smiled up at him, but he kept his eyes on the crowd.

"I don't think this conversation is productive. Towards anything. I think we should just move on."

Clara noted his frustration with satisfaction. She definitely won that conversation.

36 CARVER

Carver couldn't lie about that topic convincingly enough. There was a part of him, a specific part of him, that very much wished to resolve the sexual tension. Because it was definitely there. And it was driving him crazy.

Her constantly bickering with him wasn't helping either. If it was up to him, he'd kick her off this assignment. He was a spy. He'd figure out how to get in and get out without her. She was an accessory he didn't need. A distraction he didn't need.

They joined the masses of people who were wandering towards the center of town for the festival. As frustrated as he was with Clara, he was grateful their cover forced her to hold his hand. Otherwise, he was certain they would have been separated already. People crowded around them, bumping and knocking as they got closer to the center.

"What do you think we'll see?" Clara asked, her voice barely discernible over the din of people.

"I'm not sure." He practically shouted back. Then whispering against her ear, "Hopefully something that helps us." She smelled nice, and he immediately regretted whispering.

She nodded though, unaware of the way his heart was pounding from his foolish action.

They reached the first set of vendors, and the stream of people seemed to separate as they dispersed towards the activity or vendor they were here for. The noise, however, only increased. The vendors shouted out their wares, everything from shell jewelry to what looked like...preserved body parts?

They paused at that table, and the vendor proudly displayed a dried finger that ended in a claw. "It's from one of the wolf-men that died. Authentic. It'll bring you good luck!"

Clara looked like she was going to be sick, and Carver felt just as disgusted. "How will a dead man's finger bring good luck?"

The man drew back and gave him a dirty look, "It's not a dead *man's* finger. It's from one of the wolf-men. They're not human."

"What do you mean they're not human?" Carver tried his best to keep his tone casual, but he wasn't doing a great job.

The man looked overly frustrated at having to answer, especially since by now he'd realized they weren't about to buy anything. "They're creatures. They can't be a creature and be human. It's the finger of a *creature*."

The emphasis on the word pissed Carver off. Marsh had filled them in on what little she knew about the creatures, and he knew these "creatures" were only genetically modified *humans*. But they were still human. Somewhere, at some point, before these atrocities were committed against them. It wasn't their fault science decided they could mess with them.

"No." Clara snapped at the man. Carver squeezed her hand, inwardly begging her to keep their cover and not be far more outspoken than a Calyndor girl would be. He saw the anger flare in her eyes and knew his hopes were absolutely worthless. "They're not creatures. They're human beings that were altered by a psychopathic scientist with a god-complex."

The vendor looked her up and down, stroking his gray beard as he examined every inch of her. Carver resisted the urge to pull her behind him. "Girlie, I don't know who you think you are, but you have no idea what you're talking about. I suggest you move on and keep your mouth shut before you get yourself into trouble. No one around here cares about the emotional words of a Calyndor girl."

Clara opened her mouth to give what Carver was sure would be a vehement rebuttal, but he pulled her away before she could. He wrapped his arm around her shoulders, pulling her close to him so he could keep her from fighting back.

"Keep your girl under control!" The vendor shouted at them as they walked away, causing Clara to struggle harder against him.

"We can't fix anything if we get arrested or kicked out of the city." He hissed in her ear as they walked away.

She reared against him, catching his chin with the back of her head and making him lose his grip on her. "Dang it, Clara." He muttered, grabbing his chin.

"Don't try that kind of crap again."

He grabbed her wrist, spinning her back towards him. He knew his grip was harsh, but she didn't shirk away, just glared at him. "The assignment first." He reminded, leaning into her personal space.

She looked up at him, and he wished for the thousandth time that things could be different. "Don't assume I am incapable of following that on my own. I don't need your help to maintain my cover."

He scoffed, "Yeah, you do. You almost blew it with a vendor."

"Just leave me alone."

"Can't do that." He held up her left hand, "You're my wife, remember?" *Mine.*

"If our kingdom wasn't at stake I'd have slit your throat by now."

"Then I guess I should be grateful everything is as dismal as it is. Shall we continue?"

Clara let him pull her forward, and once again slipped into her silence. Carver was relieved. He didn't want to spend the entire day fighting when they could be collecting information and preparing for what was coming. All of their attention needed to be focused on the future. Not squandered in their meaningless conversations.

They passed more vendors, and Clara paused to examine a delicate gold necklace with a small red jewel on it. It would look beautiful on her. He thought about buying it for her, or at least offering to buy it for her. He decided any attempts at kindness would be thrown back in his face. He was worn out enough as it was.

A large crowd was gathered around a massive glass cage. They waited until a group walked away and wove to the front where they could see. He tightened his hand over Clara's, and she didn't pull away. If the man's words earlier sickened her, he could only imagine what the sight before them was doing to her.

A woman, at least, it had been a woman, was in the cage. Her skin was a pale green color, and patched with scales. The backs of her hands, the tops of her feet, her forehead and cheekbones, all covered in scales. She snarled at the crowd, sharp pointed teeth. Her hair grew only in patches.

Her footsteps remained light in the cage, and when she could move freakishly fast. The cage was just big enough for her to sprint across it and back, and the crowd oooed and ahhed as she did so. The louder the crowd became, the more frantic the woman's energy grew. After a couple minutes, she ran to the glass and ran up the glass. Pausing at the top of the enclosure when she reached the ceiling.

Carver's jaw dropped. That shouldn't be possible. To have practically seamless intertwined DNA in a way that actually functioned. This was what that report had talked about. "I don't like this." Clara whispered.

"It's fascinating," was all he could reply, fully entranced with the being they were watching.

Clara tugged at his hand, "Let's move on."

The creature seemed to look right at him, her pupils more slit than round. She slid down the wall of the cage, and he could have sworn he saw the agony in her expression. Eventually, he allowed Clara to pull him away.

37 CLARA

"It's fascinating? That's your response to those atrocities?" Carver shook his head, but Clara didn't give him the chance to respond. "It's disgusting. It's a perversion. People playing gods. Or now that you've seen one in person, are you suddenly on the side of the scientists?"

"Keep your voice down," he said, voice low.

She smacked his chest, but he caught her hand and gave her a stern look. "We're surrounded by people. This is a conversation we need to have later."

She hated that he was right. She wanted to tell him that, but doing so would most likely attract the attention of those around them. Already she could feel the stares from curious bystanders wondering why a Calyndor girl was picking a fight with her husband. So she smiled, and kissed him on the cheek like it was all a big joke, hating him and herself for every fake moment. But as she pulled away she whispered, "I hate you. So much."

His eyes were sad when he smiled, sympathy lacing his tone, "Darling, I don't believe you actually hate me."

Her forced smile faltered, but she shook off his words and became the image she needed to maintain. Forcing a laugh she ignored his words and said, "Let's find some food."

He swung her hand gently as they walked, and she thought through all the various ways she could make him pay. Stab him in the middle of the night, strangle him with a piece of wire, suffocate him with a pillow. Any of those would work. He was sleeping in the same room as her. It would be so easy to end him.

A dull pain echoed through her chest. He had been her best friend. The love of her life. And here she was, contemplating all the different ways she could kill him. She should be ashamed. But she wasn't. Actually, she was proud of herself for not falling for him again. For keeping her head on straight.

They found a stand selling finger foods. Supposedly the deep fried items were a delicacy. Clara gagged on the first bite and Carver burst out laughing.

"Not your thing?"

She tentatively took another bite as he watched. "Just haven't had anything like this."

"That's what this festival is for, my dear. To try new things."

The second bite was better, and by the time she finished it, she claimed she enjoyed it.

"What else do we want to see?" Carver asked her.

"What else would be beneficial?"

A bell rang, and people rushed towards a stage that had been set up on the other side of the square. "No idea. But that could be interesting." He nodded towards the group.

She tucked her hand behind his elbow, preferring that to holding his hand. Holding his hand brought up too many old memories she needed to keep buried.

"I'm sorry." He said as they walked towards the stage.

"For?"

"All of this. I know it can't be easy." Almost the same words they kept throwing back and forth. The only admission allowed regarding what this mission was costing them.

She didn't respond, and they wound their way through the crowd, people pressing against them on all sides as they drew closer to the stage. A man in a top hat jumped on stage and with a shout said, "Welcome, to the event that surpasses all events. My name is Holden and I am here to amaze you with the moment you all have been waiting for. The demonstration of the scientific prowess Noxvalis possesses." Every word was accompanied by motions, and even with the crowd of people his voice remained clear. Clara was certain it was being amplified, but she couldn't figure out how.

"You've seen our beautiful Lizzie," she nearly gagged again at his nickname for the woman he had seen, "And now, we have another proud creature to show you. After months and months of edits, and multiple failed attempts, may I introduce Maximus!"

The crowd burst into applause, and to Clara's shock the center of the stage separated, and another cage came up. This one was bars instead of glass. Inside was a man, his mouth open and unable to close because of the teeth protruding, his lips stretching to contain the canines. He sat back, crouched on his back legs with his fists on the ground in front of him. He snarled at the crowd, and the front row shifted back nervously.

"Now folks, you don't need to be afraid. Max is fully aware of his position here. He was engineered with a gorilla. He's capable of ripping metal apart with his hands."

"What's to stop him from ripping the bars of his cage?" One of the women in the crowd called out.

"I'm so glad you asked." Marcus replied without missing a beat. He sauntered to the front of the cage, and though the creature snarled and gnashed its teeth, it didn't lunge at him. "He's programmed to respond to our prompts. Specifically engineered to obey."

The terms were so scientific. So dehumanizing. Because the creature wasn't human. Not fully. Not anymore. Clara's stomach flipped and she regretted eating as much as she had. She had mutilated people before. She knew exactly what it was to strip someone's humanity away. But not like this. Not in a display. Not without a reason.

"Then why is the cage necessary at all?" A man yelled.

Marcus hesitated for the first time, apparently not having prepped for that specific question. "It makes it more of a display, of course! That's why we host this festival. Everyone here views the riches of our kingdom, the scientific prowess we pride ourselves on. Is everyone sufficiently impressed?" He raised his arms with a flourish, and the creature behind him stood with him, raising his arms to grasp the bars that formed the top of his enclosure. Hairy knuckles and massive palms desperately closing over the metal. Maximus's eyes screamed murder, but no one noticed or no one cared.

The crowd erupted in applause.

Anger burned in Clara's chest, fierce and biting and impossible to ignore.

38 CARVER

It took Carver less than 15 seconds to see the red flare in Clara's eyes and know he had to move her before she caused a scene. "Darling," he whispered, his voice tense, "We need to go."

She grit her teeth and resisted his pull. "I will pick you up and throw you over my shoulder if you don't follow me right now."

"Someone has to do something." She responded, desperation clear in her tone. Her eyes were glued on the cage, and he could practically see her brain tripping over ways to get involved.

"I agree." He wrapped his hand around her wrist, surveying the people around them and preparing to do exactly as he had said, "And we are doing something. But if you cause a scene now, we won't have the option of doing something."

He felt her relax a little, and tried to pull her wrist. She came with him willingly, but her eyes never left the creature on the stage. He led her into an alley that was far enough from the center that it was devoid of people. "What the hell Clara? You have to prioritize the assignment. I can't spend this trip keeping you from starting fights!"

Her eyes snapped to his, and he stepped back at the force of her glare. "Don't tell me what to prioritize. Those are people, *people* Carver!"

"Not anymore, they're not." He scoffed, running a hand through his hair. It was the wrong thing to say. He knew that the moment the last word left his lips.

He still wasn't prepared for her to slap him. His face stung instantly, tears filling his eyes from the shock of it. He flexed his jaw, hand gingerly coming up to his cheek, waiting for the reflex of tears to fade enough he could respond. "The hell Clara!"

She crossed her arms over her chest. "You're a jerk. Completely and entirely a jerk! You don't even care that they're people."

"You don't get to tell me what I care about." Every word was controlled, his voice dangerously low.

"It's so obvious. You want to stay perfect Mr. Carver Vaughan." She held her hands in front of her, mocking him with every word. "Complete the assignment and return like none of this happened. Like we didn't see anything. None of this even matters to you. Just another check box on your list of things to complete."

He clenched his teeth, determined not to give her the response she wanted. But she didn't stop there. "We were content. We were happy. Until I did something that would have messed up your perfect image. Right?" She threw her hands up. "You couldn't date a soldier. Would have ruined everything. I was supposed to stay the gentle rich girl. Perfect for you. Someone to show off. But I didn't, did I? So you ended it."

Thoughts stopped running through his head, and before he knew why or what he was doing, he had pinned her hands above her head, holding them there as his face hovered above hers. "That's not what happened." He panted out, unsure why he was out of breath. She was breathing hard too.

His nose bumped hers and neither flinched away. "No?" She

whispered, less violence in her voice. Her eyes searched his. He didn't know what she was looking for, but he hoped she found it. And then she kissed him. It felt like the world was spinning. He didn't know what was happening. Just that it shouldn't be.

He felt himself lean into her, a motion he couldn't stop. He needed her. He needed to be even closer. He pressed her further against the wall, his body squaring against hers. Further, further. It was everything he knew he shouldn't do. Everything he had wanted to do the past several days. Everything he would never forgive himself for doing since he was supposed to keep his distance.

Finally, his thoughts caught up with his actions and he pulled himself away from her lips long enough to look into her eyes.

Her eyes were wide, her lips still parted. Then she placed both hands on his chest, and shoved him away from her. Heat still raged within his body, and he wasn't thrilled with the distance she had created. She held her hands out in front of herself. "You stay there." She ran a hand through her hair, it was entirely falling from the pieces she had pinned back that morning.

"Clara," he whispered, taking a step back towards her.

"I mean it, Carver." He stayed where he was. "I don't know what that was, but it can't happen. We can't happen."

"Just the sexual tension Marsh warned us about," he attempted to lighten the mood.

She laughed, but there was no mirth in the sound. "I'm such an idiot." She muttered.

"You're not an idiot."

Her eyes flashed as she raised her head. "Carver, you're my partner on this assignment. I can't kiss you. I can't like you. I can't do anything but protect you and do everything in my power to accomplish our assignment."

She was right, but his resolve against their relationship crumbled the moment she pressed her lips to his. All he wanted was to resume that moment. No matter how foolish, no matter what the cost. "Why can't it be both?"

She scoffed, "Uh, I don't know. Maybe because you abandoned me? You broke up with me for absolutely no reason. I walked into the Vipers section broken, wondering what I did that was so bad you couldn't stay with me, assuming that even with everything I had done to prove I was strong, somehow you still only saw me as weak."

His heart plummeted. How is that the way she saw what happened? "That's not true. I was trying to protect you. Everything I've ever done was to protect you."

"So you've said. I don't believe you." Her words were curt. Precise.

He didn't have a response. There were no words he could offer to prove his sincerity. A broken promise was all it took to shatter words, and he knew he couldn't easily come back from that past mistake.

"We should get back to the festival." With that, she turned and walked out of the alley.

Carver took a deep breath, attempting to cool himself off from the heated moment and the painful conversation after. He would do anything to erase the past. She was right, he couldn't protect her. And he wasn't sure she needed his protection anymore anyway.

She had joined onlookers at another stand, and he sidled up behind her without a word.

39 CLARA

The rest of the day passed without another incident. She tried to ignore the fact she kissed him–ignore the surge in her chest every time she looked at him. She wanted to chalk it up to a mistake, a lapse of judgment, over-exhaustion, anything that would prove it wasn't something she actually wanted. Unfortunately for her, part of her remained rebellious to all of her reasoning. Her logical excuses couldn't quite prevail over the desire to kiss him again.

He fell asleep much faster than she did, and the sound of his breathing frustrated her even more. It wasn't fair he could sleep so easily on the floor (he said she could have the bed; she decided picking a fight wouldn't end well), and she couldn't fall asleep no matter how she tried.

After tossing and turning for a few minutes, she slipped out of the room. With no direction in mind, she ended up in the kitchen and decided a cup of hot tea might help enough that she could sleep.

She filled the kettle and turned the stove on. Then she leaned over the sink, stretching her shoulders and wondering what was wrong with her. After everything, how could she still care about him as much as she did? Because that was the damning reality.

She still cared. She still loved him. Somewhere under all of the callouses. Under all the bad memories of the last few years. That flame had never gone out, and now he was here. The proximity was stifling, causing the debris to be pulled away and proving that the fire was still there.

"Can't sleep either?" She hadn't heard the footsteps behind her, but years of practice still kept her from startling as Marsh entered the kitchen.

Clara turned, "Long day."

"That's an understatement." Marsh slid into a chair at the table, her robe untied as she leaned back and relaxed. "Boil enough water for me to have a cup as well?"

Clara nodded, and when the kettle screamed, took it off and poured the two cups of tea.

"So," Marsh gingerly took a sip of tea, "You and Carver."

"Me and Carver, what?" Clara asked calmly, hoping this conversation wasn't headed the direction it seemed to be.

"You have history?" She asked the question gently, nosy but pretending not to be.

"That's an understatement." Clara smiled lightly, and Marsh did the same at the reference to her earlier phrase.

"What happened?"

"Ah, you know. Men and their commitment issues." Clara tried to shrug it off, but even those words felt like salt in an open wound.

"Really." Marsh deadpanned. She leaned back in her chair and took another sip of tea. "He doesn't read like the one who would have commitment issues."

"What are you implying?" Clara's defenses rose, and though part of her knew it wasn't fair, the other part was shouting that Marsh had no right to ask her any of these kinds of questions.

"I'm not implying anything." Marsh shrugged, "No offense, but you seem far more likely to be the one with commitment issues. You walk around with like a million walls up; I don't even think I've seen you smile outside of when you're 'in character.'"

"I'm an assassin." Clara deadpanned, "What do you expect me to smile about?"

Marsh took another sip of tea, and for a moment Clara wanted to strangle her. Who was this woman to act like she knew her? "So he ended things then?" Was all she said.

"He did."

"Huh." Marsh let them slip into silence, and Clara couldn't help but feel like she was being judged.

"What?" She blurted, irritation coating her voice.

"Just confuses me a little." Marsh replied casually, adding absolutely nothing to the conversation.

"What does?"

"He is absolutely obsessed with you. Why would he end things with you?"

Clara tried to make sense of the words, "What do you mean 'obsessed with me?'"

"Well, don't hate me, but when he came down the other day I was definitely flirting with him." Clara wanted to lash out, but knew any movement or expression on her part would only prove Marsh's point, so instead she put the tea to her lips, watching Marsh from over the rim of her cup.

"He didn't even notice. All he could talk about was you. How amazing you are on this assignment, the plans you both had for breaking in, the brilliance he's witnessed." Marsh paused as she downed the last of her tea, but Clara wouldn't show whether or not the words hit home. They did. "I don't know what you did to that boy, but you've got some kind of hold on him."

Marsh set her cup in the sink, and left Clara alone in the dim kitchen. She didn't mean to have a hold on him. She didn't mean to be anything at all. "He's obsessed with me." She murmured to the darkness trying to wrap her mind around that idea.

There was no way to reconcile it. She couldn't understand him obsessing over her and him ending things with her. His insistence that she was weak, while bragging to others of her strength. He had become two different people in her mind, and she didn't know how to bring them back together. Which man would he be today? The one she kissed in the alley? She grimaced at that thought.

Or the one she almost slapped when he said he wouldn't be her crutch?

She closed her eyes and let herself relive that moment. She felt the excitement from having been assigned to special ops. The joy of wanting to celebrate it with the person she loved the most. Her heart was pounding as she ran down the hallway to reach him. She threw her arms around him, practically jumping into his arms. And he sat her down and pushed her away.

Her heart sank at his stern look. Then he tore into her. He said she was weak. He said he wouldn't be a crutch for her. "You need to grow up! Stop being so weak. It's pathetic. I can't do this anymore." His final words and he walked away without looking back. He didn't give her a chance to interject. Didn't give her a chance to change his mind, to explain her choices. Just walked away down the hallway she couldn't follow.

She had stood there for what felt like hours. Too numb to even cry. Too upset and shocked to process anything beyond the fact there was no longer a person in front of her. When she finally found the strength to walk back down her own hallway, she resolved within herself that she would never be weak again. If he ever saw her again, he wouldn't recognize her.

Did she accomplish her goal?

40 CARVER

Nothing had changed on the map over the last three hours they spent staring at it. Carver took another drink of his black coffee, and grimaced at its lack of warmth. How long ago had he poured this cup?

The logistics of the mission were close. Close enough they might work, but just far enough it could be a complete disaster.

Minutes. That was the amount of time they would have to pull everything off. Which meant that every second mattered. Marsh had thoroughly timed the guards. However, the festival was an added element. With the additional people came additional security. Would their switches become more precise or less? It was an element they couldn't prepare for. The best they could do was hope everything went according to plan.

"Okay, I officially have a headache." He groaned.

Clara scowled at him, "Can you just focus? We have to figure this out."

He took her tone in stride, accepting the distance she was creating. "I've been focusing. Now I need to not focus so I am able to focus again. I'm going for a walk. You're welcome to join if you would like. I want food from the festival."

"I'm good. Thanks." He could tell she didn't approve of his choice to go back to the festival, and honestly, her disapproval was fair. He couldn't blame her for not wanting to celebrate inhumanity.

He walked out through the front, stopping by the front desk to say hi to Marsh. The bookstore was relatively empty, and she asked if he would bring her food back. He agreed. "How's the planning?" She asked before he had a chance to turn away.

"It's going." He didn't have the energy to provide a jovial tone, and he could tell she understood.

"Clara being a bitch?"

He flinched, "I don't think she would like to hear you call her that."

Marsh laughed, "Oh absolutely not, but hey, if the shoe fits."

It was said so lightly he felt the need to defend Clara. Sure, she was hard to get along with, but that wasn't entirely her fault. "She's not being a bitch. We just have vastly different training, which produces entirely different ways of looking at things."

"Need a third opinion?"

"I'm not sure that would help."

"Ah, yes, Clara's obvious dislike for me. Though, we did have an interesting conversation last night."

"She doesn't dislike you." Carver shook his head, "A conversation about what?"

"She does, and that's perfectly fine. I'm not her biggest fan either. We're all just playing the roles required of us." She stopped speaking, not answering his second question.

"Well said." He replied, deciding not to press though his mind was spinning.

A man came to the front and asked Marsh if she had a certain book in stock. She directed the man towards the back, and followed him to help him find the edition. Carver used the chance to slip out the door. He enjoyed talking to her, but he didn't enjoy bashing Clara.

It was a weird in between. He agreed with a lot of what Marsh said. Clara wasn't very nice. She was hard to get along with. She was so opinionated on every. Single. Thing. She definitely didn't like Marsh. But for Marsh to speak so harshly about Clara? It felt like some sort of personal offense.

Here he was, still trying to protect the girl who absolutely did not want his protection.

The festival was louder today. Every beat of the drums playing on the corner resonated within his chest. He had never struggled with anxiety, but he felt the enormity of their assignment weighing on him in a way he couldn't verbalize.

He found a stand that sold sandwiches, and bought three–the extra one for Clara, even though she had said she didn't want anything. She would change her mind when he got back with the food. Plus, he would rather come bearing food and her not want it, than come empty handed and be ostracized for not having read her mind. Women.

He wasn't ready to go in just yet, so he wandered back to the stand they stopped at the day before. The one with the gold necklace and red jewel that Clara had liked so much. It was still there. He was relieved. He wasn't sure when he had decided that he would be coming back to buy it, but it felt like something he had decided a long time before. He saw her with the necklace, knew how pretty it would look on her, and subconsciously knew he would come back and buy it for her.

She'd no doubt be mad at him for it. Claim they could have spent their money better elsewhere. Claim he was only doing it to make amends.

The last part was partially true. He did want to make amends. But he wasn't stupid enough to believe a single necklace would fix all of their past issues. "How much for this necklace?"

He asked the woman behind the counter. She grinned at him, "Ah, for your wife?"

"No, just a friend." *If she could even be called that.*

"A friend?" The woman didn't sound like she believed him. *Yes, a friend. Well, no, my partner. She kissed me yesterday, but today she wants to murder me. Oh, and we have to get along or our kingdom will be destroyed. But yeah, a friend.*

"Yes ma'am, how much for the necklace?" Carver didn't have time for the back and forth debate on the status of his relationship. He also wouldn't be talked into buying anything else.

She gave him a look, but also gave him a price. He paid it, and waited as she put the necklace in a delicate box. It was just small enough that it fit in his pocket. He thanked her and headed back to the bookstore.

Marsh had slipped the closed sign over the door for lunch. He walked to the back and let himself inside silently.

"You don't have to act like this, you know." Marsh's voice was raised, and Carver instinctively shrunk against the wall to continue listening as he inched towards the kitchen.

"I'm not 'acting' like anything!" Clara's voice was also raised. *This should be interesting.*

"I only want to help."

"Oh, your help is so appreciated. You want to help yourself right into Carver's bed, I'm sure."

A glass was slammed onto the counter. "Clara, for gods' sakes, get your head out of your rear and back in the mission! I have no desire to have your boyfriend."

"He's not my—"

"I do not care. You cannot come into my house and constantly disrespect me. You don't have to like me. We don't have to be friends. But you do have to respect me, in my home, which I opened to you."

"Respect goes both ways."

Marsh laughed sharply, "Hon, a lot of things go both ways. But if you attempted to act like a normal human, you'd find that interactions aren't actually that difficult. Shocking, right?"

As much as Carver wanted to continue listening to the fight, he also didn't want them to reach a point where there could be no resolution. So he stepped into the kitchen with, "Ladies, I come bearing food."

"I told you I didn't want any." Came Clara's despondent response. He resisted the urge to repeat her mockingly.

"Thank you," Marsh sighed, taking the sandwiches out of the bag.

"You're welcome," he responded to Marsh first and then turned to Clara, "I got an extra sandwich for you, but if you don't want it, I will happily eat it. I'm starving." *There, nice and civil. Nothing she can yell at me for.*

She didn't respond for a long moment, pondering his words. Then her stomach rumbled, and though he would have liked to tease her about the pink climbing her cheeks, he just handed her a sandwich. She accepted his offering, and even gave him a slight smile and a quiet, "Thanks." Finally, a moment where they could be at peace with each other.

Or at least it could have been. Until Marsh jumped in with, "See Clara? It's not that hard to have decent manners."

That was all it took for Clara to push her chair back and storm out. At least she took the sandwich with her.

"See what I mean? Such a bitch." Marsh was quick to comment.

"You weren't exactly helping."

"Oh, so now this is my fault?"

"I didn't say that." Inwardly, he groaned. Why couldn't women just get along? "I just meant, if you know she's a bear then why poke her with a stick?"

Marsh grinned, "Because it's fun."

Carver groaned, out loud this time.

41 CLARA

Clara intended to eat the sandwich and wait until Marsh was back in the bookstore before rejoining Carver. She couldn't explain the fury that bubbled up within her everytime she was around Marsh. Too distracted to notice anything about the sandwich, she finished it and decided to lay on the bed for just a few minutes. She was extremely disoriented by the time Carver was shaking her awake.

He held his hands up in surrender when she opened her eyes, "I didn't want to wake you, but we need to finish these plans before we run out of time."

She rubbed her eyes, "How long have I been asleep?"

"About two hours."

"Crap, my bad." She rolled off the bed, and stretched, trying to wake herself up enough to focus.

"All good. I figured you were exhausted."

She yawned, "Yeah. Haven't been sleeping the greatest this trip."

"Same."

"You don't have to sleep on the floor, you know. We can switch so you can sleep a little better."

"I'm good." His tone left no room for argument, and truthfully, she didn't want to give up the bed.

She followed him downstairs where they resumed their planning. Marsh had left a pot of coffee out before going back to manage the bookstore, and though Clara wouldn't admit it, she was grateful. "While you were asleep I walked towards the edge of town to scout out the entrance and the guards."

"And?"

He shook his head, and she could sense his frustration. "It's far enough back that we will be out in the open when we approach. There's no way to get there without being seen. Which presents an additional problem. Because we won't actually have a full four minutes. We'll have to use half that time just getting there, or it will be far too obvious that we're heading somewhere we aren't supposed to be."

She groaned. "This assignment is a headache."

He nodded. "I haven't had one like this before."

"I don't think our kingdom has ever been at stake like this before. We're their last ditch effort." This thought wasn't a comfort. How was their kingdom so desperate that two twenty-three year-olds were the only ones who could save everything? She thought back, and realized after training all of her mentors just ceased to exist. She reported to Command, and one or two home-base leaders. Had they actually all died? The war was brutal enough.

"You think so highly of us." Carver pulled her back into the present.

"I don't see the point in romanticizing a death wish. No one sane would attempt this. We're practically asking to die—or worse. Be honest, can you think of anyone older than us still alive in our divisions?" She could think of Spiders, but that was only because their lives weren't constantly at risk.

"Special Operatives aren't promised a long life. Anyway," Clara took a sip of coffee as Carver brought the conversation back to an actual plan. "I know we talked about going in the middle of the festival when there would be the distraction of people, but we might be better off at night. At least then we could approach without being seen. There are at least trees there, so we might be able to get within a few hundred feet of the entrance. Otherwise, I think we're screwed from the start."

"Okay. When is our best bet for this?"

"Not tonight. We don't have enough time to get everything together for that. And the festival only lasts two more days. We're definitely better off leaving during the raucousness of the festival."

"So tomorrow night."

"Ideally." Carver closed his eyes after muttering the word.

"None of this is ideal."

"Yes, tomorrow night."

She leaned back against her chair, taking him in. He hadn't shaved in days, and had quickly surpassed the 5 o'clock shadow. It was hot. She couldn't help the second of thinking how it would feel to run her fingers across it. Or kiss him again, and feel the roughness across her own face.

Subconsciously, she brought her hand up to her face. She shouldn't think about him like this, but dang. He leaned against the table, wearing only a thin linen shirt. She could see every line of his arms tensing beneath the shirt as he tried to figure out what they should do.

She cleared her throat, and he met her gaze. "You haven't actually told me what your strengths are. We've talked about a lot of random things, but we haven't planned out our individual roles for this assignment."

"That's fair." He relaxed enough to take the chair across from her. "What do you want to know about my skills?"

She shrugged, "I don't know. Maybe tell me what you're capable of within this mission."

"Picking locks, pretending to be someone else, disabling security, sneaking in, sneaking out. Quite frankly, this assignment is more akin to my strengths than yours. I'm not sure why we were both instructed to come." For once, his commentary towards her wasn't demeaning. Just factual. And to a point, he was right. But Command anticipated there would be bloodshed, and he was utterly unprepared for that. Command also wanted the king assassinated. That wasn't something Carver could handle either.

"You haven't killed anyone." The admission hurt her. Another reminder of why he was better than her. And there was nothing she could do about it.

"What does that have to do with anything?" His tone was immediately defensive.

"You think this is gonna be easy? You won't be able to slip in and out. There will be other guards inside. Scientists manning their posts. Lab assistants keeping everything operational." She explained calmly, taking another drink of coffee.

"You're not serious." Carver scoffed.

She blinked. Her voice was barely audible as she replied, "Carver, why do you think they asked me to come?"

"You can't take innocent lives like that!" He shouted, standing and pacing away from her. He ran his hand through his hair.

Clara closed her eyes tightly, trying to press back the memories those words withdrew. "They're not innocent," she replied with her constant justification.

"So they deserve death?" He paused in front of her, hair sticking up in places, and she longed to smooth it back down.

"I didn't say they deserved death. But when it comes down to us or them, it will always be us. I will always choose us over them. You have to accept this." Her voice rang in her own ears. Far too calm. Far too calculated. When had she become so calloused to death? When had she stopped feeling the weight of blood on her hands?

He stared at her in shock. She almost touched her head to see if she had suddenly grown horns. Her appearance must have changed in some way. He was looking at her like he no longer recognized her. "So this is who you've become." His voice was quiet but harsh, and she felt it rip through her.

"I warned you," she wouldn't defend herself. She knew she had become a monster. She knew she wasn't the same person he had once loved.

"Clara, they're people too. You can't just murder them." His voice was pleading now, and he sat back down, staring at her as though that would change anything. She wished she could reassure him. She wished she could tell him it would be okay, that she wouldn't kill them unless they actually threatened them. But that wasn't the case. No witnesses meant no witnesses. Command had given specific orders. There was a reason she was the assassin picked for this mission.

"I'm not murdering them. Murder is premeditated with an assigned target. It's just killing. We're in a war. Death is part of war. Have you learned nothing the past few years? I will do my job, Carver. Nothing you say will stop me from completing my part of the assignment."

He thought about it for a moment, and then glared at her with a new ferocity. "Then you won't go with me."

"That's not how this works. You can't just decide I'm not coming with you. You need me for the assignment."

He pushed back from the table, his chair scraping across the floor. Clara flinched at the sound, too tired to push the reaction away. "No, I don't. I can figure out how to do it without unnecessary death. We're not doing this your way."

"It isn't *my* way. It's the way Command has instructed. I was told no witnesses. We can't have witnesses, Carver. Don't you understand that? You're acting like this is something I enjoy!"

"Well don't you?" The disgust in his tone shouldn't have surprised her, but she couldn't find a rebuttal.

"No," she whispered, but it didn't matter.

"I can't even look at you right now."

He stormed out, leaving towards the bookstore in the front. Towards Marsh.

Clara slumped back in her chair. She thought he understood with what she said on their trip here. She thought he would have figured out why an assassin was partnered with him. Why else? If it was only stealing something, then stealth would be all that was required. Carver, the perfect spy, could slip in and slip out.

It wasn't that simple. It never was. He was more innocent than her if he still saw the world in black and white.

42 CARVER

Carver did, in fact, leave to find Marsh. He needed to rant. He needed someone else that viewed things the same way he did. He needed the solidarity Clara would never give him. What could he do? What could he offer?

He still believed murder was wrong. That was what this would be. It would be murder because she was going in and she was taking the lives of people who had never directly harmed them. Right? Surely, he was right. *Killing on a battlefield is different than killing someone in a lab.* He reasoned. But why? *If the lab created weapons that will kill us, doesn't that make the lab a battlefield?*

Carver's head was pounding. All of this was too overwhelming. So much more than it was supposed to be. Assignments were supposed to cost something, yes. Physically, psychologically, emotionally, mentally. He knew the drill. He knew what Nate said. This was a final test. Him and Clara, pushed to the brink. Would they break?

They were special operatives. There was a reason most operatives, no matter how good they were, had a limited number of assignments under their belts. There was a reason they were pulled after a certain number. Command didn't want to deal with a bunch of fully broken soldiers.

But he had been the best. He was still the best. He was able to categorize every assignment into boxes in his mind. Open them only when necessary for debriefs and move on. Sure, he had seen terrible things. But he had never hurt anyone, had never killed anyone. The process of categorization was easier that way. That's why they kept sending him. He was able to deal with it all.

Would this be the assignment that broke him? He could feel the fractures it was already creating within him. One after the other. They had started slowly. Seeing her face. When she crashed into him on the train and he held her for a split second. Defending her when that man was trying to touch her. Each moment a fracture.

He cared way too much to watch the girl he loved become a monster. Maybe he didn't get it. Maybe he couldn't understand what the past three years as a Viper had molded her into. Maybe she had killed people already, like she claimed. But he couldn't prove that. He hadn't *seen* her kill anyone. In his mind, she was still the same innocent girl he loved. She was just so much stronger.

And yet, he knew she had become someone different. He saw how she treated people. She didn't care about anyone else's emotions. Her sympathy for the creatures was the only time he truly believed she cared about anything. Outside of that event, her guard was always up. She was always waiting for the next punch to hit. What a terrible way to live.

He walked into the bookstore, hoping Marsh would be closing soon. She had closed early every day, using the festival as the excuse. She was flipping the sign to "closed" and locking the door as he walked in.

"You look exhausted." She said, but there was no malice in the words.

"Yeah." His voice came out gruff and he cleared his throat.

"There's a chair behind the counter, sit. I'll finish locking up and we can talk."

He nodded. He sat in the chair, pulling it close enough to the counter he could lean his head in his hands. It hadn't even been a week but he felt like he had aged years.

He heard her light footsteps coming his way, but didn't look up. Her hands found his shoulders and she began massaging the tension away. He almost groaned with how good it felt. He leaned back into her touch.

"Everything okay?" She asked.

He didn't know how to respond. "Clara is an assassin."

She paused her massage, "Yes?"

"Like, I knew that. She told me she had killed people."

"But now you're surprised that her plan is to go in, guns blazing?"

He exhaled loudly. "When you say it like that I feel a little stupid. But yeah. I don't know. I felt like she would have more qualms about murdering someone."

"Is it murder though? And Carver, why are you surprised? That sounds like naivete on your part."

He almost interjected, but she resumed her massage as she kept talking, "Do you have qualms about doing your job? That is all she is doing. The job she has been trained to do. It wouldn't be different for you if you had ended up an assassin. You would go in and do your job. Don't blame her for doing the same."

"It's frustrating that you're siding with her."

She smacked his cheek lightly, and he smiled. "I'm not siding with anyone. I'm trying to knock some sense into your stupid head. You both care about each other so much, and you can't admit it. It's annoying."

He stood up, and she dropped her hands down to her sides. "It's more complicated than that."

"Really." She deadpanned. "Don't tell me about complicated. Do you know how much I want to find someone? But I can't. Because if I end up in a relationship with anyone here, I will spend the rest of my life lying to him." She bit her lip, and then stepped closer to him, placing her hands on his shoulders. When he didn't pull away, she lifted one to stroke the side of his face. "That's why I couldn't help being attracted to you when you got here. Even knowing there is no possibility for long term. Sometimes being seen by someone for even a moment is worth whatever it costs when it's over."

She stood there, hands laced behind his neck, waiting. She was beautiful. Gorgeous even. He didn't pull away, and after a moment she stood on her tiptoes and kissed him. Hesitantly, waiting to see how he would respond. That was all it took for him.

He gave her a hug, and then stepped back. "I'm sorry, Marsh. I can't do this. Not even for a moment."

She nodded, "Now you understand why it's annoying."

He smiled awkwardly, hand coming up to the back of his neck, not knowing where to go from here. "My advice?" She said, recovering quickly, "Tell her that you care. At least tell her that. Don't live the rest of your life wondering what if."

"I just want to protect her."

"That's not your job."

"Of course, it's my job!" He protested.

"No, Carver. Your job is to tell her the truth. Be honest with her. She's a hell of a lot stronger and more capable than you seem to believe her to be."

He tried to smile at her, "I'm sorry."

"For what?"

"That I'm not the man you were hoping I would be for you."

She shrugged delicately, and there was a part of him that could see how better suited they would be. A woman he could protect instead of a warrior that stood by his side. But how long until he charged into battle and would be overwhelmed with fear for her safety? How long until he too would need a warrior by his side watching his back? Marsh was absolutely right. Clara had become that warrior whether he liked it or not.

His heart pounded as he walked up the steps to their room. He rehearsed the words over and over in his head, but couldn't quite land on the right ones. *I'm sorry? I know I didn't trust you but I want to make things better now? I love you?*

None of those felt right, but as they neared the time to complete their assignment, he knew he had to say something. "Clara, I've been a jackass," *she would like that*, "I'm so sorry that I didn't trust you. I'm so sorry I didn't believe how strong you have become. I'm in love with you. I always was, and always will be. I want nothing more than to go back and change my decisions. I was trying to protect you, but I see now that more than protecting you I should have been supporting you. I hope you will give me the chance to make that better now." He stood outside the door, whispering under his breath. Yeah. That wasn't too bad. He could say that. She might even respond amiably.

"Okay, you can do this."

He pushed open the door, ready to confess. But the room was empty. His heart plummeted. "Clara?" He called out, but there was no response.

43 CLARA

She wasn't surprised Carver went to Marsh to complain about her. Of course he had. The second he left, she knew that's where he was headed. She knew that's where he had headed the second he left. It infuriated her, but in a way it was also fair. Carver didn't belong to her. She didn't have any kind of claim over him. And Marsh was attractive. Gorgeous, actually. She was soft in a way that Clara never could be, yet independent enough that Clara knew she was appealing to Carver whether he admitted it or not.

What she hadn't prepared for, was to see Marsh's arms wrapped around Carver's neck as she kissed him. Clara quickly backed away from the door and slipped out the back. Fury flared hot through her veins and she wanted to punch something. She pressed her back against the brick of the building, breathing heavily as she tried to calm down. She couldn't punch the brick. She'd break her hand. That wouldn't help anything. She considered it anyway. *Mission first.*

She had to do something.

After very little deliberation, she began winding her way through the festival and to the guarded lab. She just wanted to scope it out. She needed something constructive, and what better than a head start on their plan.

A couple drunk men bumped into her, and one almost propositioned her, but when she glared he realized she might be more than he was bargaining for and he moved on.

The sun was setting in the distance, and instead of the caged creatures brought on stage, there were performers. Flame throwers, acrobats, anything to amuse the people. It didn't take much to amuse the primarily drunk crowd. It was late enough in the day that most had been drinking for a few hours. It was certainly a party.

Clara thought they were all foolish. Idiots. So blinded by their own comfort they would never notice the desperation and pain of others. Much less defend them.

She walked through an alley, putting herself towards the back of town square and nearing the lab. There were enough trees she was able to stay in the shadows, but she couldn't quite see the guards. She approached close enough she could hear them talking. These guards weren't as stoic as the ones at the front. They sounded bored and chatted about all the things they had witnessed in the festival so far.

Clara figured their talking, plus the wind that was blowing through, would be enough to cover the noise of her climbing the tree so she could see down over them.

She was careful as she grabbed the bark. Far enough away that from their vantage point, they would never know she was there. She was still in the stupid Calyndor skirt, so she was taking extra precautions to avoid catching the fabric and landing herself in an awkward position. The wind blew through, and she desperately wished she was in pants.

The branches grew thinner as she climbed higher. She managed to inch herself out over one that she could just barely see the guards and the entrance. The two guards stood on either side of the door, but they were barely aware of anything happening. Perhaps they assumed the inside security was enough to make them irrelevant.

A man approached, a scientist she assumed by the look of his white coat. The guards froze and saluted him, both parties exchanging greetings. The man punched in a code and swiped a card. Electronics.

Clara inwardly groaned. Electronics were not a strong point for her. She knew they were easily contaminated, but wasn't sure how she could disarm the system. A bullet perhaps? That should short circuit everything and allow her access. Would that be too loud though?

She thought through other possibilities. What weapons would Marsh have had? A knife might work, but it might not be destructive enough to actually fry the circuitry. A taser would definitely work. If Marsh had that. Clara couldn't imagine that would be easy to come by, but maybe. Worst case scenario, she would make a little too much noise and pray to the gods that no one heard.

The man slipped inside, and unfortunately she couldn't see anything beyond that. After a few minutes, one of the guards swiped his card, punched a code in the keypad (she mentally noted where his fingers landed), walked inside, and returned a few minutes later. "Everything is good," he reported. Marsh hadn't warned them about guards checking the inside. Was that an added precaution with the festival?

The guards had a card. That would be even better. If she could get a card and figure out the code, she wouldn't have to go through any destruction. She shimmied down the tree and headed back to the festival.

She stopped at a vendor, and spent the precious few coins she had taken with her on alcohol. She swallowed one drink of it, just enough so it would be on her breath, and poured the rest on herself. She now reeked of alcohol. She walked unnoticed to the back of town square again. Making sure there was no one watching, she hiked her skirt up a little higher, high enough she could feel the air blowing across her butt. She tugged her shirt lower, using what little she had to her advantage.

She stood behind the tree she had climbed, taking a deep breath in. She could do this. She staggered out from behind the tree, swaying and laughing loudly until she crashed into one of the guards. He stabilized her, holding her up by her arms. She used the opportunity to snag his card.

He glanced nervously at his friend, not sure what to do. "Ma'am you can't be here."

"I thought this was the festival," she giggled, pitching into him again.

He looked very annoyed and turned to his friend, "I'm escorting her back to the festival. I don't think she'll make it there alone."

Turning back to her he continued, "Ma'am, do you have friends at the festival? Or somewhere I can take you that you can spend the night?"

She hadn't thought this far ahead. She couldn't appear too sober when answering his questions, but she needed him to actually leave her somewhere. "Just take me back to the festival," she laughed again, and he looked positively disgusted with her, "I want to see the flame throwers!"

She stumbled, falling onto her knees and tucking the key card into the waist band of her skirt so he wouldn't see it. The guard muttered to the other guard, "Flames sound like a terrible idea for her."

"At least she won't be our problem anymore." The second guard laughed.

"Okay, come on." The first guard muttered as he grabbed her

arm and roughly pulled her up. He walked her back to the festival, and though he seemed unsure about leaving her, he seemed to decide staying with her would be worse. He ensure she was steady enough on her feet, shook his head at her, and walked away.

She waited until he was out of sight before she jumped into motion. She wound her way through the crowd, making sure she would be fully hidden if he realized his card was missing and tried to find her again. She took a roundabout way to the bookstore, just in case she was being followed. The chances of that were slim, but it wasn't something she felt like she could risk.

She felt the key card press against her waist and smiled to herself. Carver would be so proud of her. This was what they needed to get inside. He'd have to admit that she was capable and deserved to be on the assignment after this. He couldn't keep rolling his eyes at her and treating her like some stupid child.

A bounce returned to her step in a way she hadn't felt in years. She enjoyed the feeling of hope and excitement. This assignment was far more than she had bargained for, but maybe it would be worth it. Maybe all of this would be worth something greater. Something better.

At the bookstore, she slipped in the back door, closing it quietly behind her. "Carver!" She called out, unworried about being heard. The bookstore would have closed hours before, and only Carver and Marsh should have been on the premises.

No response. "Carver!" She shouted again, as she flipped one of the lights on. No one was downstairs. Upstairs then? The sun had fully set, and she was careful as she walked up the stairs in the dark. She didn't feel like turning on all the lights, assuming Carver would be in their room with the lights already on. But he wasn't there either.

Confused, she decided they must have gone out to get food. She quickly changed her clothes. Black leggings and a tight red shirt.

Not exactly inconspicuous, but frilly enough to be considered Calyndor clothing. Vastly different from her other outfit in case the soldier came after her.

She enjoyed the night air on her skin, feeling lighter than she had in years. She felt capable. They would actually succeed. She couldn't wait to show Carver her success of the night. A smile crept across her face. For once it had nothing to do with being Calyndor, and everything to do with how she was feeling.

Happiness was something she hadn't experienced in a long time. She could feel the energy bubbling across her skin, and she didn't want the moment to end.

The bar she had gone the first night was as packed as ever, but she had a gut feeling Carver and Marsh would be inside. Sure enough. They were crammed into a tiny booth at the back. Marsh threw her head back and laughed at something Carver said, then swatted his arm.

Clara stood there, frozen in the sudden shock of the moment. She was trying to keep from jumping to conclusions when Carver leaned over and kissed Marsh. Marsh kissed him back, and Clara's heart plummeted. She knew it was coming. She reminded herself. She had disliked Marsh from the beginning because of this right here. Carver was too distracted from the mission. That's why she was mad. Because of the mission. Not because the small amount of joy she felt only moments before was sucked up and replaced with her broken heart.

She stumbled backwards. She had to get out of here. Go somewhere else. Anywhere else. She bumped into someone and mumbled her apologies. She looked back at Carver as he looked up. His eyes met hers and she thought she would throw up. He looked as panicked as she felt, though why she couldn't say, and he started to stand but she was already leaving.

This time she truly did stumble into an alleyway, hands on her knees as she tried to breathe. Just breathe. This was exactly what she knew it would be. Why did she think he would be proud of her? Why did she even care?

After several moments, she straightened and resolved that she didn't need him to complete this assignment. He obviously didn't want to be a team, and she obviously didn't need him.

44 CARVER

Carver sat on the bed, stunned that Clara would disappear without telling him. They were supposed to be partners. They were supposed to do this together. Together they would be strong, invincible, able to cope with everything that would inevitably be thrown at them.

He messed up when he tried to cut her out of the assignment. He told her he didn't need her. He said things that would hurt her, that were meant to hurt her. Guilt weighed heavily in the pit of his stomach, but on the other hand, wasn't it a lot for her to expect that he would casually accept her killing a bunch of people? She knew he never killed anyone. She should know he wouldn't be okay with this. Was what she said truly Command's view on the situation?

He didn't know how much time had passed before Marsh knocked on the door, but the sun had already descended and he was hungry. She let herself in, and sat next to him on the bed without a word. "She just left." He said evenly.

"Maybe that's your answer." Her voice was soft as she replied, but Carver could feel the question in it. If the reason he wasn't with Marsh was because he was in love with Clara, and Clara had made her decision, what was stopping him?

His gut told him it was a bad idea. Anything to do with Marsh would inevitably lead to heartbreak on both of their parts. He would be leaving as soon as the assignment was over, and they would never see each other again. Clara would never forgive him if he had anything to do with Marsh. *She won't forgive me anyway,* the voice in the back of his head reminded. And, it was true. Clara had already chosen. She decided on her own she didn't need him. She had become someone he couldn't protect. Maybe it was okay.

He used every justification that ran through his head as reason enough when he slipped his arm around Marsh's shoulder. She nuzzled into him. "I know I'm not her. I'm okay with that."

If the words were meant to assuage his guilt, it didn't work. But he didn't care anymore. He didn't care. None of it mattered. They'd finish the assignment and all three of them would go back to the lives of hell that war created.

He pulled Marsh closer, and for a moment allowed himself to just enjoy the comfort of being with someone. It wasn't something that had happened in the last three years. He was so focused, so driven, so intent on not thinking about Clara that he hadn't let anyone else in either. It was time for that to change.

His stomach rumbled, and Marsh laughed, standing and pulling him with her. "Let's get some food."

"Works for me."

She didn't let go of his hand as she pulled him down the stairs and out the door. Thoughts of Clara came rushing back when they entered the bar he had attempted to save her in, but he recalled how that story ended—with her hating him even more. His every attempt to protect her or show her he cared was thrown back in his face, so maybe it didn't matter. Maybe none of it mattered. Maybe he should give up.

So he held Marsh's hand a little tighter, and squeezed in on the same side of the booth with her. The guilt in his gut was mounting. He was using her to forget someone else, exactly what he had avoided doing for the past three years. But she knew he was doing that, and she chose him anyway. What did that say about both of them?

She leaned against his arm as they ordered, and he relaxed. The loud sounds of the bar drowned out the thoughts he was trying to remove anyway, and he forced himself to focus on the present. He ignored Clara, ignored the assignment, ignored all the chaos constantly plaguing his mind.

"I've never done anything like this." Marsh said as their drinks arrived.

He took a sip of his, and it was strong. "Like what?"

"I've never been on a date–never had someone that I genuinely cared about. Actually, that's not true. I went on a date once. He was from here. He was so proud of everything that Noxvalis was achieving, and my stomach churned the whole time he was talking. All I could think was how little he cared for the lives that were being so fully disregarded. It was irrelevant to him. What are a few lives for the sake of progress?"

"I've only dated one person." He offered, trying to relate to her.

Her eyes widened, and he saw his mistake, "Clara."

"Yes. We dated, but only because we ended up practically living together. It was all neat and tidy. Perfectly arranged, if you will." He tried to laugh it off, but he could feel the tightness in his smile.

"Okay, moving on." Marsh took a big gulp of her drink, "What's your favorite color?"

He laughed, "What do you mean?"

"I mean, we're sitting here. We have at least some form of

attraction to each other. We both have elephants in the room we're trying to avoid, so I'm suggesting a safe topic of conversation that will steer clear of all things gray." She gave him a pointed look, "If you say your favorite color is gray I might actually hit you."

"No, no. My favorite color is orange."

"Orange? What shade of orange? Like the fruit?"

"Like the sunset. When the sky looks slightly burnt. In between the orange and red as everything begins to fade."

"Why?"

Because, Clara and I would watch the sunset together. Because, she would lean her head on my shoulder, and the darkening sky would tint her in an array of color. It was safe. It was everything I wanted. All he said was, "Something about the sunsets."

Marsh waited for him to expound on his statement, but when he turned his attention to his drink, she jumped in with her own favorite color. "It's green. Like my eyes. I'm sure that's a little narcissistic, but it always reminds me of nature and how no matter how bad things get, everything still has the ability to grow back."

"That makes sense. You've seen a lot during your time here, haven't you?"

"Yeah."

Their food arrived, and diverted both of them from the conversation. He was even hungrier than he thought he would be, and he devoured his food.

They each ordered another drink, and Marsh sighed, "Can we just stay here for a while longer? It's nice to be out, and to pretend that things are different than they are."

"Sure."

She grabbed his face, turning him to look at her. She stroked his jaw, waiting to see how he would respond. "You're attractive," he whispered.

"Oh yeah?" She grinned impishly, and waited to see what else he would say or do. He shifted in the seat enough to kiss her.

He lost himself for a second, pretending she was Clara. But it only lasted a second, before he was opening his eyes and pulling away. He couldn't do this. Not actually–for her sake. He took another sip of his drink, trying to look like he was still enjoying their time.

His eyes scanned the room, and landed on a very shocked Clara. *Crap.* That was not how this was supposed to go. He started to stand, but she was already bolting out of the door.

Marsh noticed, and pulled on his hand. "You can explain later. Please, stay a little while longer. At least finish your drink."

He was tempted to down the drink, but as kind and lonely as Marsh was, he knew she deserved a little bit more from him. So he sat back down and played the part she wanted from him: the casual boyfriend.

His thoughts weren't in the moment. Clara took all of his concentration with her. There wasn't a good way to explain this. She was most definitely going to be pissed. Not ideal.

45 CLARA

Clara ran a couple laps through the alleyways as she calmed herself and generated a plan. What she really wanted was a punching bag. There wasn't anywhere she could go for that. So she stuck with running, hoping that would be enough to clear her mind. It almost was.

By the time she was back at the bookstore, her chest was heaving, and she wanted water more than she wanted to slam Carver's head into the brick. Well, almost more.

Why did she care anyway? He didn't mean anything to her. She shouldn't care who he kissed. But she did. She realized that, the moment she stole the card and couldn't help but think she would win Carver's pride. She wanted his affection back. She wanted to be his. She had always wanted to be his.

He was right on one count; it was why she ended up in the army. She did follow him. She stayed for her, but she joined because of him. She couldn't stand the thought of being separated from him in that way. Couldn't stand the idea of him being in danger while she lived a perfect life, safe at home. She wanted to be there with him, wanted to stand by his side and face whatever would come.

He never understood that. He called her selfish, weak, conceited. Believed she did it for the sake of control or whatever else he had called it. If only he had listened to her for long enough to actually understand. Though, she had never been good enough at verbalizing. She might have tried to tell him everything, and still missed vital points.

She downed a glass of lukewarm water, and ate some cold leftovers. Carver and Marsh still weren't back, and she debated what to do. He definitely saw her. She could stay awake and confront him when they got back. It would make her look stupid, it wouldn't accomplish anything, and it would only frustrate her more.

Or, or, she could get in bed and pretend to sleep. Once he came in and went to bed, she would be able to slip out, break into the lab, and retrieve the weapon herself.

No, that would be foolish. Or would it? Her mind spun over the idea, and the longer she waited without Marsh and Carver returning, the more convinced she became that she could do it. She'd scare the crap out of Carver by disappearing, and then prove to him that not only did she not need his protection, she didn't need his help either.

She also wouldn't have to worry about leaving him to his own devices. She'd have the opportunity to scout the lab without his concern for innocent lives. She could kill every person in the lab, retrieve the weapon, and be back before Carver noticed she was missing. She'd keep him from dying and fulfill Command's orders. The Raven would no longer be her concern.

She changed into black leggings and a tight long sleeved black shirt. Her shoes were set by the door, socks in the tops of them. She'd be able to grab them on the way out the door without nearing Carver.

She slipped the key card into the pocket of the leggings, ensuring that it was secure before she climbed into bed. Though she was warm in the outfit, she kept the covers fully covering her body so he wouldn't see what she was wearing. He wasn't stupid. He knew her well enough that if he saw her clothing, he would assume what she was planning to do. She couldn't take that risk.

She heard footsteps on the stairs, and her heart pounded. Acting was not her forte, and making Carver actually believe she was asleep wouldn't be easy. She closed her eyes, and counted her breaths to keep them slow.

"Clara?" He whispered as he eased the door open.

He moved silently across the room, and she almost jumped out of her skin when he laid a hand on her shoulder. But she kept counting breaths and didn't open her eyes. *Please let this be believable.* Now that he was next to her, the idea of fighting with him was so frustrating, she couldn't stand opening her eyes to do that.

He stood there, hand on her shoulder for what felt like an eternity. "It was supposed to be you." He finally whispered, and then removed his hand. She heard him flick the switch in the bathroom, and risked opening her eyes to confirm he had closed himself in. She rolled over, his words replaying in her head. *It was supposed to be you. Me. It was supposed to be me?*

What the hell did that mean? It was supposed to be her instead of Marsh in the bar with him tonight? It was supposed to be her? As in, they should still be together? Her mind spun over the words, but when the bathroom door opened, she resisted the urge to toss and turn. She was supposed to be asleep.

He laid down on his mat, and after a few minutes, his breaths evened out, and she knew she was close to home free. She wanted him to fall into a deep enough sleep that she could leave without him waking, so she laid there running through her plan for close to thirty minutes.

She'd slip out, and go through the back alley until she reached the tree. The branch she had been on was almost directly above the entrance. She would wait there until the guard shifted, and then hopefully drop down. That specific branch was a little too high to drop down, but she was hoping she'd be able to drop to a lower branch and then to the ground.

She had the key card, so that at least, was in her favor. She didn't know the code. But she remembered the pattern the guard's hand had gone in when he entered it. She hoped it was simplistic enough that it would be enough. It had to be enough. She could do this. *This is stupid, Clara.* She couldn't help but think. She pushed the thought aside and kept planning. Once inside, she would retrieve the weapon, hide until the next guard change, and then slip out. Silently, she slid her hands over her body accounting for all of her knives. It would have to be enough.

She didn't even allow herself to consider what would happen if one of the pieces failed. She would find Marsh's weapons before she headed to the lab and add those to her collection. She was fully capable of taking on enough guards to protect herself. She didn't need help. She would be able to do this.

She kept reminding herself of this, letting the plan run over and over, until it felt more like a choreographed performance than something she was trying to figure out.

She counted to a thousand before she slipped out from the covers, her bare feet landing lightly. She grabbed her boots with one hand, and eased the door open with the other. She waited in the hallway to make sure Carver hadn't woken to follow her. After enough time had passed to be safe, she tiptoed down the stairs.

Remembering that Marsh had pulled out the hand drawn map from a book on the shelf, Clara wondered what else had been stored on the shelf. An extremely thick book with some meaningless title stood out to her first. She pulled it out, and when she opened it found a small handgun. She wanted to tuck it in the band of the leggings, but guns would be too much of a risk. The lab was secluded, and the noise of guns plus the high oxygen levels wouldn't end well for her. She wasn't willing to risk an explosion.

She found another gun, a small taser, and a set of knives in other places on the bookshelf.

Feeling more confident with the weapons in her grasp, she slipped into her boots. She needed to get out of here. Sorting through the books had taken longer than she had planned for, and knowing that neither Marsh nor Carver regularly slept through the night, she needed to leave before they woke up and found her.

Once in the alley, she took a deep breath, feeling adrenaline already pumping through her veins. This was the excitement of an assignment–the ability to push yourself to the brink and truly see what you were made of. She would. She would push herself to the brink and find out exactly what she was made of. No matter what it cost.

46 CARVER

He stood next to Clara's bed with his hand on her shoulder for far longer than he should. He wasn't sure what he was expecting. Maybe there was an insane part of him, because he would have to be entirely insane, hoping she would open her eyes and invite him to slide in next to her. Hoping she would say she understood and she cared about him too.

It was supposed to be her. It was always her. Whether she knew it or not, from the first day they sat on the roof he had known he would never love anyone else the way he loved her.

He opened the box with the red gem necklace, and wondered if there would ever be an opportunity for him to give it to her now that he had so royally screwed up. He slid the box under his pillow and locked himself in the bathroom.

He couldn't believe he kissed Marsh–especially in public where Clara was able to see. If he could go back and rewrite that moment he would. He would tell Marsh that she was very sweet, and very pretty, that he liked her, but his heart belonged to another. And whether that other ever acknowledged him or not, his heart would remain true to her.

He turned the shower on and stepped in. If only he could go back.

He mind fixated on how crushed Clara looked in the moment he met her eyes. As the water in the shower ran down his back, that moment replayed over and over until he thought he was going insane.

He shut the water off, and quickly changed. Should he wake her? Could they have this conversation and move on? They were supposed to be prepared to accomplish the assignment tomorrow. They had wasted almost all of today. The assignment was first, right? That was the rule. *And we've done such a good job of following the rules.*

As he stood next to her bed, debating waking her, he couldn't. She looked too peaceful, too calm. And he was too tired to want to fight with her. It would be a fight. In some ways, it would be fair on her part. Whether he was committed to her or not, the rules did say that he wasn't supposed to flirt with anyone. He broke them and it wasn't even for the sake of the assignment. Because he was stupid and craved something more than the absence he constantly felt.

Surprisingly, he fell asleep quickly.

And plunged directly into a dream.

Clara had knives in both of her hands. They were in the hallway of the lab. They passed these young lab assistants on either side. Kids. They couldn't have been more than 16 or 17. She didn't hesitate as she lashed out in fluid motions and slit their throats.

Blood pooled on the white floors as they slumped. Carver gagged, but kept moving. Even with the brutality, he had to complete the assignment or it would all be for naught. He had to get the vials. He had to get the vials.

It kept repeating in his head like a mantra. He had to get the vials. He had to save Quorath. More teens stepped out in white coats, and again, Clara didn't hesitate. Again, he gagged, but again he kept moving.

He glanced over at her, and her face was impassive. The carnage, the blood shed behind them didn't seem to faze her in the least. She was fully focused. Fully determined. Nothing would stop her.

A man stepped out of the shadows as they reached the lab. He wore a dark coat, and Carver's heart dropped. Something was wrong. The man threw out two weapons, Carver couldn't tell what they were, but he heard Clara scream almost immediately and everything inside of him fully panicked.

He turned to see Clara had fallen to the ground, her wrists pouring blood. The man had cut off her hands. "It was a silly thing, you tried to do here, boy."

Carver fell to his knees, warmth soaking through his pants as the blood continued to pool. He gently wrapped his arm around Clara's shoulder, determined to save her if nothing else. Soldiers poured into the lab, standing at attention behind the man in black. They weren't going to fulfill the assignment. There was no way they were getting the vials now. At best, he could get Clara out of here alive. So that was what he determined to do.

"You were never going to win. We always knew you were coming. Do you think the festival was just to showcase our scientific endeavors?" He grinned, and Carver almost recoiled. The man's canines had been carved into points, and in that moment he looked more animal than human. His voice, however, still carried the distinct mark of royalty. Every word perfectly spoken, and with an air that you couldn't help but listen.

"No, we're not that prideful. It was an invite."

Carver slipped his hands under Clara's shoulders, trying to help her stand, but she had passed out. Her dead weight caused him to pitch forward, both of them ending up back on the ground. Her blood was soaking his pants, coating his hands, coating her, and he resisted the urge to gag yet again as nausea churned in his stomach. He wouldn't show weakness in front of this man.

"Don't you want to ask what the invite was for?"

Carver forced himself to stand, leaving Clara at his feet. He couldn't get her out with these soldiers at his back. Best to face them head on and protect her while he still could. "What was the invite for?" His voice sounded flat even to his own ears.

Again, the man grinned. Feral. "To see who would be brave enough, or foolish enough as it turns out, to attempt and steal from us."

Carver gaped, wanting to throw up a defense. All of the plans were foreseen. They were expected. "You got further than we expected, actually. That girl of yours, she's bloody brilliant. Tougher than we expected. And now, you've reached the end. Thank you for showing us the weaknesses in our labs. We appreciate it."

The man snapped his fingers and guards stepped forward in unison. Carver didn't even have a weapon to lash out at them. He stepped over Clara's body, determined to do something, anything. The man froze before he left, "Take her to the creature labs. With the loss of her arms, she'll be a perfect candidate for our new bio engineering program."

Carver yelled, standing his ground even as the soldiers came within feet of him. "Kill the boy."

One of the soldiers lifted his gun and fired.

Carver woke up, completely soaked in sweat and panicking. It was just a dream. It was just a dream. He was certain he had been screaming. His throat felt raw, and he was surprised Clara hadn't shaken him awake or wasn't glaring at him from the edge of her bed.

A sickening feeling crept into his gut. Clara. He scrambled off of his mat, his feet tangling in his blanket. He tripped and crashed into the edge of the bed before he was able to right himself. "Clara?" He didn't bother to whisper or be quiet. He needed to hear her voice, needed the reassurance that she was okay.

There was no response. He saw her hands falling. He saw the blood pouring from the stumps. Her falling to her knees and passing out. "Clara!"

He threw open the bathroom door. She wasn't there. He flipped on the light in the room. Her bed was empty and her shoes were gone. "No, no, no." He groaned. Where would she have gone in the middle of the night?

He slipped his own shoes on as he rushed down the stairs, not bothering to tie the laces. Maybe she was only in the kitchen? Maybe she had gone for a walk and was getting back? The adrenaline from the dream still flowed through his veins, and even if those were the more likely options, his body was still telling him that something was wrong. Something was wrong. Something was very wrong.

Clara was in danger.

She wasn't in the kitchen. He rushed out the back door, forgetting to close it as he surveyed the alley. No sign of her. "Carver?" Marsh shouted from the doorway.

He turned, barely even registering her frame. "It's Clara. She's not here. She's in danger."

"You don't know that. She probably just went for a walk. I'm sure she's fine. Come back inside." Marsh yawned, crossing her arms over her chest.

"I can't come back inside. She's in danger. I know it." He paced back and forth through the alley. Where would she have gone? Where could he look?

"Even if she is in danger, you have no idea where she is. Go back to bed, and I'm sure she'll be back by morning. She's tough, remember? She doesn't need your protection."

The man's words from his dream resounded through his head, renewing fear within him. They knew Carver and Clara were here. Somehow that man knew.

Carver knew he wasn't being entirely logical. He couldn't even prove that man was a real person. He had been having nightmares for years, and none had come to fruition. He had no evidence that this one was different. But it felt different. Somehow. He knew that something was wrong.

"I have to try and find her." He emphatically responded.

He started at the bar. No sign of her inside. It was late enough that a lot of the patrons had cleared out already. He stopped the bartender and described Clara, hoping that maybe he had seen her. There had been no sign of her.

Where else? He walked through the town square, a few drunk groups stumbling and laughing here and there. The shops had closed up, and the stage was now entirely empty. No sign of Clara.

He exhaled heavily, pushing his hair back off his forehead. He slowly spun in a circle, surveying the area and trying to think where else could she go.

No. No. She wasn't stupid enough to try and steal the vials on her own. No way. Was she? His heart sank. Maybe not stupid enough, but she was stubborn enough, and sometimes those two went together. He exhaled, trying to shake the anxiety grasping at his chest, and sprinted across the town square to reach the edge of the alleys.

He crept along the forest line, pausing behind the trees that were big enough to hide his body so he could listen for any noise.

He was close enough to see the guards, and silently laid on his stomach so he could watch them without being noticed. Nothing seemed wrong. Everything seemed like it was okay.

The guards were talking quietly, looking thoroughly bored with their evening. Carver couldn't blame them. Guarding an electronically guarded door frame in the middle of the night must have felt like a pointless assignment.

He tried to see behind them, desperately wishing he had binoculars. He couldn't spot anything out of order. His heart rate slowed, and he started thinking maybe Marsh was right. Clara did like to expend energy through exercise. Maybe she couldn't sleep, and so she went for a run. She was probably back already, and her and Marsh were mocking him for his over protectiveness.

Yeah, that was what would happen. He'd get back, they'd be in the kitchen with tea, and he'd get laughed at. He'd pretend to be frustrated at their laughter, but truly, he would enjoy every minute of it because it would mean that Clara was safe and his nightmare was just a dream.

He was about to crawl away and head back to the bookstore, but something inside him convinced him to wait another moment. The guards burst out in laughter, talking about something he couldn't make out. Then the alarms went off.

47 CLARA

Climbing the tree in leggings was much easier than the frilly skirt she had climbed in earlier. She checked the watch she had stolen from the kitchen, and estimated the guard change to occur within an hour. Then it would be a matter of retrieving the vials, waiting til the next guard change, and getting the hell out.

She flexed her fingers, preparing to grasp her daggers. This was another mission, and she had her orders. She would do whatever it took, and kill every person that stood in her way.

Her heart pounded as her thoughts rushed through her mind, but she kept her breaths even and stayed as calm as she could. A small amount of doubt remained in the back of her mind. This wasn't the smartest move. She wasn't too far in. She could go back, and her and Carver could continue their plan and accomplish what they needed to. Although, their current plan had Carver executing everything and her sitting on the outside because he didn't believe she should do her job.

With that in mind, she stayed in the tree and continued watching, waiting for the guard change. There was another branch a couple feet below her, and she decided she could drop to that one and then drop to the ground without injury. It was the best she could do with what she had.

A few minutes after midnight, the guards shuffled away. They weren't as precise on timing as she hoped they would be. She'd have to work with whatever she was given, regardless of how much their inconsistency increased the chances of her being caught.

As soon as they were out of ear shot, she dropped to the branch below, barely catching herself before swinging to the ground. She rolled when she landed, using her full body to absorb the impact and then ran to the door way. She swiped the key card and when it lit up with green, she copied the motions she had seen the soldier do. Denied. She swiped again, and again entered the code. It beeped at her this time, "Denied. One attempt remaining."

"Shit," she whispered. She wracked her brain, but the only thing she could think was one of the numbers had been doubled. She zoned in, surveying the damage on the keys. Was one slightly more worn than the others? Would that provide the additional move-ment? The two had more indention, but she remembered the guard's hand starting there and not coming back. She'd have to go with it.

"Access granted." Flashed across the screen.

The door began to open, just as she heard the footsteps of returning guards.

She slipped in, and hid in the first alcove she could find, hoping they wouldn't come inside. She didn't want to start killing people already. But she would.

The door closed, and she stayed a few minutes before contin-uing into the lab. No one followed her, and as late as it was, there were very few sounds present. The hum of machines, the roar of air coming on and shutting off to maintain the necessary temperature.

All of what she assumed were normal sounds, but her heart

raced at every one. She stayed close to the wall as she walked down the hallway. Presumably, the vials would be stored in the deepest part of the lab. Closed white doors marked the hallway on both sides. Most of them were dark underneath, but a couple had lights shining through and she was cautious as she passed those.

It occurred to her, that if she had incurred a white lab coat, she would have a believable cover. As it was, her fingers tightened around the knives she held, and she knew that would be the only way she could protect herself. She was glad she hadn't brought the gun. It would have been too loud, and the ricochet against the lab walls was far too much of a liability.

One of the doors on the left was open, and since she had three hours before the guards would change, curiosity prevailed and she slipped inside. The room was filled with machines, and wires, and though no one was inside, a chill ran down her spine because something about it felt very...alive.

She reached the first container and covered her mouth with her hand to stifle a gasp. A baby boy wriggled inside the container. Surrounded by fluid, he was kept alive through the tubes running in and out. But it wasn't just a baby. Even as small as he was she could see fur growing on the tops of his feet and hands. The legs were elongating and bent in a position that was markedly animalistic; the fingers curved more than they should in preparation for claws.

Her stomach churned and she swallowed hard to avoid gagging as she tasted bile at the back of her throat. Every container around the room held much of the same. Genetically modified. Babies. Children. One of the larger containers held an adult, kept in stasis as the scientists performed the modifications—the experiments. It was wrong. It was so wrong. And for the moment, there was nothing she could do about it.

She would come back. She would take this information to

Command, and eventually, eventually they could burn Noxvalis to the ground. They could destroy the labs. They could stop evil people from playing gods.

An extra lab coat hung on the wall, and she gratefully lifted it off the hook. She'd at least be less conspicuous now. It was too big for her, the sleeves covering her hands entirely. At least it made hiding her knives easier. Definitely would've fit Carver better.

The thought popped in unwarranted and unwelcome, but it was there nonetheless, there with the quiet piece of chaos she pressed down that reminded her this was wrong. She should have waited for him. Orders were orders, and she had defied hers. Something she had never done before. An offense. But an offense she could remedy as long as she was successful. So she had to be successful.

Footsteps echoed through the hallway, and she pressed herself against the wall next to the door and waited. Either the person would pass by and she would continue on, or they would enter this room and she would slit their throat.

Her hands tightened around her knives and she breathed lightly. In and out as the footsteps grew closer. It was too late to shove the sleeves up, and she hoped they wouldn't get in her way when it was time to move. The man, heavy footsteps and long gait, paused at the door, and she wondered if he found it curious the door had been cracked open. She certainly wondered when she found it cracked.

His hesitation didn't last long, before he pushed the door open and stepped inside. His pace remained slow, and with his head down he didn't even notice her standing there. She waited until he closed the door behind him before she moved. He wasn't much taller than her, and in one swift motion she slit his throat with one hand, bracing his body with the other so he slid down against her silently.

The blood gurgled for a moment, but it was barely audible in the room over the hum of machines. No one else would have heard it.

She laid him to the ground, stepping back to examine the room and her work one more time. She cursed at the blood on her sleeve, but she had done the best she could. She rolled it up, and by the third layer she managed to cuff it so the blood was barely visible. She matched the cuff on the other side.

Clara inhaled deeply, forcing herself to take in the details of the scenario rather than the dead body in front of her. Deep breath in, deep breath out. She had learned how to push the bodies aside and dissociate entirely from the deaths she caused. It was what made her the best.

He wasn't young, but he wasn't old either. His facial hair was unkempt, and the only article of clothing that looked professional was his lab coat. It opened to stained pants, and an even more stained t-shirt. The man's key card was clipped to his coat. She noticed this detail long before it clicked into place that she would need the key card to access the weapons lab. Of course she would. She had lucked out with this door being open; she highly doubted the next one would provide her the same favor.

She clipped the key card onto her own lab coat, straightening the pieces of her outfit until she could convince herself that she belonged in the labs. If she didn't falter, maybe if she ran into someone else they would believe her disguise. She only needed them to believe long enough for her to end them.

The closer she moved toward the center of the lab, the more noise there was. The air was on all of the time, machines rumbled and beeped, others hummed constantly. She stuck to the shadows, prepared for whatever would come.

It surprised her, actually, when she reached the doorway at the end of the hall. She had expected to end up in a massive lab, or something that was obviously correct. The door was marked with a red symbol, "Biological weaponry. PPE required."

She rolled her eyes even as her stomach churned and her brain reminded her that she could, in fact, be exposing herself to something dangerous. Personal protective equipment wasn't something she had time to find. It was far too late to think about that.

She swiped the key card, and the light on the tab flashed red, red, red, and finally, green. She heard the click of the lock, and anxiety swirled in her gut as she pushed the handle down. She'd arrived. The door clicked softly behind her as it closed. She felt no relief. She'd made it this far, but still had to find the weapon and get out. She could do this.

The room was lined with temperature controlled cases. Each case had a glass front, and labels on the vials. She was looking for one labeled "DF23." Beyond that, Carver would know the details. All of the details needed for this part were probably in his brief. Command was so forceful about the two of them working together. So determined that they be in the lab at the same time.

It was her job to get them this far, and his job to get them out. She squared her shoulders. She was capable of both. Of course she was.

She glanced through all of the labels of diseases and antidotes, fear creeping its way into her stomach. They had far more than Quorath had even dreamed possible. If Command knew the kinds of weapons Noxvalis possessed, would they even believe the war was something that could be won?

She reached the back of the room before she spotted it, a tray of vials labeled DF23. Success. She carefully opened the case, and pulled the tray out. She held up a vial to the light from the case. It was light purple. How could something so small cause such large issues? She didn't even want to think about the consequences of Noxvalis using this kind of biological weapon.

She looked around the room for a bag, or anything that she could use to carry these. She found a cloth sack and carefully set the vials inside as she did so. They clinked against each other, but the glass was thick enough that she thought they would be fine. She'd grab a towel and wrap them in it for better piece of mind. She counted each one as she folded them within a towel. 9.

There were only 9. There were supposed to be 10. If what Command said was true, even one vial could wreck havoc. She scanned the case, hoping that maybe the vial had gotten mixed in with something else.

The vials in the case were all different colors. Blood red, vomit green, blue, yellow. She didn't know what kind of formulas would cause the array of colors, and truthfully, the idea of understanding terrified her. There wasn't another one that was purple. Not even close to the same shade.

She groaned. Not good. But what could be done about it? She glanced at her watch, and was shocked to see over two hours had passed. She'd spent more time in that room with genetics then she had realized.

It was too late to find the vial. It could be anywhere. It could have even been removed from the lab. They could be planning on using it already. It could be ready for deployment, and the festival a cover for the biggest weapon unveiling yet. Her brain spun and she forced herself to breathe and focus. In and out. In and out. What was next?

She had to get to the door and be ready for the guard change. She had to get these out of the city, and warn Carver about what could be coming.

She resisted the urge to run down the hallway. Though she had encased the vials as best she could, she couldn't afford cracking a single one. Again, she didn't run into another person. The lab continued through its endless slew of noises. A living, breathing mechanism of its own.

She reached the door way and glanced at her watch. The guards should be changing within the next 20 minutes. She slipped into the first alcove she had hidden in, waiting to hear any sign of movement outside. Her heart pounded, but she smiled. She had done it.

Well, basically. She had the vials, she was at the extraction point, she was successful. She heard movement outside, and stood to let herself out, but instead the doors opened. Lights in the hallway flickered on, and deafening alarms began.

48 CLARA

She felt the panic climb her throat. Instantly. She had never been caught—never triggered alarms. She was always in and out. She was always invisible. The shadow. The Eclipse. Never expected and never revealed. Pure destruction with no warnings and no discourse.

The alarm resounded through her head as she ran. She kept the bag slung across her body, knives in her hands. She wouldn't have time for subtlety or hesitation. A picture flashed across her mind. Carver, as he muttered "I can't do this anymore." And walked away. He hadn't given her the chance to respond. Three years ago and she still hadn't responded.

She had to make it out of this alive. And when she did, she would tell him exactly what she thought of him. She would tell him off at every point and explain precisely why what he did was so wrong. She would bring him to reason, and then she would be the one to walk away.

She was almost to the door. She could hear boots behind her. She didn't get a chance to press the button and open the doors. The hallway narrowed as it led to the doors, allowing only one soldier through with ease. The first soldier calmly stepped into the hall, standing mere feet from her. He held a knife, casually tossing it in the air. No guns in the labs. She flipped her own knives in her hands as she faced him. "Hello," she grinned.

The one in front curled his lips at her. "You're who they sent?" The other soldiers didn't advance behind him, leaving him standing in the hallway's entrance. Clara couldn't see how many soldiers were behind him.

It was only a matter of time until the soldiers outside the door responded to the alarms, at which point the doors behind her would open and she would truly be surrounded. She needed to dispose of the ones in front of her before that happened.

"Surprise." She shot back.

He laughed, and she almost dropped her guard at the shocking sound. "I thought our enemies would have at least given us a challenge."

She batted her eyelashes, "Oh, they did." She took the bag off of her shoulder, setting it off to the side. He watched her curiously, as though she would be easily disposed of. Little did he know.

The second the bag hit the ground, she tossed the knife in her right hand, hitting him in the neck. He groaned, grasping for the knife but she was already there. She removed it and finished the slice across his throat, entirely tuning out his gasping.

He slumped to the floor and she was already prepared for the next soldier. It became repetition. Duck, dodge, launch, whatever it took to make that final slice. She couldn't keep count of the soldiers. Her own breathing came in gasps as the metallic scent overwhelmed her lungs, but she couldn't stop. One after the other, she made it.

Adrenaline fed her veins and ran through her brain. None of it felt real. All she knew was it was her or them.

The doors behind her opened, and it was the first moment she recognized since the soldiers had started trailing in. She threw a knife at the next soldier coming into the entryway, and it glinted off his cheek buying her just enough time. She grabbed the bag and threw it over her shoulder, grateful she added the towel to protect the vials and hoping nothing broke.

The two soldiers who entered through the door looked shocked, but they didn't have a chance to react as Clara threw two more knives. Neither landed where she aimed, but both hit enough to distract. She grabbed two more from her waist, aware she only had only two more knives.

She needed to run. She had the vials. She needed to get the hell away from here.

"Clara!" The voice barely flicked into her recognition, and she turned. A form ran out from the trees, a gun held out in front of him. Everything about the hand position was wrong. Had he ever held a gun?

He fired at a soldier behind her and the noise snapped her back into the moment. Run. She needed to run.

"Clara!" He called again, "Run!" He stopped running towards her, planting his feet as he aimed at another soldier behind her. The boy who had never killed anyone. She didn't have time to contemplate that as she sprinted past him, through the alleyways, winding back to the bookstore. She wadded up the lab coat and threw it in the corner of an alley, adding her bloodstained shirt to it.

Her tank underneath provided enough coverage as she ran back to the bookstore. She had to get back. The door came into sight, and she opened it, practically slumping against it as she fell inside.

She groaned as she kicked the door closed behind her, head spinning.

"Clara? Clara? My gods, Clara, what happened?" The lights

flashed on as Marsh knelt next to her, hesitating before shaking her shoulder. "Are you hurt?"

Clara groaned again, blinking against the bright light. All at once she seemed to come back into herself. First, noticing the concern and fear in Marsh's eyes. Second, feeling for the bag and breathing a sigh of relief when she found it. Third, "Where's Carver?"

Marsh's eyes widened, "He went after you."

Clara's head pounded. "I don't...I..." She squinted, trying to remember. "He had a gun? I don't think he's ever shot a gun. He," she breathed in, grimacing at the pain in her side from the motion. She could feel the adrenaline fading, and everything became more painful. "He was still there," She finally said. Entirely numb.

"What do you mean he's still there?" Marsh's voice was harsh, and Clara flinched.

49 CARVER

Carver had only felt panic twice in his life. Usually, he was the first person to respond with reason. He was capable, level-headed, and unruled by his emotions. He was calm and able to take whatever came his way.

The first time he ever felt true panic was when Clara had slipped off the roof at 17. He felt his heart fall with her, and though it was only one story, he had been convinced she would be dead or require medical care. He rushed down the side of the roof, almost falling in the process but not even noticing, so desperate to reach her. She had landed hard, the air completely knocked out of her lungs, but by the time he reached her she sat up and was laughing. The worst of her injuries were soreness and bruising.

The same form of panic hit him now. All concern for his own safety banished, and he was halfway out from behind the tree, holding a pistol out in front of him, before realizing he hadn't shot a gun in years. His first shot was wildly off, but still the guards ducked and he kept moving towards them.

The door opened, and he saw Clara. Her eyes wild, knives held out in front of her, surrounded by blood and carnage. He kept moving, ready to fire again. "Clara!" He yelled. She didn't seem to notice. "Clara!" He yelled again.

The guards from the outside posts charged at her, and holding his gun out with one hand he hoped against hope he could land the shot. It grazed one soldier's arm, just enough to slow him down. "Clara, run!"

Her eyes snapped to his now, and she scrambled out of the doorway. He planted his feet, holding the gun out with two hands and fired consecutive shots. He barely aimed. It wouldn't matter. His only goal was to help Clara get away.

This was all his fault. He had broken the rules, and now he was paying the price. He knew from the moment he saw Marsh she was just attractive enough to cause problems. He couldn't blame her for this. It wasn't her fault. He blamed himself. He was so stupid to leave Clara to her own devices.

She'd always been reckless. Why did he assume training had tampered that? If anything, it only further convinced her of her ability to do whatever she wanted.

His gun clicked, and he knew that was the end for him. The soldiers had increased in number, and were running towards him. He looked behind him, unable to see Clara, and grateful she had gotten away. That was his only goal.

Everything moved in slow motion. He felt each beat of his heart in his chest, in his throat, in his hands still tightly wrapped around the gun. Had she done it? Had Clara gotten the vials and made it back alive?

He knew she wouldn't come back for him. He wouldn't ask her to. Her role, her entire goal was to save Quorath. And because of him, she could. A small amount of pride swelled in his chest. He, too, had accomplished his mission. He saved Clara.

He dropped the pistol and held his hands up at the guards

approached. "Where is she?" One soldier gruffly motioned to the others, "Spread out and find her! I'll take care of him."

The soldiers dispersed, but Carver knew Clara was long gone. They wouldn't find her. "On your knees." The soldier ordered and Carver complied. Whatever happened to him now was irrelevant.

"I should kill you right now." The soldier muttered, instead cuffing Carver's hands behind his back. The metal bit into his wrists, but Carver barely felt it. The butt of the guard's gun came down on his temple, and Carver's world turned black.

50 CARVER

"I can't do this anymore." He watched himself say the words. He watched his form turn to walk away. He watched Clara's face crumple and her shoulders fall.

He watched as he again walked away like all of those years ago. He tried to yell at himself, tried to tell Clara that wasn't him, he wouldn't hurt her like that. But his mouth wouldn't form the words and everything hurt. The pain rushed in like a tsunami until it covered every inch of him and became the only reality.

He tried licking his lips, but his mouth felt incredibly dry and he couldn't figure out what was happening to him. This couldn't be right.

His heart rate spiked, and his only thought was he couldn't breathe. The air felt weird. Almost thicker somehow. Clara's image swam before him until she was no longer Clara. She was gone and there was nothing but black.

Had he gone blind? No. His eyes must be closed. He was then brought back to the awareness of his body. Every nerve in his body was on fire. His brain was fully consumed by the pain.

He tried to open his eyes, but the most he could manage was a twitch. He tried harder, pushing the fear aside for determination.

What happened? Where was he? Why couldn't he open his eyes?

"Subject is waking up. Shall we administer another dose of anesthesia?"

"No, no. Let him wake up."

"Yes sir."

Straps rubbed across his wrists and he tried to squirm against them but they wouldn't budge. His eyelids resisted heavily as they opened, and he blinked against the harsh light in his face.

"Dr. Nathan, do you feel it necessary to blind my subject? Please, allow him the courtesy of adjusting to the room without the surgical light directly above his irises."

"Yes sir."

The light was removed and when Carver opened his eyes again, everything blurred in front of them but he could see.

The bed shifted until he was brought to a sitting position. He raked his tongue across his lips, but his mouth was far too dry for it to be beneficial. He flinched at small pinches near his elbow, and tried to yank away but the straps around his wrists continued to hold firm. Instead, he could only stare as the two people in blue uniforms removed the needles.

The one on the right dabbed roughly at the blood that pooled after removing the needle, and Carver gritted his teeth to avoid cussing. "Where am I?" His voice grated out and he tried to clear his throat. The nurse on his left held up a cup of water, allowing him to swallow a couple mouthfuls unsteadily, the excess dripping down his chin.

He tried to remember before—before the blaring lights, before the straps, before the all-consuming pain. How had he ended up in a hospital? Was that even where he was? No. He wasn't sure where he was at all.

"Mr. Vaughan, yes?"

He swallowed. The fog in his brain finally allowing him some semblance of memory. Clara. She had been in the labs. The cool metal in his hands. A gun. He allowed her to escape. He was not as fortunate. He preferred it this way.

"Who wants to know?" His voice was clearer now, but even he could hear the weakness in every word.

"My name is King Herring. Perhaps you've heard of me?"

Carver hissed as another needle was inserted into his arm. King Herring stood in front of him, eyebrows raised. He was prematurely gray. That was the first thought Carver had. Although he was a monster, and everyone knew him to be some heinous ruler, somehow that was the first thought he could make sense of. He must be severely drugged.

King Herring could have been considered handsome. Not much older than 30. Broad shoulders, and he carried himself with all the regality and authority befitting his station. His hair hit his shoulders in a straight cascade and every single piece was gray.

"It is unwise to anger a King, Mr. Vaughan."

"What do you want with me?"

King Herring tsked, "Now, Carver, I know you are smarter than that. Do you actually expect I will answer your questions?"

"Worth a shot," Carver spat back.

He yanked his wrists and thrashed against the bonds, but nothing moved or gave any leeway. "Ooo, he is feisty," the king chuckled. "That bodes well for surviving our experiments."

Carver froze momentarily. Until that moment he was convinced his capture was his death warrant. But there were far worse fates than death. Images flashed of the creatures he and Clara had seen at the festival. Was that what was to become of him? Another creature? No longer human in the eyes of others? Someone for Clara to pity or revile?

"That got your attention."

"I'm not an experiment." Carver growled.

"Not. Yet."

King Herring stepped back from the table and took a seat in a plush chair in the corner. With a single motion he ushered everyone out of the room. Carver had to awkwardly lift his head from the bed to fully see the king.

"Tell me about yourself. Name? Age? How you came to be in my lab?"

"Go to hell."

"Believe me, Mr. Vaughan, you do not want to make this difficult for me."

He moved his thumb across something in his hand and Carver's veins erupted in a fiery sensation. Whatever poison was in the needle spread through his body, and every nerve was on fire. He groaned, unable to resist the sound as he tried not to succumb to the darkness again.

He squinted his eyes as he attempted to breathe through the pain, but to no avail. He tried to recall all of his training, all the he had endured, but the pain was too great to form a complete thought. A scream clawed its way up and left his throat hoarse before the king relented. The second he stopped whatever he had been doing, the pain faded to a dull ache. Carver's entire body ached, and each breath hurt.

"Now, are we feeling a little more chatty, Mr. Vaughan?"

Carver closed his eyes tightly. What could he say that wouldn't compromise Clara? What could he reveal that would still protect his kingdom? He'd rather die than harm Clara. Unfortunately, he may not be given that option. "No?" King Herring moved as though to turn the dial on again. Carver's entire body tightened in preparation, and he tasted stomach acid at the back of his throat.

"My name is Carver Matthew Vaughan." He slowly answered, the words sticking in his throat.

"Carver Matthew Vaughan. A strong name for an albeit underwhelming boy."

He was in too much pain to take offense, but his vision cleared enough to focus on the king's leering smile. "Tell me, Carver Matthew Vaughan, how did you come to be in my labs?"

He grunted. "I got lost."

The searing pain entered his veins again, and he could barely hear himself screaming. When the king relented, he did so with a laugh. "You shot at my soldiers. Wounded three. You helped a thief escape."

Carver groaned again, unable to think straight enough to provide a response.

"You gave no attempt to escape. It was shocking, almost. Except that the thief was a girl. Someone you cared about perhaps? Maybe you thought yourself capable of protecting her? We have not found her yet, in case you were wondering." The first bit of relief Carver had felt. "But do not worry, we will. She must be something else. Truthfully, she got further than anyone would have considered possible. Our security system is top tier, but her little rendezvous has let us see just how far we have fallen. Times of prosperity do bring complacency, it is true. But we will use her endeavor as a framework to redesign our security. Rest assured, a break in will never again be possible."

Carver gritted his teeth, his vision nothing more than sparks. Everything hurt, and all he could hope was that King Herring was wrong and Clara was long gone. Surely, she wasn't stupid enough to try and come back for him.

"I will leave you to recover, Mr. Vaughan. I hope our future conversations will be much more fruitful. We shall have *many* such conversations imminently. You should take the opportunity to consider what type of experiment you would like to become. There are options. You have seen our creatures, I'm sure. But something so benign does not seem like the ideal for you. Perhaps you could be in our newest idea for experiments. We are creating a line of super soldiers. You have the build for it. Your body should respond well to the...well, let us call it what it is, Mr. Vaughan, invasion. And with a little more training you will be made to comply."

The door shut behind the king and Carver closed his eyes.

They did it. Clara had the biological weapon, and she could make it back to Quorath without him. She was safe. The price of saving their nation was only his life.

It was a price he was more than willing to pay.

EXCERPT FROM COST OF ATTAINMENT
CLARA

Three days. They'd been back for three days. They'd been out of Noxvalis for a week. And still, none of it felt real. Clara felt the world pass by in a blur.

She stood at attention. She answered the questions Command presented. No, there hadn't been 10 vials. Only 9. No, they hadn't had an opportunity to stop Carver from being taken. Yes, she had seen the experiments. Yes, they were atrocious. Yes, Quorath had every reason to fear what Noxvalis was capable of. No, she hadn't seen the king. Yes, she had failed on the private assignment they had given her. She, of course, presented her deepest apologies, though her heart wasn't in it.

She could tell they didn't believe her. Her heart ached, but not from their disappointment.

She was halfway through the questioning on the third day, and she was drawing on all her training to stay focused. "I have reason to believe Noxvalis presents a greater threat than the vials would indicate. Their biological experiments are terrifying, to be sure, but they have the items they need to dirty bomb all of Quorath."

Every person in the seats for Command leaned forward, "And this is the first time you are mentioning it, Operative Harris?"

"My apologies," Marsh lowered her eyes in deference, "I wanted to ensure we answered all of your questions on our first assignment before I addressed another problem."

Clara could have sworn the woman rolled her eyes. "Continue, Operative Harris." She said firmly.

"The last shipment came in two days before Clara and Carver arrived. I had heard rumors they were creating dirty bombs, but I thought it would be impossible for them to get that much of a radioactive substance. I also heard rumors they bombed a few towns a couple days from Noxvalis. I didn't believe those rumors to be true."

"But?" The woman prodded, clearly annoyed by Marsh's run around on information.

"We passed through those towns on our way back to base. They were ghost towns. It looks as though people packed up and left. It's possible some of them were warned, but for the rest...families don't leave photos of their children on the mantle by choice."

Collectively, Command seemed to shrink away from them, desperate to put a few extra inches of air between them and the Operatives standing before them. Clara turned suddenly, staring at Marsh as though she didn't recognize her. Not once during their trip did Marsh mention anything to her about this theory. The entire trip, she made it immensely clear she wanted nothing to do with Clara. But this? This was information Clara had a right to know!

"The only form of radioactive material they would be able to obtain and stabilize has a half-life of 74 days. It isn't long enough to remain a risk. By the time we passed through, the effects would have been nonexistent." Marsh clarified.

"If what you say is true, what are the effects of this type of dirty bomb? Wouldn't you have found bodies in the towns, Operative Harris?"

"They have enough materials to bomb all of Quorath. The first effect is shrapnel. Bombs exploding in every town will cause mass panic. And the effects of the radiation? Burns and weakness at best, acute radiation poisoning and death at worst. They will weaken us, allowing Noxvalis to swoop in and decimate us. I can't imagine Noxvalis wants us to know how close they've gotten to us. I'm certain they removed the bodies either to burn or for their own experimentation."

"Hmm. How confident are you in this information? You did say it was information you collected from rumors." Aside from the one woman, all of Command sat perfectly still. Clara barely breathed, anxious that anything she did would make this situation reflect poorly on her as well. This was Marsh's problem to deal with.

Marsh lifted her chin, "I was right about the vials. I am right about this. I would stake my life on it."

"In a war, it may come to that. You are both dismissed, for now. You may resume a normal life on base until further summoned."

Clara turned to leave, but Marsh didn't budge. "I'm not kidding about the bombs. I know which lab their materials are stored in. We have to do something, or they will wipe us out."

"Your concerns are heard, Operative Harris. Please follow your orders. If you are needed, we will summon you."

Marsh's fists clenched, and Clara waited for another outburst. Instead, her shoulders slumped, and she turned to follow Clara.

As soon as the Command doors closed behind them, Clara turned on Marsh. "What the hell was that? You knew those towns were abandoned by radiation? Don't you think this was information I had a right to know?"

"I'm not doing this with you." Marsh chuckled mirthlessly. She began walking down the Raven hallway, but Clara grabbed her wrist and spun her back. Marsh broke her hold and stared her down. "I suggest you return to your sector."

"What else do you know you aren't telling us?" Clara searched Marsh's eyes, not sure what she was looking for.

"I watched you leave your partner to die. Do you really think you're the person I'm going to trust with anything I know? Go to hell, Clara." Marsh spat her name like it was bitter in her mouth.

Clara felt the words like a knife in her chest. The guilt she carried for days came back in a rush of pain, and she had to remind herself to breathe. Marsh continued walking away, down the hall to the Raven sector. Into the sector Carver belonged to. But he wasn't here to follow her.

ACKNOWLEDGMENTS

I am guilty of skipping the acknowledgments page in almost every book I read, but I find my book doesn't feel complete without mentioning those who helped me reach this point.

To my mother. You fostered my love of writing at such an early age, edited my book, and offered valuable insights and suggestions. If you hadn't let me commission a cover for the book I wrote at 11, I may never have ended up here.

To my best friend. You listened to the roughest drafts of this book, and helped me brainstorm every time I was stuck. I can honestly say, this book wouldn't be what it is without you. You inspired so many pieces of *Rules of Engagement* and I am forever grateful for your constant support.

To Hannah. You've been reading, editing, and critiquing my books since 14. How does it feel to know your best friend finally published something???

To all of my friends and family. I am grateful for all of you. I wouldn't be who I am without you. I hope you enjoy this book!

To my ARC readers. Thank you for your feedback and suggestions! I appreciate every one of you, and am grateful you were willing to read my debut novel.

To my readers. I hope you enjoyed this book. Maybe you saw pieces of yourself or those around you. I hope you stick around for the rest of the journey.

ABOUT THE AUTHOR

Alex Lane started writing at 11 and is beyond thrilled to have published two books. She loves all things fantasy, romance, sci-fi, and dystopian. For more information, and to keep up with coming releases follow her on social media (@alexlanecreative) or visit her website:

www.alexlanecreative.com

Sign up for her newsletter to receive bonus content from the Rules Duology!

9 781966 978015